A SUMMER OF HOPE

- Croc Brothers Romance - Book Three

Donna Munro

Warm Witty
PUBLISHING

Warm Witty Publishing

Sunshine Coast ☺ Queensland ☺ Australia

A SUMMER
OF
HOPE

- Croc Brothers Romance - Book Three

Donna Munro

Warm Witty Publishing

Sunshine Coast ☺ Queensland ☺ Australia

First Published – 2020 - Elephant Creek
This edition published 2022 by Warm Witty Publishing
Sunshine Coast, Qld Australia
www.warmwittypublishing.com.au

The National Library of Australia Cataloguing-in-Publication

Creator: Munro, Donna, author.

Title: A Summer of Hope / Donna Munro.

ISBN: 978-0-6452629-4-0 (paperback)

Subjects: Romance fiction.
                 Contemporary fiction
                 Adventure Romance
                 Australian fiction.
                 Romantic suspense fiction.

Typeset in Times New Roman 12pt by Warm Witty Publishing.
Cover artwork by Donna Munro Graphic Design.
Printed and Bound in Australia by Ingram Spark.

Chapter 1

Emma craved an illusive love. Not the settled-for-boring-financially-secure kind of devotion. *An easy-to-be-with, my-sense-of-humour, same-values, adores-only-me sort of guy.* Could Wade become that man?

The sun dipped over the western sky, painting amber colours on the smooth waters of Currumbin Creek, flashing through the gum trees lining the road's edge. Street lights blinked. She switched the car headlights to shine down the tar road, though it was yet dark. A full moon rose low in the eastern sky casting silver light over the tranquil creek, humming with a twilight bush concerto.

A chill prickled goosebumps down her neck. She tried shaking the peculiar feeling by rolling her shoulders, but it remained.

Bing! Glancing to the glovebox, she shook her head. Another phone message. *Wade.* She met him on Tinder which was sort of embarrassing. *A cliché or what?*

Good-intentioned girlfriends loaded her profile, only revealing it to her after it was online for all to see. Out of dozens of possibilities, Wade aroused her curiosity. His dark, sexy looks made her go *phwoar!* A few nice dates followed — dinners, beach walks and a kiss here and there. Though a little guarded, Wade seemed normal. Not crazy, or a sociopath, though Jessy warned her of the possibility. Her sister was happily married and held no regard for Tinder daters. The thought made Emma laugh and shake her head, watching the road ahead.

Wade was a muscular, handsome guy with a dark fringe, often masking hazel eyes. It made him look like a rock star and younger than his thirty-seven years. He was hot but not as smoking as some.

Emma really needed to stop her infatuation with Mr Sizzling Hot and join the real world. She smacked her forehead. Wade was available and keen. *Yeah, okay, he wasn't Mr Sizzling Hot, but he was close.*

1

Emma couldn't quite put her finger on what bothered her about Wade. Sometimes he was aloof and quiet. She'd tried downplaying her chatty nature long enough for him to say something, at least. Longing for effortless conversations and comfortable silences wasn't too much to ask.

As the car passed lush acreage properties, with a wistful look, Emma admired some of the new homes facing the creek with sandy banks and jetties anchoring boats and jet skis.

She'd never been the picket-fence kind of girl, but lately, she felt an urge for a companion. Maybe her biological clock was ticking. She was twenty-nine after all. Unfortunately, most guys didn't rock her boat, make her womb tingle or heart ache with desire. *Was it so wrong to want bells and whistles, not to mention a fair amount of lust?*

Jessy said she was too picky, though at least their mum disagreed. Ali would say, 'You'll know when the right guy comes along.' *I bloody well hope so.*

Turning her attention to the road, she rounded the next bend.

***

Derick smiled, patting Sasha's broad head. The dog sat on the worn passenger seat with her tongue lolling towards the window breeze. 'Picture perfect, eh, girl?'

The sound of the battered ute broke through a squawking flock of white corella's swooping through the sky to their roost for the night.

'Don't let on to Crystal I let you sit in her seat,' Derick said to the dog, chuckling to himself and watching the road. The tan Staffordshire Terrier turned, with a wide gummy-fanged smile, panting and wagging her tail, so it thumped against the door.

Derick was a cautious driver watching the road from every angle, checking his mirrors as well as what was on the road in front. He always drove under the speed limit. He did so because he'd often held precious cargo; his wife, kid, grandchild, and beloved dogs.

Placing his left hand on Sasha's stomach tumour, he frowned, wiping a curled finger under welling eyes. Seriously, he was becoming a sook in his old age. Well, he wasn't exactly old, but he was turning 68. It seemed a hell of a lot older than 28, but he didn't feel much different, despite a few aches.

'Should give up the ciggies too, eh girl?' he said, glancing at the cigarette packet on the dash.

Sasha barked sharply. Derek glanced at the dog for a second. She nipped a red dot of light on the armrest. Yapping excitedly, she scraped her paws, trying to bite it with her teeth.

2

Derick slowed the car. Perplexed, he glanced up the road to headlights coming his way. A blinding flash forced him to shut his eyes momentarily. His foot hit the brake, and the car skidded, veering to the side of the road near the creek. Blinded except for the violet light burning under his eyelids, he lifted one arm to shield his eyes. With white knuckles stained with nicotine, he gripped the steering wheel, maneuvering on a road he could no longer see.

Tyres screeched. Gravel crunched, spitting from the wheels. The steering wheel spun from his hands though he grappled hard for control. The windscreen shattered, glass cutting his hands and face.

As the airbags slammed into his chest, Derick felt his lungs explode with the pressure. The metal walls of the car closed in around him.

The last things he heard were Sasha's high-pitched yelps and terrified screams for help.

***

Emma heard the screech of tyres and a thunderous bang as she rounded the bend. Eyes wide in shock, Emma's heart staccato to a beat barely contained in her chest. Her arms tingled with goosebumps. 'Oh, jeez. What the hell?'

Slowing the car to stop, she stilled shaking hands, gripping the steering wheel with trembling sweaty fingers.

Twisted metal littered the bitumen like a junkyard. Glass from the windscreen and headlights dropped on the tar-like falling pebbles. Engines hissed and whirred to a stop as fuel, and burnt rubber stunk the air.

Peeling her fingers from the wheel, Emma wobbled as she stepped from the car.

The sound of a barking dog made her jump and clutched her heaving stomach. Shaking, she glanced up the road with no other headlights in sight. *I don't want to do this on my own?*

The ute was wedged close to the creek edge. Its engine hissed with steam rising. The bonnet, like a can of beer under a booted foot, was crushed and twisted. Miraculously, the occupant shook his grey head, slowly opening the driver's side door.

A crumpled small red sedan's headlights were like empty eyes in a broken skull. A young man dragged himself away from the wreck, his legs twisted at odd angles.

Running to him, Emma ignored her fear. 'Are you okay?' Her voice croaked. Biting her lip, she held back tears.

With desperate eyes, he peered to the driver's side; pain etched in his pale face. He screamed, 'Where's Callum? Fuck! Where's me, mate?'

'Stay calm. I'll check on your friend.'

'My legs. My legs are busted.'

Lifting her hand in a stop sign, she said, 'Stay still. I'll be back.'

She took a steady breath, edging to the driver's side, momentarily shutting her eyes. *I'm scared to look.*

Another young man was pushed nearly into the back seat from the force of the collision. A deep wound gashed his forehead, pouring blood down his face to his chest, staining his t-shirt. Barely breathing, his closed eyes twitched as if caught in a nightmare.

Emma's hand shook, reaching for his shoulder, touching cold skin — smelling blood, petrol and fear. Bile rose in her throat, but she quashed it, trying to stay brave.

The other young man cried out. 'Callum, mate? Dude, talk to me. Callum?'

Emma pressed her fingers on the driver. 'Hi Callum, I'm Emma. Can you hear me?'

His eyelids flickered. Slight tremors shuddered his shallow-rising chest. 'Stay still. I'm calling for help. You're going to be okay.' She hoped it wasn't a lie.

Running back to her car, she grabbed the mobile phone from the glovebox. She rang triple zero, sniffing the mounting petrol fumes hoping the cars weren't about to catch fire. She gave the responder details about the crash in a calm voice, watching the man stagger beside the ute. Thankfully, he seemed stunned but unhurt.

Clutching her queazy stomach, she blinked at the tragic scene. 'Not sure. I think three people. It's only just happened. Hurry.' Putting the phone in her jeans back pocket, she strode to the older man who looked about to fall over. Taking his elbow to steady him, she smiled as she urged him to the curb. He was elderly with a thatch of thick grey hair, a portly stomach but sinewy tradie or farmer-type arms. He gave her a weak smile, but his grey eyes showed kindness and a hint of tears.

'Are you okay? Do you know what happened?'

'I — I'm' He rubbed his temple where blood pooled on a small wound. With moist eyes, he shook his head. 'I'm fine. Those people? Jesus. Oh, God, I hope they're okay.' He glanced towards the sedan, slumping to the ground, his head in his hands.

Emma's throat caught, and she gulped. The boy on the road went silent and looked to be unconscious, head resting on the road. 'They're hurt, but I think they'll be fine. The ambulance is on its way. You should stay sitting.'

The gentleman looked at her, a baffled expression on his craggy face. 'It was the light. It was so bright. It —' He sobbed into his hands.

'The moon?' Emma asked, furrowing her brow. The moon was so bright it seemed unlikely to cause such a tragedy.

4

'No. Red. It was a red light.'

A whimper sounded in the otherwise quiet air. The man called, 'Oh, Sasha, Sasha, where are you, girl?'

Emma frowned, feeling a chill, turning her attention to the young man with injured legs. He glanced up, regaining consciousness, his eyes clouded in confusion and pain. 'The ambulance will be here soon, so hang in there,' Emma said with a sad smile.

A groan escaped his lips while he twisted in pain, gripping his legs. 'Don't let us die.'

'You'll be fine. I know it hurts. Just hold on.' If only she had a blanket or towel to wrap him in because he seemed to be in shock.

The sound of sirens grew as they approached from the east.

Emma checked the driver. 'Callum. Stay awake. Come on. You can do it. They're nearly here.' Gently, she touched his shoulder, feeling sticky blood on her fingers and cold skin. 'You'll be okay.' She bit back tears as her bottom lip trembled. He was in a really bad way. *Oh, my God!*

Shuddering, she kept a reassuring hold on his shoulder. Squeezing his clammy skin gently, she said, 'Stay with us, Callum. Fight it. Stay with us.' She kept talking, trying to keep him conscious until help arrived.

Sirens blared. Red and blue lights flashed blending with the moonlight to create an eerie Halloween disco. Vehicles pulled up around them. The ambulance paramedics and police attended to the boy in the car and the one on the ground.

A fire engine parked with a hiss of its brakes. The troop of firefighters ran to their tasks as their captain assessed the trapped boy.

An officer questioned the older man with an open notebook in his hands but didn't stay long. He came to Emma with a reassuring nod.

'I know you're probably in shock, so if you forget anything, you can tell us at the station tomorrow when you give your statement,' he said.

Emma's mind tumbled with everything she'd witnessed. Trying to keep from turning into a blubbering mess, she bit her bottom lip, answering what she could.

The boy on the ground screamed while they lifted him onto a stretcher, even though he sucked the life out of the green stick of Penthrox.

It took longer to free the poor young driver from the vehicle. The emergency services concentrated on him as Emma sat beside the gentleman. Both were in their thoughts as they watched the rescue unfold, and onlookers began to pull over to find out what happened.

'Are you okay, young lady? It's a horrible thing for you to see,' the man said, turning to her with soft, kind eyes.

'Not really, I guess. It's a shock. What about you? I wish the paramedics would hurry up and check you.'

'They will. Those young men are worse off than me.'

Emma nodded, glancing at a senior paramedic shaking her head as she spoke to the fire chief about the trapped boy.

Turning to the older man, she realised he was clutching his chest.

'Oh, no.' She screamed, 'Quick, someone. I think he's having a heart attack.' Sirens blocked her voice.

Collapsing on his side, the man gasped for breath.

Glancing at the busy paramedics, Emma acted quickly. Turning him over, she checked his airways before compressing his chest with her palms, screaming again to the ambos for help.

Pumping his chest, she watched his screwed up, terrified face turning grey. His lips were blue.

Emma pressed as tears spattered her hands stained from the blood of the young man. What seemed like minutes was probably only seconds, when someone crouched beside her and said in a soothing voice, 'It's okay. You've done well.'

A paramedic hooked up a defibrillator. 'Move aside. We'll take over. Good work. You've probably saved a life.'

Emma stayed on the ground, crawling back on her haunches, watching them work on the man.

'Here, sweetheart. You'll be in shock,' a woman said, draping a blanket over Emma's shoulders.

Neighbours lined the road. Some to help, others morbidly gawking.

Through a foggy cloud of numbness, Emma watched the scene. It was like an episode of Chicago Fire without the hot guys. *I wish it were a TV show instead of real.*

Police huddled near the mangled sedan talking in hushed tones. One seemed most affected, tears streaking his face as he held the hand of the young man in the back of an ambulance.

A fresh-faced policeman walked from the group striding towards the creek. He threw a small object into the shimmering water. Emma heard the little splash, wondering what he threw. An odd feeling swept over her. She pulled the blanket tighter, curling her fingers in the comforting fabric.

Sirens screamed from the ambulances driving off at high speed. The fire truck drove east, as did the police cars. The sounds of the bush, cicadas, owls and frogs replaced the chaos.

A dog whimpered nearby.

Emma stood under the full moon shivering in a stranger's blanket, wishing she could unsee the night. A fish made a splash, making her wonder what the policeman tossed in the creek.

6

Chapter 2

'Why couldn't you have left after speaking to the cop?' Glancing at his watch, Wade rolled his eyes, tapping the face. He sulked, a frown twisting his handsome face.

Emma bit the inside of her cheek, choosing her words carefully. 'I couldn't. I sat with the old man while they tended to the boys. We were in shock. Lucky I did since he had a heart attack.' She sighed, twisting her fingers around the napkin on her lap. She hoped to fall into his arms, finding comfort, not confrontation. *Don't turn out like all the other doofus I've dated.*

'Whatever.' He waved his hand dismissively. 'I'm disappointed. Forget it.' He lifted a wine glass to his lips.

Emma's fingers shook when she lifted hers and placed it down again. Wade didn't seem to notice. 'Well, at least we got served. I made it before the kitchen closed.' She reminded him. 'I'm just going to the toilet before the meals arrive.' Rising slowly, she strolled towards the loo, passing Mr Sizzling Hot. He was married, so her crush on him would remain a fantasy. But gosh, he was easy on the eyes.

Their shoulders brushed as he bent his arm to fish a mobile phone from his trousers.

'Sorry, luv,' he said in a smooth, deep voice, smiling, but his brilliant eyes flashed sudden alarm. Turning away, he held the phone to his ear, striding outside to the quieter deck.

His electric touch lingered on her skin. In the bathroom, she wiped her face with a wet hand towel, dousing the flame he always stirred. *That guy is so hot he's a mid-summer heatwave.*

He had a wife, of course. Usually, he stand-up paddled the creek with his little girl, sometimes a dog perched on the front of the board — a family for sure.

Smacking her head with a flat palm, she groaned. *Stop thinking about him when a lovely guy waits in the restaurant.*

The mirror reflected her pale cheeks. Dark circles curved under her green eyes like the dark side of the moon, making her frown. Even makeup couldn't conceal how she felt. *Why didn't Wade get that?*

Wade insisted on keeping their dinner date despite the shock, even though she pleaded she wasn't feeling up to it. Instead, she would have gladly curled up in front of the television, with tissues and chocolate watching a chick flick.

He looked forward to her company, so she couldn't be annoyed by that. The accident was making her overreact to everything. If only he'd been more understanding about her horrible night, she would be able to relax a little.

Walking towards him, she took in his profile. Good looking enough to garner second looks and hushed giggles from the women seated nearby.

Wade glanced up, flashing a perfect smile. She smiled back, wanting to feel happier. Images of the accident played on a loop in her head. Shaking her shoulders to rid the shiver sweeping down her spine, she flicked a napkin over her lap. She eyed the Pesto Chicken with a lurching stomach.

'Food smells delicious. You must be starving,' Wade said, tucking into his own, scraping the ceramic plate with his knife, making Emma flinch.

The door to the deck slid open. Mr Sizzling Hot ran towards the front doors with his ruggedly handsome face flashing concern. Emma wondered what made him look so concerned. *I hope his little daughter is okay.*

Emma stabbed the meal but didn't cut the meat. She lifted the full wine glass, hoping to settle her nerves. A dreadfully fruity taste assailed her taste buds. She was tempted to spit it out but swirled it in her mouth, eventually swallowing. Observing Wade's handsome face as he ate gave her an odd feeling. Preoccupied with the food, he barely glanced at her. If he looked adequately, he would have seen she was pale and upset.

Taking a nibble of a hot potato chip, she frowned, feeling sorry for herself and wanting to ring her mum. The main person she could turn to in a crisis—*good old Mum.* Instead, Emma longed for there to be a partner she could turn to who understood her — someone who would know at a glance how she felt.

Finally, with gravy on his chin, Wade asked, 'Emma, are you alright?'

'Mmm. Yeah. I don't know. Maybe I'm in shock.'

'Well, toughen up, Princess.' He laughed. 'We have some dancing to do. Band's started already.'

Wade took another bite of his steak, oblivious to Emma barely touching her plate. 'Hey, it's late already. Could we skip the dancing? I'd rather head home,' she said. Usually, one to love dancing, it was the last thing on her mind.

8

'Emma, if that's what you'd prefer.' A glint of desire flashed in his hazel eyes as his eyebrows rose.

Emma picked up the handbag draped over the back of her chair. *Really! He wants sex when I feel like shit.* Her thoughts were on sleep, not shagging.

Earlier dates had only led to deep kissing and groping. It had built desire, but Emma felt exhausted, not horny. As they left the RSL Club, Wade possessively took hold of her waist. She wanted their first night of lovemaking to be romantic, not her stressed and upset by what she'd seen that afternoon.

During the taxi ride home, he hungrily kissed her lips. Losing the energy to deny him, she kissed him back. Perhaps it would be good to release the sexual tension building between them. Though yet to adore him, she hoped to, and maybe once they made love, the horror of the day would disappear. She hoped it would build the connection she craved.

During the short ride home, Emma's head lolled on Wade's shoulder. Shaking her, he said, 'Wake up, sleepyhead. How about I carry you to your door?'

With her body like jelly, Emma let Wade scoop her in his strong arms. Smelling his masculine scent mixed with expensive cologne warmed her to the idea of a tumble in the sheets.

Wade placed his lips on hers before putting her on her feet at the door. Fumbling with the keys, she let them in. A skateboard in the hallway almost tripped him. He swore before picking it up.

'Yours?' he asked, placing it on the floor.

'My nephew, Jai's. Sorry. I told him to put it away. He probably forgot, rushing to the next sporty thing he wanted to do.'

Wade pushed her against the wall, pinning her hands and kissing her lips. 'Bloody kids. I don't know why you have him stay here so often.'

'He's my nephew. I love him. Why wouldn't I?'

'I'm not a kid person.' He said it as if most people weren't. 'Where's your bedroom?' The skateboard rolled down the hallway.

'Upstairs,' she answered. *Why doesn't Wade like children?* Alarm bells rang, but she ignored them.

The accident scene flashed in her mind; fear, blood, petrol, broken bones, sirens. 'Now?' she asked, shaking her head to clear the images. Wade seemed in no mood for a nightcap or foreplay. 'You have a condom, right?'

Wade answered by taking her hand, squeezing her fingers tightly almost crushing hers. She led him to her room, where he pushed her onto the bed a little forcefully. Kissing her with teeth clashing, he tried to push his tongue deep, while his hands tore at her clothes. There was no tantalising lead-up building her juices. No time to admire his buff body. His fingers roughly stroked and poked inside her for mere minutes before he pushed his cock inside her.

'Condom?' she asked too late. Slowly she relaxed, letting her body respond until she met each thrust of his hips with the same intensity. Before she could build to a climax, Wade grunted his release. *Thank God for the pill.* As he groaned his satisfaction, she felt unsated.

The accident scene flashed in her head. Wade panted on her shoulder while she stared at the ceiling with tears wetting her cheeks.

Chapter 3

'Jeezus, Dad, you gave us a scare,' Noah said softly, stroking his father's sun-spotted hand, avoiding the catheter in his wrist. 'You don't do things by halves, eh?'

'How long you been here?' Derick asked in a scratchy voice, glancing to the window streaming sunlight.

'About eight hours. I was at the RSL when I got the call from Mum. We got here as quick as we could after I dropped Hope at the babysitter. How are you feeling?'

'Son, I'm fine,' Derick said, a croak to his weary voice. Blinking, he gazed around the private hospital room. 'Where's your mother?' Panic rose in his voice.

Noah patted his hand, standing to stretch his arms over his head, yawning. 'She's gone to find a couple of coffees. Neither of us slept, worrying about you.'

'Take more than a car accident for me to see the pearly gates.' Derick sighed. 'I wonder how those young men are.' His eyes were moist.

Noah couldn't meet his father's eyes. 'I'm sure they're fine. They were taken to the university hospital. You're at John Flynn. You know that, don't you?'

'Thought it looked a bit posh.' He raised a grin before coughing.

'Mum always looked after things like that. She took out a private cover as you aged.'

'Whose aged?' He laughed before wheezing. 'She's such a clever woman, your mum,' Derick said, touching a hand to his heart. 'Guess this means I'll have to give up the ciggies.'

Noah nodded, smiling with raised eyebrows. 'You could at least try.' He chuckled. 'When Mum returns, I'm going to head home and pick up Hope. I'll check the road for Sasha. It wasn't far from home. With luck, she'll probably greet me when I arrive.'

'Check on Smelly too, son.' Derick closed his eyes, falling asleep with a gurgling snore escaping his open mouth.

***

Noah collected Hope from the babysitter. As he strapped her into a booster in the back of his twin-cab ute, he asked about her sleepover.

'I got to play with Sammy's cat. Why don't we have a cat?' she asked.

'I suppose, Hopey, that's because we already have a dog, guinea pigs, cows and an elephant. Oh, and your gorilla too.'

Hope giggled a delightful laugh, her whole face lighting in the process. He watched her through the rear-view mirror full of pride and love as she shook the toy gorilla in her hands. 'Poppy coming home?' she asked innocently. 'Why you looking out window all time?'

'Ah — just checking for wildlife,' he white-lied, 'you know how often they stray on the road.'

'Yup. Silly wallies,' she announced, giggling again.

Stupid drivers.

Noah kept an eye out for the family dog. He told Hope Sasha went for a walk, not wanting her to know the shocking details of what happened to her grandfather. She would understand little due to her Down Syndrome, but she was a smart little girl in other ways. Hope possessed a deep sense of kindness some able-minded people didn't.

Sasha was nowhere. Hopefully, she was lazing on the verandah with her tongue hanging out, waiting for them. Her tail would thump, thump, thump on the timber as she wagged it before pulling her tired old body up to greet them eagerly. It didn't matter if they were gone five minutes or five hours; the level of keenness never waivered.

Turning down the winding driveway, two narrow concrete paths, he watched the bush for signs of movement.

Looking past his small home, more a shed than a house, his eyes scanned the wide-veranda of the main Queenslander house. He narrowed his eyes for their missing dog. Frowning, he parked the car in the carport. Hope fumbled with her seatbelt.

'Sasha, not here, Daddy?' Hope stared at the timber deck.

'She'll be somewhere nearby. Don't you worry about the old girl.'

'Okay, Hope, no worry. Sasha with Stinky.'

'Probably, sweetie.' He pulled her from the car. Her little hands curled around his neck, one still gripping the toy gorilla. Snuggling her head into his neck, she kissed his cheek. He kissed her hair, squeezing her. 'I love you, Hopey.' A small child for a ten-year-old, she was girly but loved the outdoors — a tom-boy who looked like an angel. He never understood why some people couldn't see Hope the way he did.

'I love you too, Daddy.' She lifted her head, screwing her nose. 'You smell funny.'

Noah sniffed his shirt. The antiseptic smell of hospitals. 'Yup, I need a shower don't I?' He pinched his nose, putting her down at the door. She copied, looking ever so cute as she did it. 'How about you unpack your overnight bag. After I get clean, we'll have a breakfast cook up.'

Hope clapped her hands. 'Pancakes?'

'Sure, for you, sweetie, but I've got a craving for bacon and eggs.'

***

Emma waited for Wade to leave. He didn't take the hint about her having plans for her day. If only it were a weekday, she would have the excuse of work. Finally, he left at eight. She shut the door leaning with her back to it, feeling sick.

She wanted intimacy with Wade; unfortunately, her expectations were high, and he fell well short of the mark. She couldn't put her finger on why.

The accident shook her, and she wasn't her usual happy self. On their first night together, she probably didn't rock his boat either. Was it her fault the stars didn't align because her mind was elsewhere?

In hindsight, she should have told him they couldn't meet up. It would have been the honest thing to do instead of pretending everything was hunky-dory.

Gulping back the lump in her throat, she rang her mother. Ali answered on the second ring. 'Emma, are you okay?'

'Hi, Mum. I'm — um no—' The last words wobbled with the tears spilling onto her lips.

'I knew something was up. What happened on your date?'

'No. It wasn't the date.' Wiping her face, she told her mother about the car accident and going to dinner afterwards — nothing about ending up in bed with her date.

'You poor darling. He shouldn't place you in such a position. He could have understood and rescheduled.'

'Oh, Mum. It's not his fault I felt fragile. I hoped meeting with him would cheer me up.'

'Did it?' Ali asked in the matter of fact way she always used with her children.

Ali's husband, Shaun, was sure to be in the background smiling. Shaun adored Emma's mother. He was a wonderful, kind man, and Ali deserved a lovely guy like him after everything she'd been through. *Could Wade ever be that guy?* She took a while to answer. 'Kind of. Maybe. I don't know.'

'Do you want me to come over so we can chat over tea?'

'No, Mum. I'll be fine. I think I'll drive by where it happened and get some clarity. I want to find out if the people involved are okay.'

13

'There was a small announcement on the radio. I'm sorry to tell you, darling, but one of the young men passed away. The other received a spinal injury and the man had a heart attack. It must have been horrible for you.'

Emma clasped a hand over her mouth, letting the tears fall again.

'Emm, are you alright?'

'Yep. Oh, dear. I'd hope —'

'I know, honey. You did your best. Ther would have been nothing more you could have done for that poor boy.'

'Any cause?'

'Not that I heard. Further investigations are underway. There'll be an update. I'll keep listening and let you know. Are you sure you want to go back?'

'Yes.' She nodded, knowing she should. The lovely man had seemed more concerned about her welfare than his injuries. His kindness melted her heart, and the anguish on his face during his heart attack did something to her soul. To mend her own fear and aftershock, she needed to find out if he was okay. She also wanted to let him know what she'd witnessed. Deep down, she felt there was something more sinister going on.

***

'Eat up, Hope,' Noah urged, forking the last bite of bacon into his mouth.

Out the window, a Wattle Bird's *poo kak poo kak* sounded the morning alarm. A tractor on a nearby property rumbled over fields, and a crop plane flew overhead.

Hope cut the pancake with her hands at awkward angles. She precisely placed slices of banana in a circle with two pieces in the middle, leaning together. She smiled at him as if she'd constructed a pyramid.

He grinned. 'Hope, don't play with your food. Eat it, please. I'm already finished.'

A car engine neared. His heart raced. *Who? Katie's people?* It was always in the back of his mind. She'd remarried. He should feel safe, but the years in hiding jaded him.

Standing quickly with his eyes to the road, he nearly toppled over a chair. *It's her — the paddleboarding chick.* Righting the chair, he glanced out the window. The distinctive yellow sedan drove down their driveway. Her long hair flowed out the open driver's window. 'Stay here, Hope.'

'Okay, Daddy.'

14

Noah strode to the car. He'd been avoiding the woman for a good reason. *She's fire and I can't afford to be burnt.*

She glanced at him with a smile, stepping from the vehicle. Slender tanned legs in cut-off denim shorts sent his imagination into overdrive. *Vavoom!*

The sexy girl usually wearing a skimpy swimsuit, he saw most days paddling on the creek. He sucked in a breath. *Fuck she was even cuter up close.* 'What are you doing here?' he asked, narrowing his eyes. He'd practically dreamt of her nightly. The thought made him want to step closer and run at the same time. *You only need Hope.* A woman was a complication he didn't need, no matter how much he was attracted to her.

'Is this Derick Redman's place?' She strode to the side of the car.

'Yep.' He folded his arms over his chest, giving a slight nod. The words, 'it's none of your business' stayed on his tongue unsaid. She turned to open the car's back door.

Noah heard a dog whimper. *Sasha!* He pushed past the girl to get to his dog. 'Sasha! Wow! Hey girl.' He patted Sasha's flank. She wagged her tail and licked his cheek, trying to leap into his arms. 'Where did you find our dog? We've been searching for her.' He turned. The woman was so close he could smell shampoo, making him think of summer days and a roll in the hay.

A tear dropped on her cheek under red-rimmed eyes. *Damn, she looked vulnerable enough to hug.*

'I heard her last night and came back to the — accident site. She was curled in nearby bushes, licking her foot and whimpering. I've given her water.' She blinked.

Noah turned his attention to Sasha, gently testing each leg. She tried to lick his face, and her tail beat on the leather seat. The dog pulled a front paw away. 'Probably ligaments. You're okay, girl. I'll get a better look at you once Hope says hello,' he said to Sasha, trying to ignore the kind woman who brought her home.

'Yeah, I think so too. Should probably see a vet to be sure.'

Lifting Sasha, he met the woman's gorgeous green eyes. 'All good. I'll take care of her.' He strode towards the veranda.

'I read the name tag. Derick had been calling for a dog at the accident when we were talking — before — um.' Noah glanced back to see her bottom lip wobble. 'Is he okay?'

'He's fine. Thanks. You can go now. And shut the gate on your way out.' He ignored how vulnerable she looked, not willing to play with fire.

***

Slamming the door, Emma followed Mr Sizzling Hot's ass in snug boardshorts as he walked up the stairs. His legs were muscular and tanned a deep latte. Broad shoulders stretched the thin t-shirt allowing muscles to flex underneath. She longed to get closer even though he was about as approachable as a shark near burley. Anyhow she didn't need two damn annoying men in her life.

With hands on hips, she glared at him, waiting for him to put the pet down. He did so slowly, gently rechecking each limb and speaking to the dog in a soft voice contradicting the mean exterior. A little girl of about eight opened the sliding door, running to Sasha with open arms.

'Sasha's back!' The child hugged the dog, receiving slurping licks to her mouth and nose. She looked up. 'Who you?'

Mr Sizzling Hot stood aside with a half-smile on his handsome three-day-growth face.

'Emma.' She smiled. 'Who are you?'

The little girl kissed her pet's forehead before leaving Sasha to leap at Emma, almost toppling her over with an exuberant hug.

'Ank you, Emma. I, Hope.' The child kneeled back beside the dog, receiving a slurpy lick on her face, making her giggle.

'Is this your dog, Hope? She's a beautiful animal.'

'Yep. Sasha. Sasha safe.'

A smile tugged at the man's thick lips, but it soon turned to a frown at Emma. 'Thank you for bringing our dog.' He stood, running a hand through his hair which nicely showed off his more than ample biceps. Fascinating green-blue eyes scanned over her with an unreadable look. A more stunning, sexy man she'd never seen. *Too bad, he was an A-Grade asshole to women. Though, he did seem kinda cute with animals and children.* He's an enigma. *What is his problem with me helping?*

Emma could smack herself in the head for it, but pitifully she couldn't help staring at him, even though he was shooting daggers her way. Bravely, she stepped close enough to feel his fresh breath on her face. Conjuring a coherent thought seemed impossible, but she pushed on. 'I came about Derick, so please hear me out.'

'What about Dad?' His jaw twitched.

She contained the urge to run a finger along his thick kissable lips in case he bit it off. He had no reason to be mad. Perhaps he was angry with the world.

Damn, I want to kiss his smug face. I'm losing my shit.

'I'm worried about him. Do you want to know what happened, Mr Cranky Pants or not? I was there at the accident,' she asked, poking him on a firm shoulder.

'Cranky Pants?' He smirked, raising his eyebrows. 'Dad already told me. I don't need it from a stranger.' His chiselled jaw twitched.

Hope grabbed the man's t-shirt, tugging for his attention. 'Daddy, why are you angry with nice lady?' Sasha's tail thumped on the timber deck.

16

'I, I'm not, Hope. Hey, why don't you take Sasha inside and give her some dry food. I bet she's starving. Check the guinea pigs have food too.'

Hope's eyes lit up. 'Okay, Daddy.'

'Emma's leaving now. Say goodbye,' he said, grabbing Emma's elbow leading her down the stairs.

'Bye, Emma.' Hope waved.

The man growled in her ear, 'Don't upset my daughter.'

'Seriously?' Emma jerked her elbow free, storming ahead of him. Swinging to face him, out of earshot of Hope, she asked, 'What's your problem?'

'You.' Raking his hand through his hair, he stared at the sky. 'Anyway, forget it. Go home.' He opened her driver's side door. 'I don't like my daughter hearing adult stuff. What could you tell me that I don't already know?'

'There was no adult stuff. Seriously you're a pain. I'm here about Derick.'

'What about Dad? Spit it out already.' His hand rested on the door. His other ushered her into the car. She ignored him to stand under the carport, shading from the summer sun.

'You have a problem, mate. I'm here to help. Your dad may not remember since he seemed out of it.'

His jaw twitched. 'Remember what? Anyway, it was a minor attack as far as heart attacks go. He only needs one stent. He'll be fine.'

'Well, that's a relief, but you haven't heard what the police are insinuating.' She glared at him, but her bottom lip wobbled. His cold stare was about to make her cry. Since she'd never been a crier in front of strangers, it was disconcerting.

'What's that?' He stepped into her personal space staring down at her. Her hands shook, but something about him wasn't threatening, even if he was sending a million stay-away vibes. It was such a weird contradiction, she stepped away from his heat, choosing survival mode. *He's only a guy. A stupid, cranky, hot guy who loves children and animals — just a friggin guy.*

'I heard them saying they would charge your father. One threw an object in the creek. It was weird. They were cagey when I asked what it was.'

'What are you saying? Someone's setting my father up?'

'Maybe. I'm only telling you what I heard and saw.'

'So?'

'A radio report this morning said the policeman's son survived. Robbie Trobia.'

The guy's eyes widened. He slammed her car door. 'Are you sure?'

17

'Yes, why would I make it up? Seriously? I care about your dad. He was lovely to me. Something suss is going on. You need to do something about it.' She threw her hands in the air.

'Fuck.' he raked his hair, swearing softly. 'Sorry, I'm protective of Dad and my family.'

'You can protect your family without being Mr Cranky Pants, surely?'

A small smile tugged at his lips, betraying his hard exterior.

'You need to know there's more. Your father seemed genuinely puzzled by how the accident happened. He wasn't speeding. I think whatever they threw away was important. Your dad said he saw a red light. He was blind to the sedan.' She gulped, watching his jaw twitch and mesmerising eyes harden. Opening the door, she got in the car, turning the ignition.

He was silent but nodded.

'When your dad feels better, if he has any questions, I'd be happy to answer them.' She passed him a business card. Big, strong hands took the card with an electric touch. Feeling the warmth of his fingers, she noticed scars over them and callouses on his palms. *It was best to look at them instead of his hypnotic eyes.*

Pulling his hand away, he glanced at the card, mumbling, 'Okay.' His Adam's apple bobbed. The glance in his eyes flashed warmth for a moment before his guard came up again.

Hope waved from the verandah, the dog circling her legs.

Glancing in the rear-view mirror, he stood in the driveway, a million miles away in his thoughts. *Hell, she hadn't even asked his name.*

A thick canopy of trees shaded the driveway where bush grew thick. Something grey swayed the scrub — a big animal lumbering behind the grove of avocado trees. *Hallucinations? Accident stress? Elephants living in Australia? No way.*

Driving by the accident scene, a chill crept along her spine like boney fingers with long scratchy nails. *What the hell had the police thrown in the creek?*

18

Chapter 4

'Hi, Mum.' Emma opened the door to her mother and nephew. 'Jai, you bought Cheetah too, of course?'

Her curly-haired nephew grinned. He was a nine-year-old ball of energy, followed by his dog, Cheetah, the brindle Staffordshire Terrier.

Emma embraced her mum. Jai raced down the hallway toward a cupboard where she kept his playthings: basketballs, footballs, skateboards, cricket sets and kicking tees.

'Aunt E, you gotta call me Lion. Can I take the skateboard over to Cam's place? He's built the sickest skate bowl ever.'

'Put your pads and helmet on first — Lion,' she said, knowing the little thrillseeker would strip off the safety equipment once out of sight. Thankfully he rarely got injured.

'Sure,' he said with a wicked wink in his dark blue eyes. Donning the helmet, he didn't bother clipping it under his chin.

Ali laughed. 'Jai, I mean, Lion, you only have half an hour. This is a quick visit because I have to get back to meet up with Grandad Shaun.'

Jai bolted out the door, the dog trailing eagerly behind, tail wagging. The longboard skateboard looked too big for him even though he was tall for his age.

Emma shut the front screen door. 'So funny he wants us to call him by his nickname..'

'I guess it's a phase. It's an Aussie male thing, wanting a nickname. Anyway, how are you?'

'I told you I was okay, Mum.' Emma shook her head.

Ali stepped forward, wrapping her arms around her daughter. Emma burst into tears. She cried for a few minutes before pulling away, wiping tears. 'I guess we need a cuppa,' she said, half smiling.

'Tea solves most things,' Ali said, filling the kettle. 'At least the conversation that comes with it.'

Emma placed mugs near the kettle, popping a teabag in each. 'I don't know why I break down when I see you, Mum. I've been keeping it together. Really.'

'I'm sure you have, my brave girl, but we all need support in times like this. You've witnessed a tragedy. Later you could probably do with

19

counselling, but at the least, you have me. Even if you don't want to talk about it yet, you know I'm here when you do.'

Emma poured the teas handing Ali a mug. They sat at the small café setting on Emma's patio overlooking Currumbin Creek. It was a lovely townhouse complex. Each unit allowed a view through the parkland of tall gums and open grassy spaces, plus access to the creek via a timber pontoon. Emma enjoyed paddleboarding on the water most days. It was a release from the deadlines of graphic design.

Ali patted Emma's hand. 'It's okay to say you're not fine, you know.'

Emma closed her other hand over Ali's, biting her bottom lip. 'It was awful.' She chewed the corner of her mouth. 'I'm sure I'll discuss it soon. Not yet. At this point, I only want to help the older man. Poor guy was visibly upset. Helping will be good for me.'

'That's a nice thing to do, but how do you go about it?'

'I found his dog on the side of the road near the accident site — a much older tan version of Cheetah. The poor old girl whimpered in the bushes. She wasn't badly injured, only traumatised —' she paused, 'I could relate to it, I guess.'

Ali sipped tea, nodding for Emma to continue.

'The tag had an address. I took the dog to the property off Currumbin Creek Road. Past the old flower farm out from the duck ponds?'

'Didn't the Robinsons used to live near there?'

'Yes, but this property is a battleaxe down a winding road behind theirs. You can barely tell it's there. I gave the old man's son a bit of a surprise when I rocked up unannounced with the dog.' She smiled. 'I think they're a bit reclusive. Anyhow at least they don't need to search for the dog.'

'Turned out well, but what aren't you telling me?' Ali asked. 'That smile from nowhere.'

'What smile?' Emma coughed, almost spitting out tea before covering her mouth with her hand. *Mr Sizzling Hot.* Though she'd admired him from afar, up close was something else. A handsome face with vivid blue-flecked green eyes sucked her in like a whirlpool. Hot as he was, he'd been rude and unwelcoming. So why was she thinking about him so much?

'Emma, there you go again. That smile.' Ali pointed to Emma's upturned lips.

Emma changed the subject. 'Oh yeah. I'm trying to think happy thoughts the way you always taught me. Wade,' she white-lied.

'Oh, so that's what's making you smile. I didn't think the date went well. You like him?'

20

'Yes, of course. The date failed because of the accident. It wasn't Wade's fault. We've dated nearly a month. I think it's going somewhere.' Emma tried to convince herself, if not Mum. The mobile phone on her benchtop beeped. 'It's probably him now.' Considering he already called her three times and messaged dozens, it seemed likely.

'I'm happy for you, darling. Wouldn't it be lovely if you settled down and we couple you off with your sister and Ben.'

'Yeah, yeah, Mum. Don't get carried away.' Changing tack again, Emma asked, 'So how's Shaun going? Did he extend the eco-village on the resort he's been working on?'

'Oh, yes, he's finally through the red tape. I think Kendwa would be proud of how well the business does in Africa. We'll be leaving a legacy for Jai after those first few lean years.'

'I'm so glad. You've got a good guy in Shaun.'

'I sure have. You'll have someone one day. Don't give up on love, Emma. It's truly the best thing in life.'

'Sure, Mum.' Emma rolled her eyes over her tea. Her mother said it easily because she married a good-looking, genuine, dependable man who adored her more than life itself.

Glancing at her watch, Emma said, 'Hey, don't you have to get going? I need to make a formal statement down at the cop shop anyway.'

'Oh, did you need me to come with you? I can ring Shaun. He'll understand,' Ali said, rising with both tea mugs.

'No, Mum. It's something I need to do myself. I'll let you know how it goes.'

***

Noah looked from one policeman to the other with his brow furrowed. 'You are kidding, aren't you?' He slammed his fist on the counter, forgetting where he was, making a pen rattle and roll.

'No, sir. This is a serious matter. We will be charging your father with dangerous driving resulting in death.'

Noah gripped the counter, staring at the police officers. How could someone as kind as his father be charged with a crime?

From a side room, a female officer ushered Emma out. 'Thank you for your statement Miss Jarvis,' she said, shutting the door leading to reception.

Emma wiped her eyes before walking towards Noah. 'Is everything okay? You look kinda tense.'

'So do you,' he said tersely, regretting it springing from his lips when he noticed her bottom lip wobble. 'Sorry. It's my Dad. They're charging him.'

'We know he's done the right thing. It's okay, you'll work through it,' she said, placing her small hand on his.

Her touch sent electric shocks through his body. It took Noah by surprise, considering his father's predicament. Why would she even speak to him, let alone be kind, after the way he treated her that morning?

One of the officers coughed, startling them.

Noah raked a hand through his hair. 'They're going to the hospital to charge him. I have to get there to soften the blow.' To the officers, he said, 'Can you give me time to tell him first?'

'We can't guarantee we won't arrive before you, Mr Cooper. But we do have some paperwork to get through first,' the young officer said with a wink, garnering an angry stare from his sergeant.

'Thanks,' Noah said without conviction. Turning from the counter, he strode towards the doors.

'I can come with you if you like,' Emma offered, following him outside.

'I don't need anyone.' He fastened his pace, but she kept up, taking three steps to his one.

'Maybe I want to help your Dad. It's not about you.'

'What?' he stopped, turning quickly, causing her to stop against him. The warmth of her body and frangipani scented perfume gave him the urge to wrap her in his arms. Instead, he held her shoulders, staring into her earnest, pretty face.

'I —I want to help solve it. I was there. I know something weird is going on. Your father does not deserve charges.'

Tears slipped down her beautiful cheeks. Noah wiped them off with a thumb watching her solemn stare at him entering his soul. Stepping backwards, he rubbed his forehead. 'Look, I'm the kinda guy who works alone.' He did. It was true, but it had nothing to do with why he pushed her away. 'I have no time for this. I have to warn my father.'

'I'm coming. I can tell you what I heard at the police station on the way. You'll want to hear it. I promise.' Emma grabbed his t-shirt in her fist.

He placed his hand on her's, ready to tear her hand off, but when he clasped it, his resolve wavered. Only a tiny touch, and he didn't want to let go. 'Okay, but you're only coming for the ride. You're not seeing my father.'

Dropping his shirt, she asked, 'But why? I need to see he's okay.' Her bottom lip dropped again.

Fishing his keys out of his chinos, he sighed. 'Do you ever give up?'

'Rarely.' She smiled.

Pointing at his car to unlock it, he rolled his eyebrows at her. 'Get in.' Inside he was grinning.

***

Once they were driving on the Gold Coast Highway, Noah turned to Emma. 'So, what do you know?'

'I know your name is Noah Cooper, which baffles me because your father is Derick Redman.' *I also know you're a nicer guy than your letting on.*

Noah rolled his shoulders and shot her a glance. It wasn't an angry one, but his jaw twitched as if he were pondering. 'I changed my name. Next.'

'The sergeant is the one whose son is in a wheelchair. Probably never going to walk again. It must be devastating to their family.'

'The one at the counter, Sergeant Trobia?'

'Yep.'

'No wonder he's been hostile towards me. And?'

'When I waited to make my statement, I heard him talking to someone on the phone. His wife, I think. He said, 'Honey, I have it sorted. Robbie's in the clear.' He glanced at me and must have realised I was listening. He went quiet, covering the phone before slamming the door, yelling at everyone to close doors when investigations are underway.'

'Mmmm. He was furious?'

'Yep. Sure was.'

Noah flattened his foot on the accelerator, gripping the steering wheel. The ring on his left hand caught a glint of sunlight, reminding Emma he was a married man. *Damn it!*

Emma frowned, watching his determined stare as he manoeuvred the twin-cab ute. Stubble lined his chin like an almost beard. Thick kissable lips twitched as he shook his head. 'Fuck,' he swore as they came to a halt at traffic lights. 'Sorry,' he glanced at her with raised eyebrows and a frown.

'I have a brother who's a footballer. I've heard a swear word or two. Even use them myself.' She smiled at him.

A tiny grin tugged the corner of his mouth, exposing a dimple. His teeth were not perfect like Wades but clean and white with a small chip in one of his front teeth. His brown hair grew thick, short back and sides with waves at the top showing he'd probably have curls if he let it grow longer. Scars ran along his sinewy arms and hands. A crocodile tattoo adorned one bicep trailing up and over, its jaw in the crook of his arm, the tail whipping over his shoulder disappearing under his tight t-shirt. His scent wafted pure masculine musk and testosterone.

Flicking her a glance, he asked, 'Why are you staring at me?'

Leaving her mouth agape, she couldn't think of a retort. Instead, her face flushed as she twisted her fingers in her lap.

'Do I remind you of someone?' he asked, expertly taking the turn to John Flynn Hospital too fast for most drivers.

'Yeah — um—maybe that's it. You do look familiar.' *Because your Mr Friggin' Sizzling Hot.*

'You've waved at me on the creek from your paddleboard.' His grin told her he was teasing.

'I didn't mean that. I know I've seen you around, but you do look like someone I've seen. I'm just not sure who.'

***

'Everyone has a doppelganger, so they say.' *Except for you, gorgeous. There could be only one you.*

Emma chewed a nail, glancing at the hospital looming on the hill. She looked sweet and innocent and damn it — sexy as sin.

'Are you okay?' he asked, turning off the ignition. 'I didn't mean it about not seeing him. You are welcome to if you want. It may do you both good after the ordeal of the accident. Surely you were shocked as he was.' And Noah could tell by the way her face crumbled the trauma of it remained. It made him feel bad for being abrupt when she only tried to help. Without thinking it through, he grabbed her small hand, squeezing it. 'It's up to you. You can wait here if you prefer.' *If you keep looking at me with those puppy-dog eyes, I'm going kiss your sadness away.*

Looking down at her hand, he realised he'd held it for way too long, so he pulled it away. Her touch felt good.

'I'd like to see your dad. You go first. You need to give him the bad news. We may not have much time. Let's get cracking.' She stepped from the car, striding up the path.

Blowing air from his lips, he glanced at the sky before letting his eyes rest on her pert little butt in the same cut off shorts. *Hell, those shorts were a distraction.*

***

Emma turned to find Noah unguardedly eyeing her. Trying to still the flutters in her heart, she yelled, 'Come on, slowpoke. At this rate, the police will beat you to your dad's bedside.'

'Not a chance,' he said, sprinting past her. 'Room 24A. Second floor. See you up there.'

She watched him run like an elite athlete — nothing awkward about him. Every part of his body moved with precision. She wondered what he looked like under those clothes. *Scorching!*

Something primal about him kept her staring long after a reasonable time — *for someone who isn't a stalker*. Picturing him naked made her insides quiver. Slapping her forehead, she sighed, knowing she had to quell those thoughts and gain some decorum before she walked to his father's ward.

She came to the hospital to help Derick beat a conviction, not lust for his son. A reasonable person with morals should not let the mind go there in such circumstances.

The phone in her handbag pinged. Fishing it out, she glanced at another message from Wade. Frowning, she shoved the phone in her bag. Not one thought of Wade entered her mind while in the company of Noah.

If only she hadn't slept with Wade, it would be less confusing. But why should she give up on Wade when Noah was clearly a married man.

The words of her mother filled her brain, 'Emma, you will know when you meet *'the one'*.'

Life sucked when *'the one'* happened to be someone else's *'one'*.

Chapter 5

Screwing her nose to the antiseptic hospital smells, Emma paused at the door to Derick's private suite. Lifting her arm to tap, she took a deep breath before knocking twice.

A lady in a bright kaftan with scarfs twirling through her long grey hair answered the door. 'You're the young lady who saved my husband, aren't you?' She asked. 'So happy to meet you, lovely.' The woman's arms jingled with many bracelets down her slender arms. She embraced Emma in a warm hug. 'I'm Crystal.'

'Mum, give Emma a chance to get in the door,' Noah said in his deep, velvet voice.

Emma flushed. 'Hi, Crystal. The ambos saved your husband but thank you. I'm glad I happened to be there to support him.' Emma slowly stepped towards the bed, feeling nauseous on seeing the many wires hooked to machines and Derick.

Noah stood near an open window with his arms folded across his broad chest. Crystal moved to a chair beside the bed.

'How are you doing, Derick?' Emma asked, feeling it a stupid question.

'Aint you a sight for sore eyes,' Derick said, his eyes tearing up. 'If it weren't for your quick thinkin', I'd a been a goner for sure.'

Emma placed her hand on Derick's. 'That's an exaggeration. The defibrillator did the job on your heart. I'm glad to see you're on the mend.'

'Can't wait to get out of this place. Have you ever tasted hospital food? I could eat most of it through a straw. Though, of course, Noah here will eat anything, so nothing goes to waste.' He winked at his son, who shook his head with a grin.

Emma glanced at Noah. Their eyes met and held. Her heart squeezed tight. She could barely breathe, watching a little glint of something like fire in Noah's eyes. To top it off the delectable dimple appeared in his cheek. *How could a lopsided grin be so damn appealing?*

27

Composing herself by taking a deep breath, she spoke to Derick. 'The last time I had hospital food, I was eight and had my tonsils out. Mushy food worked for me.' She smiled, pausing. 'How did you feel about the news Noah gave you?' Glancing back at Noah, she waited for Derick's answer.

Shifting slightly in the bed, Derick shook his shoulders. 'I expected it. Someone's got to be blamed. Not much I can do. Forensics should prove otherwise. I hope so 'cause I sure know I wasn't speeding.'

'He never does,' Crystal and Noah piped in.

'I doubt you were either. Stay true to your story when the police — ' An abrupt loud knock startled her.

Noah strode to the door. He opened it, defiantly blocking the police. 'Take it easy on him. He's just suffered a heart attack, remember.'

'And one boy died,' the sergeant said, pushing past Noah. 'Derick Redman, you have the right to remain silent —'

A constable ushered Noah and Emma from the room. 'You're the wife?' he asked Crystal, allowing her to stay.

Noah paced the corridor raking his hand through his hair and staring at the ceiling as if it held an answer.

Emma sat on a lounge watching him. 'Why don't you sit? You look exhausted by all this.'

'I can't keep still when I'm stressed,' he admitted.

'What do you do to unwind then?'

***

'Exercise. Run. Climb. Surf. Paddle.' *Make love to beautiful women like you.*

'I do too. I love paddleboarding as the sun rises and the water shines smooth as a mirror.' She glanced wistfully out the window.

He sat next to her. 'You paddle well and sure look fit.' *More like beautiful and sexy.*

'Are you complimenting me, Noah Cooper? What happened to Mr Cranky Pants I met yesterday?' She grinned.

'Maybe.' He winked. 'Mr Cranky Pants redirected his irk at the police instead of the one person who's been trying to help him.'

'I am attempting to help.' She lay her hand on his knee.

It felt so damn good it made him envision it sliding further to his stiffening cock. *Woah up!* The goddam police were interrogating his dad, and he got a boner. He stood abruptly, grabbing a magazine as if he were going to read it to conceal his groin.

Emma's hand dropped. It lifted to cover the frown on her pretty face.

28

'Sorry, as I said, I need to keep moving.' Changing the subject, he asked, 'Why are they taking so long?' He slammed the magazine on the coffee table. Clenching and releasing his fists, he stormed, almost wearing a trench in the linoleum.

'Hopefully, your father convinces them, it's a mistake.'

'Nah. They're charging him. Shouldn't I get a lawyer? I'm not thinking straight.' He rubbed his bristling chin. Fishing his phone from his trousers, he asked Emma, 'Do divorce lawyers do other law?'

Emma ruffled through her bag. 'Maybe, but I do know a criminal lawyer.' She passed him a business card.

'Ivan Solver. You've got to be kidding. Really?' He raised his eyebrows.

'His name sounds comical, but he's authentic. I've designed some of his book covers. He writes surf crime as well.'

'There's such a thing?'

'I think he started it, but yeah.'

'I'll give him a call. I'm going to go. Waiting here is sending me stir-crazy. Do you need a lift?' Noah strode towards the hallway. Pushing her away was easier than admitting his growing dependence on her.

'I came here with you, didn't I? Jeez. I can Uber it or something if you need to do your thing.' She said it as she picked up her bag and placed her hands on her hips, glaring him down. *The girl has spunk.*

'Come on. I'll drop you off on my way home.' He curled his hand in a come-on gesture.

She smiled a happy, adorable grin with pearly white teeth and sweet lips with a shine of pink lip gloss. *Damn, that's a sexy smile.*

'I'll show you where I live.'

After driving for ten minutes, silently caught in their thoughts, Emma said, 'Turn here.'

Noah stole glances at her. Emma's luscious hair fell in waves down her slender shoulders. Glossy lips curled in a permanent smile. He couldn't help but grin being around someone so damn cheerful. Let alone the fact she was stunning. The denim shorts rode up high enough for him to see a delectable curve of bum cheek and tanned slender legs. Dainty fingers tapped on his dash in time to the radio music.

'You have access to the creek?' He asked.

'Yep. A shared pontoon, though I'm the only one who uses it regularly.'

'We have one on our property, though it's due for an overhaul after the last king tides. Something I've promised myself I'd do. Lucky a slice of sandy beach makes up for it.' A lot of conversation for him. Why did he talk so much to Emma?

29

He pulled up in front of a townhouse complex of eight. Her home at the end enabled a larger courtyard wrapping around the side. Emma stiffened in her seat, clutching the leather upholstery.

'Must take a while to get to where I paddle. You're kilometres up the creek, Noah.'

'A long paddle helps me unwind. It's a far cry from my last life.' An understatement, but why did he confess it? 'Looks a nice place.' Noah noticed a man sitting at the front stoop. Turning to Emma, he realised she stared at the man, taking a deep breath. 'Are you okay, Emma?'

'Yeah, sure. He's a friend. Been calling me all day, and I haven't had a chance to —' Her fingers shook on the door handle.

The man with dark hair and arrogant posture strode forward.

Hackles rose on Noah's neck. Something wasn't quite right though the guy waved a friendly hello. *Probably overreacting.* The green-eyed monster passed across his mind.

'Thanks, mate, for dropping her off,' the guy said in an overly cheerful voice.

'Sure. Any time.' Noah grit his teeth.

Emma nodded mutely, twisting her handbag strap in her arm. 'I can explain, Wade.'

'Sure, honey.' The man kissed Emma on the lips. Noah felt sick when she responded. He seethed, though he had no damn right. It wasn't as if he'd even asked her if she had a boyfriend.

Tucking her hair behind her ear, she said, 'I've been helping the man who was in the accident with the heart attack. This is his son.'

The man turned Emma around to face the townhouse, giving her a pat on the bum. It seemed demeaning to Noah. 'Go on up. I'll be with you after I thank your friend.'

Emma nodded, turning to give Noah a small wave.

The man approached the wound-down side window. 'Where have you been with her all day?' Wade asked, raising his voice.

Noah watched Emma over his shoulder, wondering what the go was between them. He thought it best not to aggravate a guy who seemed possessive. 'She's been helping my old man. Such a kind woman, Emma.' He knew it to be true. For some reason, he felt he needed to cover for her absence. 'She spent a long time at the police station giving her statement and afterwards went to the hospital to check on my Dad. She's been quite selfless. I think the accident impacted her and she thought to help. She could probably do with a shoulder to cry on after the last couple of days. It's been traumatic for her.'

'She has my shoulder for that.' He glared. 'So why did she get a lift home with you? I saw her car still at the police station.'

Weird the guy would check.

30

'She seemed shaken after the police interview. We were both going to the hospital. It appeared a good solution. She mentioned she needed to call you, but it was pretty full-on, and there wasn't much time.'

The man smiled, stepping away. 'Thanks, *mate*.' He said it sarcastically like he wasn't Noah's friend at all.

Noah raised his eyes to the rear-view mirror. Emma stood at a window partly covered by a curtain. She smiled a reassuring smile but even from that distance, he reckoned fear flashed in her eyes.

***

The wind wafted through the gum trees creating a rustling background to the birdlife swooping through the bushland near the creek. Noah trod carefully, taking photos with his mobile phone of skid marks and other evidence. A piece of plastic police tape flapped from a small shrub. He tore it off, swearing. Didn't the stupid police know, leaving a piece of plastic could kill wildlife living near the creek? He continued methodically scanning the area as he tucked it in his pocket.

Two adult ducks with six ducklings neared the creek bank from the water until all were waddling along the road. Noah noticed something shiny near one of the webbed feet. It would have to wait. Instead, he stepped to the street, holding a hand up to stop a passing car. The duck family safely made the other side.

The driver tooted and waved with a friendly smile and a thumbs-up. Noah waved back. He strolled to where he'd seen the thing the ducks unearthed in the sandy mud.

Leaning down on haunches, he dug under the footprint to reveal a small metal object. Washing it at the water's edge, he whistled. 'Bloody hell. Couldn't this cause some havoc!' Pressing the button, he tested the light beam. 'Damn!' A tiny ray of red light pointed across the fifty metres of creek, hitting a gum tree like a bullseye. Flicking it off, he stashed it in a small clip-seal bag, adding it to a canvas satchel heavy with other potential evidence.

Stepping back onto the road, he stood where the sedan began its skid. Figuring out where his father's ute came from, he strode over — glaring at where his father faced. He envisioned a beam of red light, hitting the dash. Sasha would have yapped and chased the light. His Dad was possibly either distracted by the dog or momentarily blinded. It seemed the police threw it in the creek, as Emma suggested. *The evidence will clear Dad.*

How could he prove it was at the crash site? Taking photos of where he found it may be enough? He couldn't chance to leave it where he found it. The military-grade laser could be buried further or washed out on the rising tide, and then there would be no evidence. *But who would believe him?*

Scratching his head as he paced, he tried to find a solution. Remembering the business card in his wallet, he fished his wallet out, opening it. First, his fingers found Emma's business card. He'd forgotten she gave it to him when she'd come by the house. At the time, he hadn't even bothered to read it. Sunny Graphic Design, Emma Jarvis, her phone number, email and website, much like the woman it was glossy and bright. It was easy to picture her as a creative type.

Slipping it back in the wallet, he found the lawyer's card and dialled the number. After speaking to Ivan Solver, Noah got back in his car. Crystal had picked up Hope. They would be at home getting dinner ready.

His father's hospitalisation and legal drama was a distraction from tomorrow. The mainstream school accepted Hope along with a teacher's aid. It wasn't a big deal for most kids, but for a little girl like Hope, the milestone was huge.

It made Noah sick to the stomach with worry. Kids could be cruel. The concern of someone bullying Hope in the classroom tore at him. He could not protect her at school.

Hope remained positive about it. She'd endured bullying when she went to speech therapy, tolerated it at physio and mostly ignored it. Going to proper school would help her progress, but it could also erode her confidence. His brave girl was willing to take the risk because all she wanted was to be normal.

But what is normal anyway? Just because Hope was born with one too many chromosomes didn't mean she wasn't normal. In his eyes, she was perfect and always would be.

His stomach churned. So many things swirled through his brain. He wanted to be around more for Hope. He needed to clear his father's name. At thirty-four, it felt time to settle down and give Hope a secure family home. And he felt he should protect Emma, though from what he wasn't sure. All three things were emotional, and he wasn't good with feelings. Give him something physical to do, and he'd nail it. Wrangle crocodiles, yep. Fly helicopters, yep. Run through dense bushland, yep. Track criminals in the wild, yep. Work with commandos, yep.

Deal with emotional issues? Nope, nope, nope!

Chapter 6

Steam hissed from the kettle as it whistled, breaking the morning silence. Emma clunked coffee mugs on the sink, slammed a couple of drawers for good measure and turned the stereo up. Still, Wade didn't rise from the bed.

It was Monday, and she needed to work. Catching a glimpse of the inviting creek, she sighed. Wade was making her miss a morning paddle. *Why not let the lazy sloth stay in bed?*

Running upstairs, she grabbed her swimsuit, sun visor, sunnies and sunscreen, all while Wade snored loudly in her bed. The sheets were half off him, exposing a muscular chest and bare hip flexor trailing to dark hair where the sheets covered his bundle. Wade's face with mouth part-open in a snore was model handsome. Why did the sight not arouse her as much as it should?

Without a doubt, if he woke, he would want sex. It was difficult enough to evade him last night with excuses of emotional exhaustion, but in the morning light, she doubted he'd take no for an answer. She tiptoed from the room, frowning over her shoulder at the man she wanted to love.

Another man broke into her thoughts, making her smile as she pushed her paddleboard off the narrow jetty into the creek.

Once the board was gliding along the smooth water, she relaxed her stance. Shaking her shoulders of tension, she dug the paddle in, sending the board up the creek. Birds whistled a symphony helping her mind clear. *Think of nothing except nature.* Breathing in tea tree, freshwater and damp sand, she sighed.

Rounding a bend, Noah paddled towards her. His broad shoulders rippled with lean muscles with every stroke. Her breath caught. If she were perfectly honest, she hoped he would be out on the creek. *Damn it, Mr Sizzling Hot.*

The little daughter Hope wasn't with him. He mostly brought her for the afternoon paddle, and the absence of Hope was a relief for some reason.

As usual, he was bare-chested and wore long boardshorts. Not bright patterned ones. They were understated navy and grey, sitting low on lean hips, revealing flexors and a defined six-pack. The tattoos along one arm weren't the intimidating bikie sort. Rather they were artworks of animals twisted together in stories she wanted to know. Everything about him was rugged but tidy. As if he tried to tame himself to be the best father he could be.

'Hey, you,' he said as he smoothly glided his paddleboard aside until their edges bumped. 'How's this hot morning?' He smiled with his face half shaded by a peaked cap.

Clearly, he had discarded the macho-man-don't-speak attitude. She almost fell off her board. 'Lovely but hot,' she said weakly, knees buckling. *But not as steamy as you.*

'I was hoping I'd see you on the morning paddle.'

Again, she almost toppled from the board. Steadying her feet, she asked, 'Why?' She was tongue-tied—a rare thing for her which had her rattled.

Spinning his board to face upstream, he said, 'Want to paddle this way while we talk?'

'Sure,' she said rather too quickly. Paddling beside Noah was her kind of bliss. He seemed to slow his usual speedy pace so she could keep up. A tiny thing but thoughtful.

***

Noah grinned to himself. Emma seemed lost for words. Maybe she liked him more than she let on. He watched her pretty face for a sign.

'So, what did you want to talk about?' She raised a perfect eyebrow.

Eyeing off her curves, he didn't bother averting his gaze. It was too damn difficult to stop. The skimpy orange swimsuit left little to his vivid imagination. He reigned in his lust, hoping she didn't notice the bulge in his boardshorts. Anyhow he had important things to say.

'Oh yeah. Sorry I was enjoying the view too much.' He watched her wobble on the board, but a small smile curved her delectable lips. 'As you were the first at the accident site, I wanted to show you something I found.' Pulling the laser light from his back pocket, he held his breath as she paddled closer.

Lifting her pretty eyes to his, she glided towards him. Her scent drifted intoxicatingly close. A frangipani fragrance of summer sunshine and shagging on the beach. *Jeez, mate, stick to your plan.* He pressed the button to show the light. 'I found it near the skid marks close to the waterline.'

As her fingers took it from his palm, they brushed like gold dust. Twitching his cheek, he tried to still his rampaging heart.

Flipping it, she pointed to a tree up creek, creating a pinpoint red dot on the trunk. 'This was the light your dad must have meant. Red, he said. How does it work if it's been in the water?' She passed it back. He felt an electric shock again.

Tucking it in his pocket, he turned sideways to paddle again. 'It's military-grade. Made to work in any environment. They're illegal. I guess the kids in the other car got it somehow. Possibly, they were skylarking with it. Not knowing the consequences. Silly buggers.'

'It's the reason the policeman threw it in the creek. They must have already known it was the boys' fault. It's so terrible Callum died — that was his name.'

Noah watched her bottom lip wobble. Drawing his board close to hers, he moved his paddle aside, placing a hand on her shoulder. 'It's okay to be upset about it. You've had a terrible shock.'

Nodding slowly, she brushed tears with her wrist, lifting her paddle, which clipped his legs. Not expecting the hit, he became unsteady. Wobbling on his board, he let go of her shoulder, but she bobbed too. A small dingy drove past, pushing a wake wave their way. Both toppled from their boards with a splash.

Rising to the surface, she grabbed a side of his board. Their wet arms brushed as he clutched it from the other side. Facing each other, they stared before bursting into laughter.

'That's better than crying,' she said with a wide grin, wavy light-brown, sun-streaked hair plastered to her damp face.

'You have a great smile.' *An understatement or what!* 'Hey, you've lost your sun visor.'

'Your cap too,' she said, tilting her head shyly.

The grin on his face must have looked corny as he took the compliment. His heart thudded, and deep in his gut, something stirred. An urgent need to kiss Emma filled him. His lips inched closer to hers.

She glanced at his hands, notably his ring, looking away, scanning the water. 'It will float. Oh, there it is. I'd better get my board.' She laughed, scooping the floating sun visor. Swimming to her vessel, she climbed aboard and lifted her paddle. 'Did you call the lawyer about this?'

Damn, he'd missed his moment.

Getting on his board, he answered her, 'Yeah. He thinks Dad will have a case now.' Droplets sprayed from his hair as he shook it. His tongue licked his lips where he would have tasted her if they'd kissed.

'Oh, that's great. Good luck with it. I've got to go. I have deadlines. Call me later if you want to nut it out further. You have my number?'

Glancing at his waterproof watch, he swore. 'Sorry — not swearing at you. I have to go too. This is one day I can't be late.' He turned to paddle but took one last longing look at her. 'I have your number memorised.'

Grinning, she made the 'call me' signal with pinkie and thumb to her ear before paddling towards the jetty.

Noah couldn't wipe the smile from his face, but something concerned him about the way she gazed towards her home. He paddled hard and fast up the creek. Hope would be wondering where he was. He needed the paddle to clear his head before he sent her off on the biggest day of her life so far. School sucked sometimes. If it were terrible for Hope, he'd pull her out, but he must let her try.

Ditching the board, he ran towards the main house where his parents lived. Running up the stairs two by two, he almost bumped into his mother standing on the deck.

'About time, son,' said Crystal with a frown.

'Sorry, Mum. Lost track of time. How's Hope?'

'Dressed and ready. I gave Hopey breakfast first so she wouldn't make a mess of her uniform.'

Kissing his mother on the cheek, he went inside. Hope grinned at him from the floor, where she tried to shove an old toy gorilla into a yellow backpack.

'Hey, sweetie. You ready for your big day?' Noah knelt beside her.

'Rilla won't fit.' Shoving at the soft toy, Hope scrunched her nose in concentration.

Gently Noah took the toy. 'You don't need Rilla to go to school.'

'What if I get scared?' Her eyes were downcast.

'Remember what I said about there being a special bench called Bench Buddy?'

'Yup. What if no one sits with me?'

Noah tried not to think of the possibility. 'Of course, someone will sit with you, beautiful girl.' Pulling her up by the hand, he bent down to hug her tight. For the millionth time, he pondered the deep love he felt for his precious child. The heartache he endured every time things went wrong in her life. How could he continue to protect her as she sought her independence in a world where not everyone was tolerant and kind?

'It's okay, Dad. I can do it.'

'I know you can.' They punched fists, linked pinkies in a heart shape and high-fived — their secret handshake.

Hope grinned as she struggled to get the heavy backpack over her shoulders. Noah watched her battle with a slight grin. She hated when he helped with the things she wanted to do independently. Finally, when she was ready, he took her hand.

'Let's get you to school,' Noah said as Crystal took her granddaughter in her arms.

'You should put a shirt on in case some of those single mums get the wrong idea,' Crystal said, passing him a neatly ironed t-shirt.

'Thank's, Mum.' He let go of Hope's hand to shrug the shirt on.

'Have fun, Hopey. I'll have fresh berry muffins for when you get home,' Crystal said playfully, flicking the tea towel draped over her shoulder.

'Thank you, Nanny.' Turning to Noah, Hope said, 'Can't hold my hand when we get near school.'

'I know. Just until we get to the end of the block.' Squeezing her fingers, he grinned down at her. The school was only two kilometres away, a pleasant stroll down country roads with white cockatoo cawing raucously overhead and the occasional wallaby feeding on the long bush grass.

Hope loved animals and possessed the kind of affinity with them most people didn't acquire. It ran in his family, his father, brother, and he had the gift too. Sometimes it seemed a curse because, though he could relate to animals on a deep level of understanding, figuring out people was far from easy.

A block from the school Hope dropped her hand to stroll in front of him. 'You can go,' she said, urging him away with a wave.

'Okay. Have a great day, Hope. Make sure you just be yourself.' *How could she be any other way?*

Watching her stroll towards the front gates, Noah wiped the corners of his eyes. A lump formed in his throat as he watched her approach girls about her age. Her wide smile engaged them, and they walked with her through the gates. He let out a breath he didn't even know he was holding.

***

Emma was startled when she found Wade still in the townhouse. Leaning an elbow on the dining table, he rested his head on one palm, reading the free local paper. It meant he'd gone out the front door and come back in. *Why didn't he keep on going?*

Smiling strangely, he folded the paper, pushing it aside to sip coffee.

'Wade. Don't you have work today?'

'No. I thought I'd spend the day with my girlfriend,' he said smirking. It made his handsome face look twisted and mean.

Baulking at his assumption, she poured a glass of water facing away from him. An unwashed cereal bowl sat in the sink. Gulping the water, she turned to face him. With a coffee cup to his lips and one hand pushing the paper aside, his eyes held a strange glare.

'Sorry. I have work to do. You should go.'

'I can just hang. You work from home anyway. I'll keep you company.'

'I don't like company while I work. I have to concentrate.'

Slamming his coffee cup on the table, he stood. In two steps, he held her arms back against the sink. 'You left this morning without something.'

Emma frowned. 'You're hurting me, Wade. Let me go.' Squirming made Wade tighten his grip on her wrists.

'If you follow me to fuckin' bed. We left things unfinished.' Hot coffee breath hit her face.

Emma opened her mouth, but no words came out. He took the opportunity to crush his lips on hers. Tilting her head sideways, she unlocked her lips and found her voice. 'Get off me this minute.' With no room to lift a knee to his groin, she spread her fingers, reaching towards a butter knife on the sink. As she considered stabbing him, he let go.

Shaking his head, so his fringe flopped over his eyes, he stepped back. 'Sorry, I don't know what came over me,' he said, seemingly mortified.

'Why?' she asked, baffled at his personality switch.

'I don't know. I — I haven't been in a relationship for a while.'

'That is no way to act,' she said, trying to hide the shake in her throat. She pointed to the hallway and front door.

'I know. Emma, I'd take it back. I would never hurt you.' Wade's voice whined.

'You did, and you're right. You never will, again. Get out now.'

He backed towards the door, reminding her of a skulking cat.

Lifting his hands in surrender, he said, 'I love you, Emma. We're great together. You can't fuckin' throw me out.'

'Wade, I'm not sure you even know what love is. You just showed me what it isn't.' She yelled, trying to avoid tears forming in her eyes. All the disappointment of another failed relationship assailed her. She took a deep breath and pointed at the door. 'Go.'

As he stepped to the porch, before she could shut the door, he said in a meek voice, 'I'll call you tonight when you've had time to calm down.'

Just like nothing happened.

'I am perfectly calm, Wade. Do not call me tonight — or ever.'

Wade's eyes held a glint of anger and strangeness. 'But you'll regret —'

The slamming door blocked his last words. She locked the door and ran to the back door to do the same. Collapsing on the chair Wade had sat on, she stared at the paper. With shaking hands, she grabbed pages of the publication, screwing them into a ball and throwing them against the kitchen cabinet.

The headline of the next page caught her attention. Speed-reading the article, worry replaced shudders of anger. The headline read *Longterm Valley Man Charged with Manslaughter*. The report said as she expected, given the discussion with Noah. Not reported was the vital evidence he found.

But it wasn't the article keeping her gazing at the page long after she'd read every word. It was a tiny column giving her chills. With wide eyes, she glanced at both doors, wondering for the first time in her life if she was safe.

Chapter 7

Hope chatted happily about the school day. 'We read, painted, played.'

Noah's heart expanded, knowing Hope not only coped with her first day of mainstream school but thrived.

'So, you really had fun, even the maths?' he asked, winking at his father sitting on the sofa with a blanket over his knees.

'I did, Daddy. I have friends. School work okay.'

'And you got Mrs Ruby. She's a lovely teacher. What about your teacher's aid?' asked Crystal, ruffling Hope's hair as she walked past with a cup of tea.

'Mr Hunt, nice,' said Hope pushing her empty plate aside.

Crystal handed Derick the tea.

After taking a sip, he rolled his eyes. 'What? No milk or sugar?'

'No. We need to look after that heart of yours, honey,' Crystal said, smiling fondly. She turned to Hope, 'Hope, you can have your usual hot chocolate, but Poppy drinks plain tea now.'

'Poor Poppy.' Hope frowned.

'Don't you side with Poppy against Nanny. You know who will win,' said Noah, taking his and Hope's dinner plate to the sink and rinsing them. 'Anyhow, I still don't know why you drink a hot drink in weather like this.' He wiped his sweaty brow with the back of his arm. 'Thanks for dinner, Mum. Come on, Hope, say goodnight, we'll head back to our place. You need an early night after a big day of school.'

'Okay, Daddy.' Rising slowly, Hope strolled over to cuddle Derick and Crystal.

Noah kissed Derick on the forehead. 'Look after yourself, Dad.'

'Oi! What's with the shows of affection. You becoming a sook?' Derick said with a wide grin.

'Just taking after my old man, I reckon.'

Crystal shook her head. 'You two should learn from the women in the family. Hugs and kisses make the world go around, don't they Hopey?'

Hope giggled, patting Sasha's head as she passed the dog lazing by the door. The half-asleep pet's tail whacked on the floorboards. Noah patted her lumpy stomach.

'Don't get up for us, Sasha.'

Hope raced ahead towards their smaller house at the front of the property. 'We say night to Stinky?' she asked. The sun was setting in a midsummer sky, casting amber light.

'Of course,' said Noah. 'She would expect it.'

As they rounded the garden bend towards a sandy goat track, they heard the low grumble of Stinky. In the grassy thicket, shadowed by tall gum trees and avocados, the pachyderm flapped its ears. It raised its trunk in a happy gesture. A low rumble welcomed them.

Hope strolled around the large animal's tree trunk sized legs. The elephant gently touched her shoulder with its trunk, kissing down her arm.

'Hey, old girl.' Noah reached to stroke the aging Indian Circus elephant's broad forehead.

Thirty years ago, she'd been a circus star, a small elephant only 1.9 metres high. It had been a cruel life, prodded, dressed up, painted and mistreated to do the tricks expected of her. The old wounds of grinding chains remained above her hooves where she'd been shackled. She lifted one for Noah to stroke.

He rubbed the area where the chain scarred the deepest. A wound festered if he didn't check it regularly. The gesture seemed to calm her from the pain. Probably horror of her past haunted her dreams, but at least the last years were calm and free.

Hope pulled at the sagging skin down Stinky's legs. 'Lost weight.'

'Yeah, Hope. She's getting old. We'll have to say goodbye to her one day.'

'Like Jumbo?' Hope frowned, cuddling into the elephant.

'Mmm. Come on, let's get you ready for bed.' Noah took his daughter's hand, leading her towards their small home. Glancing back at Stinky, he frowned, shaking his head.

Once Hope fell asleep after the fifth book he'd read, he took a beer from the fridge to sit outside. Relaxing into the plush outdoor sofa, he rested his feet on the coffee table with ankles crossed. *To Kendwa.* He raised the beer to the sky before taking a sip.

Noah felt his brother's spirit often—at least, he hoped he was around in some form or another.

When Noah hit rock bottom, Kendwa's voice echoed in his head, urging him to move forward – *live the life I never had the chance to live.*

Noah wasn't morbid, but sometimes he wished he found a soulmate instead of the wife he chose. Before Katie, he was happy, carefree, upbeat and indestructible. He'd fought the black dog of depression during his marriage.

Katie lived a wealthy, privileged upbringing where she always got what she wanted. Unfortunately, she chose Noah without their Down Syndrome daughter. When Katie threatened to institutionalise Hope, Noah shot through up north to hide Hope. He changed their names and took risky jobs to keep Hope safe.

He missed his brother, but his ex-wife ruined him. Yeah, his brother dying made him grieve. It sucked. It was sad, and it hurt him, but it hadn't nearly killed him like Katie's hate did.

After a couple more sips of beer, Noah pushed thoughts of Katie aside. It wasn't like he loved her anymore. Affection evaporated when she abandoned Hope. Though he didn't believe in hate, he felt as close as he could for Katie.

Hope deserved love. How could Katie abandon their little girl? Noah ensured Hope did not know of the rejection and kept her mother's hate a secret he would die with.

At least Katie clocked out of their lives for good. He rightly guessed she would find another sucker to marry. That's when she gave up the vendetta, signing away her rights as Hope's mother. It should have been sad for Noah, but it was a relief to know Hope would be safe finally.

It took six long years. A time where he suffered no contact with his sibling or parents in case Katie's people chased them down. Being unable to say goodbye to Kendwa killed a part of his heart. But now it was time Hope lived a normal, non-nomadic life.

Drinking down the rest of his beer, he put the empty bottle on the table. Settling lower into the couch, he placed his hands behind his head to appreciate the velvet sky and stars, listening to a frogmouth owl hoot.

The lights reminded him of Emma. A smile played on his lips as he imagined her watching the same perfect sky. He'd seen the joy in her face as she enjoyed the early mornings on the water and the beauty of nature when she smiled. She'd be sure to relish his enthusiasm for the moon and stars

Though he couldn't leave Hope, he wanted to drive to Emma's house. Realistically she'd probably reject him. After all, she had a boyfriend.

It didn't stop him fantasising about her or wishing she were free to be his. A rusty key twisted into his heart and opened it.

***

43

Emma rechecked each door and window, watching for shadows outside. She wasn't one to panic, but when Wade left, something strange flashed across his eyes, unsettling already jangled nerves.

Wade hadn't called or messaged since. The weird twisted feeling in her stomach kept her alert. She never ignored a sense like it. Wade seemed up to something.

Though she'd completed design jobs to their deadlines, she hadn't worked as efficiently as she usually did. Her mind shifted elsewhere, wondering if Wade would come back.

The article said he tended towards violence. It was weird to notice the story—a tiny paragraph. No picture, only his name. Enough information for her to know his real intention was to have control.

Boxfit and paddleboarding kept her strong, but she knew she was no match for a gym addict like Wade. Glancing at her knife block, she decided to hide the knives in case Wade broke in.

Sliding the largest from the block, she put it aside, ready to take to her bedroom and keep it under the bed.

The mobile phone rang, startling her from her thoughts. Tentatively she reached for it, relieved to see Noah's number.

'Hi,' she said, her heart hammering.

'Hey, it's Noah.'

'I know.' She smiled.

'I was just — thinking of you. I wanted to check you were okay. You seemed a little off when you paddled home this morning.'

How did he notice so much?

'I'm fine.' Even to her, it sounded unconvincing.

'Really. You don't seem like your usual bubbly self. What's up?'

Her hand shook as she held the phone to her ear. 'Nothing. Anyway, you don't really know me. I could be split personalities for all you know.'

'Doubt it. From what I've seen, you're kind, caring, spirited, fun —'

'Stop it. You don't know.'

She heard him take a deep breath.

'I want to.'

The words made her bottom lip tremble, so she bit it. It would be nice to be wrapped in Noah's big strong arms. As sweet as the image seemed, she didn't need a man. Not Wade and especially not a married man like Noah—no matter how tempting he was.

'It's not very honourable of you, Noah, considering you're a married man. What sort of morals do you think I have?' Tears slipped down her cheeks. She didn't bother wiping them away.

'Wait, you've got the wrong idea.'

'Ring on your left finger? Ring any bells?' Her voice rose as she clutched the phone tighter.

'The ring.' He chuckled. 'It's my commitment ring to Hope, my daughter. It's not a wedding ring. Remember at the hospital when I asked you if a divorce lawyer did criminal cases?'

Her mind ticked over. Holding a hand to her mouth, she took a deep breath. 'You're divorced?'

'Long time ago, in fact.'

Emma burst into tears. Holding the phone away until she found composure, she heard Noah swearing.

'I'm back.' Rubbing a tissue under her eyes, she waited for him to speak, half expecting him to hang up.

'Are you okay? What's wrong? I'm sorry I said anything. I know you have a boyfriend. I'm putting my foot in things, aren't I.'

'No boyfriend. It's the accident. I'm a mess since —' she paused, 'I guess it's an aftershock. I wish you could hold me.' There, she'd said it.

He was silent.

'Noah, are you there?'

'God, woman. I'd be there in a heartbeat to hold you, but Hope's asleep and —'

'I know. You're a dad first. I don't expect you to come to me.' She bit her bottom lip as she threw a tissue in the waste bin.

'I'm worried about you. What's made you upset? From what I know of you, you're so upbeat you're a breath of sunshine.'

'It's nothing. I'm being stupid. I'm fine, really. Just tired, I need to go to bed.' Rubbing her forehead, she knew sleep was unlikely. Wade wound her tighter than an occy-strap spring.

'It's that guy, isn't it? There's something weird with the bloke.'

Emma sucked in a breath. 'How could you know?' she blurted. Glancing at her window, she shrugged her shoulders to rid the chills.

'Come here, Emma.'

'To your house?'

'Why not?'

'We — I.'

'I'll hold you. That's all. With everything you've already done for my family, I owe you that.'

'You owe me nothing.'

'You said you wanted me to hold you. Well, I want you in my arms too.' He sounded so earnest. Though, so did Wade in the beginning.

She glanced at her front door. 'What if he's out there?'

'Shit. You're scared. I'm coming. I'll drop Hope at Mum's.'

'No, you can't do that. I'll come to yours.'

'You will?'

45

'Yes. I need to get out of my house. My garage is internal and remote control door, so I'll be fine.'

'Text me when you're leaving. I'll wait at the carport.'

'Okay. Bye.' She hung up, taking the stairs two at a time to her bedroom. Grabbing a backpack, she stuffed a nightgown and change of clothes in it along with a vanity bag, including her toothbrush.

Staring in the mirror as she brushed her unruly hair, wondering what got into her. She was running to Noah's house, not knowing why but realising she wanted to. With equal excitement and fear, she imagined hugging him or perhaps more. He'd only offered to hold her, but she doubted she could deny her attraction to him if they got close. She was too edgy to stay home, and Noah seemed to be a safe haven.

The drive to Noah's seemed agonisingly long. Each time headlights came behind her, she imagined Wade following her, ready to run her off the road. Gripping the wheel, she watched for the turn to Noah's family's property.

***

The car headlights dimmed as the engine cut. Emma stepped from her car. Reaching inside, she slung a bag over her shoulder before shutting the door and turning to Noah. Carport lights showed dark circles under her eyes, though she smiled at him.

Taking her bag, he wrapped her in a hug, kissing the top of her head. He felt her head rest on his chest, where his heart expanded. Squeezing her to him, he said, 'Here's the hug I promised. I hope it helps.'

'It does.' She sighed.

She snuggled into him further. It felt so damn good. 'Let's get you inside.'

Emma followed him into the small house. Her eyes shone, and she smiled, touching a picture on the kitchen fridge with a finger. It was covered in Hope's drawings, some with the words 'I love you, Daddy'.

'I know it's a mess, but I can't take anything down she gives me,' Noah said with a smile.

'It's beautiful. My sister's son, my nephew, does the same.' She laughed. 'Though he no longer writes 'I love Daddy or Mummy' he's too grown up for that.' She inspected Hope's artwork twisting her head.

Noah tried to keep his distance, but all he wanted was to take her in his arms again. The fact she endured something upsetting kept him in check. First, he needed to know what was going on.

'How old is your nephew?'

'Nine but going on nineteen.'

46

'Hope is ten, going on nine.'

'Oh, I'm sorry. I didn't mean — Hope's an adorable little girl.'

'I know you didn't. I'm being realistic. She'll never reach the same milestones, but she's doing well. Being one year behind works for her. She's started mainstream school. Though she has a teacher's aid, she's in regular classes. I'm really proud.'

'And so you should be.' She stepped away from the fridge towards him.

The sweet look on her face made him hope for a kiss.

Slowly she reached a small hand to his face cupping his cheek. He twitched his jaw, feeling the warmth from her touch, wishing he'd shaved.

'You're a beautiful man,' she said, her breath on his skin. Her lips brushed his cheek. He was ready to turn, take those lips in his, hunger for her tongue, release some of his pent up desire, but she stepped away. 'I should explain why I got so nervous. Seriously, I don't even know why I am here. I feel foolish.'

His heart sank. 'Do you want a wine or beer? I don't have much. There's a bottle of Cassegrain.' He lifted the bottle to show her.

He had an uneasy feeling about her boyfriend, and it wasn't going away without a good explanation. What the hell was going on with them?

Chapter 8

'Sure, wine, please. It's a hot night, might settle my nerves. I'm not normally like this, you know. I cope with things. I'm independent. It's just there's something odd going on with Wade, and I have an unmistakable feeling of dread like something horrible may happen. Have you ever had that?'

'More than a few times,' he said, passing her a glass of wine. 'Let's go out on the deck. If you don't mind sharing the sofa, otherwise I can bring a dining chair out.'

OMG, he is so thoughtful. 'The sofa is fine.'

Noah let her sit first. When he sat next to her, their shoulders and thighs touched, sending sparks. Tingles flooded her body, making her incapable of speech. Instead, she sipped the wine.

'I want to know what's going on with this guy. I know you're a strong woman and can look after yourself, but he's a bit of a weirdo. Well, isn't he?'

Squirming to reach her back pocket, she pulled a newspaper clipping from it and passed it to Noah. He lifted his gorgeous eyes to hers before taking it. Lost in their fathomless depths, she'd never seen such kindness in one look. Was there a hint of more? She wasn't sure.

His Adam's apple bobbed, and he took a deep breath.

'Oh, sorry, not the story about your Dad. The tiny column.' She leaned over him, pointing to the spot, leaving her hand over his thigh. *Subtle or what?*

'Shit. The mongrel. Five other women? He's got problems. What were your last words to him?'

'Not to come back ever.'

'Good.'

'But before I shut my front door, he looked at me weirdly. Like with hate but also with the knowledge he knew something I didn't. It seemed a mocking look but evil. You know?'

'Mmmm.' Noah scrunched the newspaper into a ball with his fist. 'Oops. Did you want this back?'

'Nope.'

Tossing it on the coffee table, he turned to her, lifting her chin. Her insides quivered. 'Let's make a plan to get him out of your life for good. He might intimidate women with his good looks before showing his true motives. He's a spineless coward. I've seen his type before. Probably doesn't even have any male friends.'

As Noah's thick kissable lips moved, she tried to concentrate. It was important to listen to him about Wade but having Noah so close was like sitting on a firecracker. 'I — um. No, I don't think so. In the month I've never met any.'

'See. That's odd. I have plenty of mates.'

'You're normal. He's not.'

He dropped her chin. Lifting his beer, he took a swig. 'What if we pretended to be a couple? I think he may be daunted by me and back off and leave you alone.'

Brazenly she stroked her hand along his thigh, under his t-shirt on his washboard stomach, trailed it up to his chest, leaving it there, feeling his heart pound double time. 'I don't think we need to pretend,' she said huskily.

Taking her hand, he pressed it to his chest, turning to her. 'I couldn't, anyway.' He crushed his lips to hers.

Her lips met his with equal desire, parting, inviting him further. Their tongues danced deeper, their passion building with each taste. His hands roamed down her backside, cupping her bottom, lifting her slightly, so her groin jutted against his hip.

Her cervix flipped. She was so wet and hot for Noah, she could barely contain her need, but he pulled away.

Standing quickly, he almost toppled her wine glass but steadied it in time. He raked a hand through his hair. 'I'm sorry. I offered you a safe place, and I'm doing this to you. You're so beautiful I got carried away.'

She stood. 'This is not about me coming to safety. I could have gone anywhere. My mum lives around the corner, for Christ's sake. I chose to come to you, Noah. I want to be with you.'

'But I don't want to take advantage of your fragile state.'

She clenched her fists into balls. 'Fragile. Don't call me that. I admitted a bit of vulnerability, and you call me fragile.' One thing she hated was men treating her like a china doll.

He grabbed her hands, drawing her to him. 'I didn't mean it like that, Emma. Bad choice of words. I was only trying to do the right thing. Maybe you'd regret it. Perhaps you think you need me, but you're just angry with him. Maybe we are rushing it.'

'Maybe you talk too much.' Her lips met his.

Stopping the kiss with a grin, he said, 'I don't usually talk at all. It's something about you.' He kissed her back.

50

'Mmmm, on a guess, I'd say you're backing off a little bit because of your past too. Don't try and talk yourself out of this.'

Silencing her with a deeper kiss, he picked her up and carried her inside to his bedroom. Dropping her softly on the bed, he said, 'This is not a one night stand. I don't do them anymore.'

'Okay,' she said, gulping as he shrugged his t-shirt over his shoulders, revealing muscles, scars and tattoos. He was an incredibly interesting, sexy man.

'Will you strip so I can watch you bit by beautiful bit?' he asked with lust flashing across his magnificent eyes.

Stunned by his poetic words, she mutely undid her blouse button by button, slipping it from her shoulders to reveal her bra.

His muscles twitched, and the bulge in his boardshorts enlarged.

Enjoying the way his eyes shone at her, she shimmied her shorts down her hips. Unhooking the bra, she smiled at him as she revealed one breast at a time.

He groaned, stepping closer, never taking his eyes from her. Ripping at the velcro of his boardshorts, he let them fall to the floor. The underwear did nothing to hide his massive erection.

She stepped from her panties. Noah crushed his body to hers, lifting her onto the bed to lie below him. Cupping her face, he kissed her deeply before trailing his lips down her neck. He kissed places she didn't know were so sensitive; behind her ears, on her lobes, the dip in her shoulder, the curve of her breast before sucking her nipple with little nips and tantalising licks.

Bucking her hips to him, she tried to contain her enthusiasm as every nerve ending sparked with fire. As his tongue explored, so did his fingers. They trailed down her stomach, across her hips to below. A finger brushed her clitoris, fueling more fire. It entered her smoothly, mixing with her wetness to dip in and out, pushing her senses into overdrive. Thrusting towards his finger wasn't enough. She clutched his thick hair as his face drew down between her legs. He glanced up at her with lust in his eyes before diving in to taste her. His warm tongue roamed languidly, inching around her wet entrance before pushing in and out as his fingers rubbed her budding clitoris. It sent her into a frenzy of delirious ecstasy, building to shudders of release and pleasure.

Wiping his mouth, he grinned. It was something that may have embarrassed her with previous lovers, but it was natural and raw with him.

'Oh, my,' she sighed. 'I can't believe —'

'I've imagined doing this to you, watching you enjoy it.'

'I definitely did that,' she said as another tremor hit her cervix.

'I have to find a condom.' He strolled to the bathroom and brushed his teeth, coming back with a couple of foils of condoms. He opened

51

one and rolled the rubber over his massive cock as she watched in awe. Though he sated her, the desire built again at the thought of him inside her.

Turning her on her side, he cuddled her from behind. His cock prodded her hip as if homing in on her core. She twisted to face him so they could kiss deeply. She tasted his mint breath and wanted more. Groping his cock, she stroked the smooth hot rod, feeling it grow larger with her touch. Cupping his hairy balls made him breathe hard on her shoulder as she relished the weight and hairiness. Guiding his cock into her felt as exquisite as his mouth, but a more significant connection meant her heart filled with more than lust. With each thrust, she felt a part of her heart join him — one more brick in her wall fell.

They rolled so she could straddle him, letting her hair fall over his chest. His hands held her hips to increase the pressure. Their eyes locked as their bodies rocked. Limbs entwined, hips ground, and liquids joined. In and out, she felt every fluid motion building to a crescendo. Harder, faster, sweatier until she came again as he began to grunt his orgasm.

She collapsed on top of him. With his fingertips, he wiped sweaty hair away from her face, kissing her. 'Wow,' he said. His heart thumped rapidly.

Kissing his chest and lips, she sighed. For a while, neither spoke. They clung together, letting what they did slowly sink in as their bodies returned to a normal rhythm.

He rose first, tossing the condom, locking his bedroom door and pulling the sheets over them. She snuggled her body into his in a perfect fit. 'Should we shower?' she asked languidly.

'Probably, but I'm kinda enjoying the smell of you on my sheets. We'll get up early and wash before Hope wakes up.'

'I guess I'd better go before she does. It might be confusing for her.'

Kissing her, he grinned before saying. 'I feel like I'm in a dream.'

'Why?' She raised her head on one elbow.

'You're my fantasy. A feisty, strong, kind, compassionate, creative, beautiful woman. Oh, and did I say friggin awesome in bed?'

Playfully she smacked him. 'You were pretty amazing yourself. I have never felt like this — ever.'

'Surely a beautiful girl like you has been loved before?'

'If you count self-indulgent males out for their own satisfaction first. I guess not.'

'You've been dating the wrong blokes.'

An understatement considering Wade.

'Until now.'

Noah grinned. 'Are we dating?' It was his turn to rest his hand on his elbow, but his other hand trailed over her hip.

'Maybe,' she said smiling — *happiest happy dance ever.*

Sealing it, they kissed intensely, creating further passion in already sated bodies.

His hands slid between her legs.

***

Miles away from their bliss Wade plotted his vengeance.

Chapter 9

Noah woke before dawn. He felt the warmth of Emma on his arm and her breath on his chest. Her eyelashes rested on smooth cheeks as her sweet lips curved into a smile. She snuggled closer, and her pretty eyes fluttered open.

'Morning, beautiful,' he said, kissing her lips.

'Hey, you.' She smiled the sweetest smile. 'I could stay here forever, but I guess I'd better get going before Hope wakes up.'

His erection pressed into her thigh. *God, he wanted her again.*

'Well, someone is definitely awake.' She laughed. 'No, really. I don't want to upset Hope.'

'Just a quickie?' he asked before taking her lips in his. 'Waking up beside you is sweet torture, you know that?'

'I doubt you have a quickie in you considering what we did last night. Was it four times?'

His bruised lips were testament to it, but it didn't stop him from wanting her all over again. He teased his cock between her legs, feeling her welcoming dampness. 'At least four, but who's counting?' His cock found its way feeling the intoxicating tight hold deep inside her. She pushed her hips into his. His need for her intensified if that were even possible.

'Oh, Noah, this is—oooh.' He loved the way she talked while they did it.

He couldn't speak as they thrust together, glued as one. Cupping the back of Emma's head, he kissed her with eyes wide open to watch her face as she built to a climax. Her legs tightened around him as she threw her head back, closing her eyes as tremors hit. She let out a high-pitched grunt before resting her head on his shoulder. He smiled at her abandonment.

Rolling her onto her back, he finished his orgasm, shuddering into her only seconds later. Without putting his weight on her, he pulled her to him, so they lay side by side again. Each panted heavily before smiling and laughing.

He spoke first. 'Wow! What a way to greet a day.'

'I'll say, but seriously, Mr Cooper, I have to get my butt out of here.' She slipped the sheet over her breasts as her eyes scanned the floor for her clothes.

Taking the sheet from her, he ran a finger over one nipple. 'Fuck, you're gorgeous in the daylight.'

She raised her eyebrows as she reached for her bra and hooked it on. 'So, I'm not so gorgeous during the night?' With her panties half pulled up, she shot him a look. He wasn't sure what it meant, but it was sexy as hell.

'Emma, you are dazzling every single second but particularly when you're undressing or dressing in front of me.' He placed his arms behind his head, admiring her.

'Thank you.' She smiled. 'Where the hell are my shorts?' Slipping the t-shirt over her head, she began pacing the room, picking up cushions, moving his clothes aside and finally found her denim shorts. As she rode them over her hips, she glanced at the empty condom packet. 'You were prepared this morning.'

He shrugged. 'I had hoped is all. You can never be too prepared when it comes to protection. More for you than me.'

'You don't have a disease, do you?' Her face didn't change, so it seemed obvious it didn't bother her.

'No way. I haven't even had sex in—shit, let's not go there.' He raked a hand through his hair and got off the bed.

Her beautiful eyes brazenly trailed over his body, and for the first time in a long time, he felt shy. It was an odd way to feel after everything they enjoye —all the hot, sweaty sex.

'Look, you go have your shower. I'll sneak out and have one at home,' she said, raking her fingers through bed-tangled hair.

'No. What about dumb ass?'

'You mean Wade?'

'What other dumb asses do you know?' His jaw twitched, and he held his temper at the man in check.

'Maybe a few,' she said laughing, 'but he's king dumb ass.'

'He could be waiting around your house.'

'Nah, he hasn't even—' She picked up her phone and scrolled through the messages. Her pretty face paled.

Still naked, he took the phone from her. 'Jeeesus! How many messages. Any voice?' He handed the phone back so he could dress.

'I don't want to listen to them, but there's eight. All from Wade.'

'Well, that's decided. Go to your car and drive up Currumbin Creek Road and stop at the duck pond. I'll meet you and follow you in my car. I'll have to wake Hope and take her over to Mum's for breakfast.'

Lifting a hand, she waved him off. 'I can't disrupt your life. I'll have to handle him myself. I'll call my mum. She can meet me there.'

'No way. I'm sure your mother is as competent as you, but two women may be no match for a guy with his history. I am coming.'

'My step-dad will be with her.'

Walking her to her car, he pleaded. 'Let me follow you. Did you mean what we said last night?'

'We said a lot last night.'

'The couple bit?' He held his breath.

'I wasn't sure if you would mean it the next day.'

'Of course, I meant it!'

She leaned into him for a hug and kissed his lips. 'Thank goodness for that.'

'So officially,' he said, grinning, 'it means boyfriends must ensure girlfriend's safety.

She raised her hands in defeat. 'Okay, you're right, and I would feel better if you came.'

'And it's about time we scared off the bully, and he went crawling back to the hole he climbed out of.'

'I hope he does.'

'You have no idea of my power of persuasion.' He kissed her cheek, relieved she agreed. 'I won't be long. Hey, can we take a photo? I want to remember the day we got together forever.'

She grinned, passing him her phone. 'Your arms are longer.'

He took a few shots, handed back her phone and kissed her, reluctantly letting go so she could get in her car.

'I'll meet you at the duck ponds,' she said.

***

Emma watched the rear-view mirror to make sure Noah's car stayed behind her when she pulled into her driveway. She didn't bother with the remote door; instead waited until Noah stood at her driver's side before getting out.

Wade wasn't sitting at her front porch as she expected, but no relief came with the realisation. He would be somewhere. She was sure of it.

'Let's go inside. I'll check it out first. You stay behind me,' said Noah, taking control.

For the first time in her life, she felt happy for a man to be the one to call the shots. There was something reliable and safe about Noah.

As they made their way through the townhouse, Emma jumped at small sounds, and goosebumps ran along her arms. Noah reached back to give her a reassuring touch now and then.

He'd been thorough even finding the knife under her bed. Holding it up to her, he asked, 'Self-protection?'

'I only put it there the other day when I got spooked by the article.'

'Good, keep it there. I think you should change your locks too.' He led her downstairs. 'In case he got a key cut. In the meanwhile, stay locked up. Until I've had a word with him, you won't be able to go on the deck or paddleboard, okay? I'll come back this arvo to check on you.'

Tearing at her hair with both hands, she paced the kitchen, nearly wearing out the tiles. 'This is ridiculous. A prisoner in my own home. I hate that guy.'

He kissed her forehead. 'It's only temporary. I promise we'll sort it out.' His nostrils flared as he smelt a masculine aroma.

'What?'

'Nothing. An odd smell. Probably nothing. I'll call you when I drop Hope at school and after I take Dad to his lawyer.'

'I can't smell anything except air freshener and the creek. How could you?' On tiptoes, she kissed him. 'Go to Hope. I'm fine.'

'I spent a lot of time up north tracking animals and people. I'm pretty good at sniffing out things.'

She saw him off at the door, waving like a love-struck teenager as he drove away. She bounced around in a bubble of happiness despite the fear of what Wade might or might not do. After locking the door, she strode to her office to check her inbox and begin work.

Fear prickled the back of her neck when she heard the back door to the deck slide open. Noah wouldn't come that way. Grabbing a metal ruler off her desk, she edged around the hallway. Her heart, so recently hammering for love, now boomed with fear. Biting her bottom lip, she glanced up the hall. Turning to the sound of a front door knock, she jumped in fright. On hearing Noah's voice, she ran to it to unlock it.

'I couldn't leave. I have an odd feeling he's here,' said Noah.

The fear in her eyes must have alerted him as he stepped in front of her. In a warning voice, he called, 'Wade, show yourself.' He whispered to her, 'Did you hear him inside?'

Whispering back, 'The backslider.' She held tightly to the back of his t-shirt.

On hearing the door himself, Noah bolted forward. When Emma reached them, Noah held Wade's shirt. His face drew close to Wade's, restrained anger flashing across his eyes. She half expected him to let out a snarl. With his right hand bunched into a threatening fist, Noah said, 'What're you doing sneaking into my girlfriend's house, you lowlife?'

Wade paled. His hazel eyes reddened with fear. 'I — I'm her boyfriend.'

Noah shook him. Though Wade was a tall man, he was no match for Noah's animal strength of bunched muscle and power. Wade may have worked out in gyms, but Emma doubted he had any real advantage compared to life-hardened Noah.

'Let's get this straight, mate. You are not Emma's boyfriend. You're not even her friend. If you ever set foot near her again, you'll have me to answer to.'

Wade squirmed, trying to release Noah's hold on him by slapping his hands. 'I didn't realise. I thought she was—.' He dropped his head.

Emma wanted to yell at Wade, to tell him how much he intimidated her with calls and texts and threats he would never give up on them.

'Well, she's taken.' Noah released him, but his jaw twitched. His stance was wide and provocative. 'You understand now?'

Wade glanced at Emma with a pleading disappointment in his narrowed eyes. 'I need to hear it from her.' He attempted to move past Noah, who blocked him with a broad shoulder.

Noah nodded at Emma.

Gulping back the first spiteful words filling her mouth, she said instead, 'I've told you it's over, Wade. You haven't been listening. Please leave me alone. Give me the key you used to get in through the back and any others you have cut. Which, by the way, is not normal behaviour.' She held out her hand.

Reluctantly, Wade slowly passed a key.

'Any more?' Noah asked.

Wade reached in his back pocket, handing Emma a copy of her front door key.

'Jeezus,' she said as she took them.

'Fuck,' said Noah.

Wade smirked.

Noah grabbed Wade's arm, twisting it behind his back until he yelped. Pushing him, he marched him to the front door. 'Go out that door and never come back. Don't come near the street. Don't follow her car. Keep the fuck away, mate, or there will be hell to pay.'

Wade skulked away as if he had a tail between his legs. With his hands deep in his trouser pockets, he didn't look back.

Noah slammed the door. Emma fell into his outstretched arms.

'It's over. He won't be back. I'll come and stay the night, not because I think he could but because I can't bear to see you so wound up.' He smiled. 'And, I kinda like the idea of staying over as your boyfriend.'

'I like that idea too.' She hugged him close. 'Thank you. What made you come back in?'

'A hunch. I've worked in some extreme situations, and you get to a point you have to follow your hunches or get killed.'

'Come on. It wasn't so extreme.' She raised her eyebrows.

'You have no idea what I've done in my life, but we'll have plenty of time to talk.'

She raised her eyebrows. 'You have me intrigued.'

Chapter 10

Ali kissed Emma's cheek as she walked in the door. 'You look happy,' she said. 'Things have improved with Wade?'

'No, Mum. That's over. I need a cup of tea, and I'll explain.' There seemed a bounce to her step and a glow on her cheeks.

Ali raised her eyebrows, relieved. She thought something about Wade didn't add up. It was confusing because Emma wore the look of love on her dreamy face. It wasn't something Ali could remember seeing in a long time.

In the kitchen, she poured teas. They strolled out on the deck to drink them as they talked, swiping at flies in the summer heat.

'So, how are Jessy and Ben going in Africa?' Emma asked, a small smile still playing on her lips.

'They had a few hurdles with the resort, but everything's smoothed over now. They employed some great staff. Jess said they should be home by next week.'

'Oh, that's good. I'm sure Jai would be missing them, especially now school is back.'

'Yeah, he pretends he isn't, but Nana and Grandad can't replace Mum and Dad. Shaun and I aren't quite hip enough for him. Shaun even tried riding the skateboard but kept falling off. God, I thought he'd break something. I don't think I've ever seen so many eye-rolls from Jai.'

They both laughed.

Ali tapped her daughter's hand. 'So, stop keeping me in suspense. What's going on with you?'

Emma grinned with a shiny look to her eyes. 'I'm in love.'

'If it's not tinder-date Wade—' She grimaced.

'Muuuuumm!'

'Well, that's what Jessy calls him.'

'I'll never Tinder again. I didn't feel comfortable with it, but you know the girls, they can be persuasive. Just because they're all married with kids, they constantly try to hook me up.'

'That bad with Wade?'

'You can't even imagine.' Emma waved her hand as if brushing away a fly. 'You know the old guy from the accident?'

'The one you saw at the hospital?'

'Yeah, well, his son, Noah and I are a couple.'

The way she said Noah made Ali smile.

'Mmmm.'

'Noah. He's—amazing, gorgeous, kind, strong. God, Mum, I didn't know I could feel like this.' She placed her cup of tea down and held her heart.

'Wow. Wonderful. I'm so happy for you, darling.'

'Oh, I have a photo. We took one this morning when —'

'This morning, huh!' Ali raised her eyebrows but smiled, enjoying seeing her daughter squirm with happy embarrassment.

'Well yeah, umm. See. How gorgeous is he?'

Ali took the phone. She tried not to drop it as she stared at the man Emma loved. Struggling to keep the shake out of her voice and her fingers, she handed the phone back. 'Oh, darling, you look so happy. How did this happen?' Luckily Emma remained in a love bubble; she did not notice Ali's discomfort.

'I've seen him paddleboarding for months. You know, Mr Sizzling Hot, I mentioned. I thought he was married. It turns out Noah divorced a long time ago. He has a sweet daughter who lives with him. I don't know his full story yet, but I've never felt more connected. You know?'

'I get it. Like Shaun and me.' She couldn't say Kendwa's name. It was unfair to Shaun, but it was also strange considering what she'd seen in the photo of Emma and Noah. 'What's his daughter like? You haven't been in a relationship for years. A child could complicate things.' *I'll say.*

'Don't be a fuddy-duddy, Mum. Look at Jessy and Ben. They adopted Jai, and no one seeing them as a family would ever know it. They love him to the moon and back.'

'I know. It's only not what I pictured for you. Baggage can be difficult.'

'Mum, seriously. I can't believe you said that. How could you call Hope baggage?'

'It's not what I meant.' Ali felt sick. She held a secret that could impact everyone she loved. Even if Emma adored Noah, if it was even his name, she couldn't. It would destroy Jessy.

Emma stood. 'I thought you'd be happy for me.'

'Of course, I am. I'm being practical. I have to be I'm your mum.'

'Hope has Down Syndrome too. Are you going to try and convince me it's all too difficult? I can't believe you, Mum. You're the kindest, most tolerant person I know. What's with you today? Thanks for bursting my bubble of happiness.' Emma stormed off.

Ali placed her head in her hands. She should have known it would come to this at some point. Honouring Kendwa's wishes would eventually come at a price. It was a long time since she opened the box with his papers and things for Jai. She couldn't even remember what his requests were but one she knew off-by heart; if Toby ever returned alive, Jai could choose to live with his uncle, and Toby would inherit half of the safari business.

Not only Jai's happiness at stake so was the livelihood of their family. She would protect with all her might.

When she heard the door slam and Emma's car drive away, Ali walked to the study with her head down, glad Shaun remained at work. It would be awful explaining to him Kendwa may impact their lives again. Shaun had been tolerant about it in the past. Now the company he meticulously helped her build could be in jeopardy as well as their beloved grandson. She doubted he'd be open-minded this time.

She took a deep breath before opening the timber box with Kendwa's last belongings. Rifling through the contents, she found the envelope containing the photos. Kendwa's wedding to Sharli. *God, they were a beautiful couple.* Jai, a tiny baby in Sharli's arms not long before her tragic death. And the one making Ali gasp. Kendwa with his arm around his best mate Toby. The same man in Emma's photo, younger, but the resemblance was undeniable. Ali's heart sank.

Placing the photos down, she searched the box for paperwork. Lifting some from the box, she filtered through them until she found the one she needed. A DNA test was taken after the birth of Toby's daughter, confirming Kendwa and Toby were brothers. Ali read further down where it said Toby's birth name. She couldn't remember, but she knew Noah was Toby. Noah. Noah Ely. Kendwa's brother.

Ali slapped the photos off the desk. Tears streamed down her cheeks. Placing her head in her hands, she tried to think of what she should do. Shaking her head, she rubbed her temple before moving the box closer to go through the other contents.

Kendwa made it clear if Toby ever resurfaced, he must have a relationship with Jai. It seemed fair enough in the beginning when they brought Jai home from Africa after Kendwa died. Now with Jai adopted by her daughter Jessy it no longer seemed reasonable or feasible. Toby, or Noah, was Jai's blood relative. He had every right to fight to have him. *And what if he did?* It would shatter them.

Ali woke to Shaun shaking her shoulder.

'Honey, what are you doing here in the dark?' Shaun asked, concern etched on his handsome face.

Bewildered, she looked around. Seeing the paperwork in front of her, she burst into tears.

Shaun knelt in front of her chair, taking her in his arms. 'What's happened?'

She pointed to the photo of Kendwa and Toby on the floor. 'He's surfaced.'

Shaun picked up the photo, standing to switch on the office light. 'Kendwa's brother? How do you know?'

'Emma's friggin' fallen in love with him, and he's gone back to being called Noah, his birth name.'

'Shit!'

'I know.'

Shaun paced, scratching thick greying hair. 'Right. It can't be all bad. He could be a nice guy and only wants to know Jai, not interfere in our lives.'

'What if he doesn't? He could ask Jai to live with him. They are blood. Jai's only blood.'

'We'll work it out.'

'Shaun, it's not simple. I've gone through the paperwork. Noah is entitled to half the business too.'

'Moon Under Safaris? The company we've built up?' He shook his head. 'No. That can't happen.' He smacked his hand on the desk, startling Ali.

'What do we do?' Ali's bottom lip trembled.

'How into him does Emma seem?'

'Ridiculously, hopelessly in love.' She rubbed her temple. *Just like me with Kendwa.*

'Shit!' Shaun paced, nearly wearing holes in the carpet. 'Right, so let's act like we know nothing. Maybe we need to see a lawyer about what percentage we've put into the company to grow it post Kendwa. I think Jai's safe. It's been over five years, and Jess and Ben adopted Jai legally. Noah would have trouble contesting even if he's blood-related.'

'Are you sure?'

'Yeah. Pretty sure. Okay, let's calm down and be rational. We'll keep Jai away from meeting him until we figure things out.'

'So, that's our plan?'

'Can you think of a better one?'

'No. Shaun?'

'Yeah, sweetheart.'

'Emma looked the happiest I've ever seen her. I can't take love from her.'

'We have to protect her too. Can you recap me on the whole story? I must admit I was so in love with you when we got together I didn't take in the Kendwa story because I was jealous of the guy.'

'You want it all?'

'Yep. I guess it's about time.'

64

'Right. So, I met Kendwa in Africa after Roger and I split.'

'Roger's an idiot. Go on.'

'When Kendwa died in Zanzibar, he'd already put things in place for Jai in case something happened to him. He knew the poachers were after him because of his stance on wildlife and trying to build sustainable safaris and resorts. Since his family and Sharli's either passed away or couldn't care for Jai, he hoped Jai could go back to Australia.'

'That's right. He was born here and holds an Australian passport.'

'I didn't realise at the time even if Kendwa didn't meet me he wanted Jai in Australia because he figured it might be a way he could find his uncle.'

'So why did Toby, I mean Noah go AWOL?'

'It's a sad story too. Toby married and had a baby girl with Down's Syndrome. The mother rejected the baby but wanted to take her from Toby and institutionalise her. She was spiteful and of old Miami money, which bankrolled her malice. About a year before I met Kendwa, Toby changed his name and took Hope up north so his ex-wife could not find them. He worked wrangling crocodiles like he'd done with Kendwa but found a niche teaching commandos how to negotiate croc-infested waters. They helped him stay hidden. Even Kendwa couldn't stay in contact with him in case the ex-wife's people tracked them north. I have no idea what happened afterwards, but it's obvious the ex-wife no longer threatens him, and he's back in town. Our town, Currumbin, can you believe it?'

'It's too close for comfort. How did you know so much about this guy if he was in hiding?'

'I asked Metra why I hadn't known about him. She told me bits over the years. I sometimes think only enough to stop me from asking questions but deep down, I was happy for him to never be found.'

'Did he know where Jai went?'

'No, because Kendwa died when Toby remained in hiding. Even Metra couldn't find him to tell him about Kendwa. Toby's adoptive parents were informed, but even they couldn't reach Toby. Everyone thought he died or didn't want to be found.'

'It's like he's come back from the dead more than once.'

'I know. I wish he'd stayed away.' Ali glanced at Shaun, feeling embraced by his love and support.

'I don't think Emma would see it that way.'

'No. I guess not. I think I'll phone Metra and get her advice before we make any decisions. Maybe she's contacted Noah.'

'That's a good idea. Is she back in Zanzibar or London?'

'Zanzibar, setting up a new shelter for women and their children. She's such an amazing woman. I'm due for a catch up with her anyway. I'll call her tomorrow.'

'We'll figure it out.'

'You keep saying so.'

'Trust me sweetheart. Have I failed you yet?'

Never. And she had to believe Shaun never would.

Chapter 11

Wade smirked as he listened to Emma's voice on the audio device. The new guy was a problem he didn't need. Grinding his teeth was like chalk on a chalkboard. He frowned, lifting his eyes to the storm clouds rolling in from the west outside his open window. Slamming it shut, he then sat at his desk, resting one elbow with his chin on his hand, pondering his next move.

Usually, the women did anything he asked, especially when he threatened them. The violence even turned some on. At least it's what he told himself. So what if the last one took him to court for breaking her jaw. The damn bitch deserved it big time.

Emma had been different. She seemed to see through him as if she could see under his mask of normality.

It seemed best to be more vigilant. They'd incarcerate him next time if he weren't careful. The thought made him cringe. Good looking men like him didn't last long in places like jail. He hated men even more than he despised women. Men intimidated him and he didn't understand why. After all, he did everything he could to look good and be a man's man, but they didn't get him. Making friends was awkward. In the end, he'd given up on them all together and filled the void with the women he could control.

Flicking the device's switch silenced the room void of personality —a desk, a single bed and small TV. He never bought the women around anyway, always preferring to scope their homes. That way, he could install the bugs and cameras.

'Fucking boyfriend,' he swore as he flipped the laptop open. He would have gotten a camera set up in the ceiling of her bedroom if only he'd found another day or two. No chance now, but at least he installed the one at the front door, so he could see who came and went. He hadn't given up because of the fuckwit turning up. The guy intimidated him for sure. A way of getting him out of the picture had to exist.

Flipping open his laptop, he played the latest video. The fuckwit stepped inside after Emma opened the door. The man kept her safely behind him as they moved out of frame. No images were broadcast for a few minutes because the camera only took in the front porch, doorway and part of the hall. He came into frame from the hallway. Even with the fuzzy image, he could see how much he cringed as fuckwit pushed him from behind.

Screwing his eyes into narrow squints, he pretended he did the pushing. When the door slammed shut, he was the one taking Emma in his arms and kissing her. He rubbed his stiffening cock. Emma was feistier than most of the women — a challenge he'd never discovered. He couldn't wait to see her beaten and bleeding with her legs spread wide as he thrust into her. If her eyes pleaded for him to stop, he'd only go harder.

A loud bang at the door made him slap the laptop shut and shift his nuts and cock.

'What ya doin' in there, son?'

'Nothing, Mum. Is dinner ready?'

'Yeh ain't getting' any unless ya do chores. Bet, ya haven't even got the board for me neither. Ya, good fa nuthin.'

He rolled his eyes but stood and opened the door. 'Sorry, Mum.' He kissed his mother on the lips the way she liked. A wicked smile spread across her ugly face. He felt her hand on his bum. At least he was too old to take her crap anymore or her unwanted attention. He only stayed because he had nowhere else to go. No family, no friends, just his deranged alcoholic mother.

His dad shot through about the time he discovered what a freak he'd married. Wade guessed he'd been about five, but he could no longer remember. Sometimes his mind did that, forgot stuff and got muddled around.

'You can be a good boy when you want to.' She giggled in the weird way she did when the second bottle of wine sat empty on the dining table.

He ate quickly, not wanting to spend more time with her than necessary.

She barely touched her crappy meal, spaghetti on toast again. Lifting the wine glass to her lips, she appraised him with unfocused eyes. 'Wanna watch tele with me?' she asked in a long slur. It seemed crazy she used to be stunning. The photo on the sideboard held testament to it, but he couldn't remember it either. The alcohol drained the prettiness out of her a long time ago.

'No, Mum, I have work to do.'

Waving the wine glass in the air, she stood wobbly. 'Watch by meself then.' She sat on the lounge with a sulky face making her look even uglier. Cheap white wine spilled on the rug.

Clearing the table, he went to the sink and did the dishes, as expected. In moments his mother lay back with her mouth wide open, snoring. He picked up the wine glass from the floor, wiped at the stain and rinsed the glass. With a last withering look, he strode to his room with a protein shake in his hand. His muscles wouldn't build with spaghetti on toast.

Returning to the laptop, he watched a new video. Screwing his fist, he punched the desk. The fuckwit was back kissing his girl. He rubbed his fingers as he watched them hold hands and walk out of frame. *Seriously, who did that?* He'd rather tie up hands than hold them.

An idea formed in his mind before evaporating. He smacked his hand on his head, hating when his brain fogged. *What was it? Revenge?* If he couldn't get Emma back, he could hurt her in other ways. He just had to figure out how when his mind was less chaotic.

Chapter 12

Loving the warm feel of Noah's hand in hers, Emma lead him to the kitchen with her fingers clinging to his. 'Tell me how your father went at the solicitor. Do you want a cold drink?'

'Water's fine, thanks. No, first tell me if your day was okay. You didn't hear from Wade at all?' He spun her around to face him.

'Not a peep from Wade.' She watched his Adam's apple bob at the mention of Wade's name.

'Good.' He kissed her as she leaned towards the fridge.

She passed him a glass of icy water, placing one on the dining table in front of her as she sat across from him.

'Thanks,' he said, before kissing her for a long, tantalising kiss over their glasses.

Taking a deep breath when they finished, she was lost, staring into his eyes. Gently, she stroked his bristled jaw. 'You look tired.'

'A lot's going on, but I'm fine. Did you get any work done?'

'Not as much as usual. My mind's all over the place. It's good though, I've put Wade out of my thoughts. It's you I can't stop thinking about. In a good way.' She smiled.

'I like the idea.' He took her hand, twisting it around gently, stroking her palm. 'Dad's solicitor is switched on. When I showed him the laser light, he asked if I could find out where they were sold. We can narrow down who may have purchased it.'

'How will you do that? Couldn't it be from anywhere?'

'It could, even the dark web. From my time up north, I have connections who know how to find these things. I'm going to ring a commando mate tonight and see what I can dig up.'

'So if you can prove one of the boys bought it, your father can be cleared?'

'In theory, but there's still a long way to go.'

Squeezing his hand, she softened her eyes. 'He'll be cleared. I can feel it.'

'I hope you're right. Hell, Emma when you look at me so, all I can think about is exploring your beautiful body and kissing your lips — and everywhere.'

'When you stare at me, making love to you consumes my mind and other parts.' Her lips parted slightly, inviting another kiss. He rubbed his thumb along the bottom lip before crushing his lips to hers.

They fumbled with clothing. Noah lifted her skirt and slipped her panties down. Emma unbuttoning his trousers, helping his cock escape his underwear.

He cupped her bottom to sit her on the table. She spread her legs wide, putting her arms around him to draw him near. He played with her entrance making her throb with desire. His fingers poked into her wetness as his cock edged closer. She grabbed hold of it stroking smoothly and leading him to her. He entered slowly, but she could tell by his scrunched eyes and rapid heartbeat how little control remained. Planting her feet on the table, she thrust her hips to him until he entered her fully.

Puffing on her neck, he kissed the hollow of her throat and whispered, 'Emma, I can't hold back.'

'I don't want you to,' she assured him with more grinding pressure and her hand trailing down the t-shirt still on his back, feeling the muscles underneath. Everything intensified to a frenzy of lovemaking. Every nerve ending tingled with her ensuing orgasm. She wanted him deep inside her, filling her and connecting in an abandonment she never felt before. *Love with a heavy dose of lust.*

Words of endearment slipped across her tongue but didn't find their way out as she shuddered beneath him in exquisite pleasure. Her climax hit like a tremoring earthquake. Noah came soon after, grunting and groaning his pleasure before collapsing over her with her arms pinned back.

He must have realised his weight was on her because he propped himself up and pulled her with him to sit. He shifted her thighs to straddle his hips and though he panted, kissed her deeply. Resting his head on her shoulder, he sighed. She felt his hammering heart blend with hers as she ran her hands through his thick hair.

As they were dressing, he said, 'I didn't want this, Emma.'

Pausing as she straightened her skirt, she eyed him as her heart constricted like a python wrapped around her lungs. 'You didn't want what?' she asked, her voice squeaking.

Wrapping her in his arms, he kissed the top of her head. 'Love, Emma. It terrifies me.'

She glanced at him, feeling his muscles tense. 'It doesn't need to. I'm scared too.'

Kissing her lips, he relaxed his stance and stroked her shoulders. 'I've been burned. I'm not sure if I'm good with relationships anymore. You might not like me as much if you knew everything about me.' He curled a stray hair behind her ear.

'I think I would. We all have a past, Noah. I've got plenty of annoying habits that might drive you totally batty.'

He raised an eyebrow. 'Oh, like the one where you bite your bottom lip when you're trying not to cry. Or the one where you do this cute little grunt when you orgasm.'

She realised he was teasing. What she was surprised by was how he observed her so well. 'You're such a funny guy. I do not grunt.' She giggled.

'You do and don't ever stop doing it.'

'I'm pretty sure I've only ever done so with you.'

'Let's order in some food before the thunderstorm outside really hits and later we'll test my theory in your bedroom.' He winked as thunder boomed in the distance.

***

After a Chinese meal and plenty of foreplay, they made love again in her bed.

Afterwards, listening to the rain on the roof, they snuggled facing each other, smiling because of another delightful copulation. *And yes, she did grunt.*

'I love the smell of rain,' she said, letting out a breath.

'I enjoy the sound better on a tin roof like mine. The tiles muffle the music.'

'I guess so. It probably means I should stay at your place next time it rains.' She stroked his chest, trying to make out the tattoos on the left side of his chest and left arm in the dark room. A ceiling fan thumped above them like a beating heart.

'I don't know where this is going, but I'm feeling damn good about it.'

'Me too, but let's go slow.'

He grinned and raised his eyebrows. 'Too late for slow.'

'I guess, but we haven't known each other long.'

'It already feels like forever. I think I'd like it to be.'

'I — um,' she didn't know what to say. Her independence was hard-fought. She'd bought the townhouse outright when her last flatmate got married, and she gave up on finding anyone else to pay half the rent. Working from home meant she could claim some tax breaks to help make her mortgage affordable, but often keeping afloat was a struggle. 'Forever is a long time.'

73

'Chill, babe. I only meant it would be nice. It's not practical. Besides, I know Hope's probably daunting for you.'

'Oh, Noah. Don't think that. Hope is a beautiful little girl. You couldn't think I'm shallow enough to let her syndrome bother me. It doesn't at all. In fact, she's a bonus.'

'Really? Most women don't see her in such a nice way.'

'I'm not most women.'

Kissing her, he mumbled, 'I sure know that.'

'It's more about me than you and Hope. Give me some time. I've been single for yonks. Why else would I have taken a chance on a loser like Wade?' She dropped her eyes.

'You're entitled to a lapse in judgement. Don't be too hard on yourself about him. He's good at his game; otherwise, he would have already been locked up. I'm not putting pressure on you, Emma. I love you, but I don't even know if I am ready for more yet. Plus some things I need to tell you about my past. It's complicated.'

'You have to tell me some things. Like, what do you do for a job?'

With a wide grin, he answered, 'I'm a vet specialising in reptiles. I work at the Croc Enclosure at Currumbin Sanctuary, but I'm on a break while Hope settles in school.'

'Oh, wow. Sounds super cool and dangerous.'

'I used to wrangle crocs all over the world, so these guys are a breeze. I'm not in any danger.'

'That's good.' She kissed him. 'It also explains the tattoo on your bicep and shoulder. She traced it with her finger.

'I used to be into the dangerous side of things, but Hope changed it all. I went back to it for a while — to support her, but I can chill a little now and be the father she needs.'

'Why did you pause? It seems like there's more to it.'

'There is, but it's for another day.'

'You're a man of mystery,' she said, kissing his chest and sucking on one nipple.

'A man of sweet misery while you're doing that.' He groaned. 'I need some sleep so I can get up early enough for Hope.'

'I know, sorry.' She gave a cheeky smile and raised an eyebrow.

'You're not sorry one bit, Emma Jarvis.' Noah kissed her deeply. When he pulled away, he gazed at her with a serious expression. 'Emma, just promise me one thing.'

'What's that?'

'Don't break my heart and please don't break Hope's either.'

'That's two things.'

'We're two joined as one.'

Chapter 13

Crystal watched her granddaughter study homework books with her nose scrunched in concentration. 'Do you need some help, Hope?'

'I can't do maths. I forget how teacher told me do it.' Holding her pencil in the air, she tapped it on her head.

'Can't help you with maths, sweetie, but I'll get you a cookie instead. That might make you think better.'

Hope giggled. 'Nanny, cookies can't make you think.'

'These might be Magical Nanny Cookies.' Crystal passed Hope a cookie topped with gold and silver sprinkles.

'Sure, look magic,' Hope said, holding the cookie to study it.

Footfalls sounded on the deck. Noah opened the front screen door, trying not to grin like a love-struck fool.

'You've been gone for three days on and off, Noah. What's going on with you? You never leave Hope this long.'

Noah turned away, from his mother, kissing Hope on the forehead and paying attention to her homework. 'How's maths going, Hopey? Sorry, Daddy's been a bit busy with work.'

'Bollocks!' swore Crystal with her arms folded over her chest where her apron still held cookie crumbs.

'Mum, just leave it will you.'

'Leave what, Noah?'

'Not in front of Hope.'

Hope raised her eyes to the adults. She exaggeratedly rolled them, used to the adults talking over the top of her.

Crystal followed Noah onto the front deck. He turned to her with a grin. 'I've met someone, Mum.' He lifted a hand. 'Now don't go making a fuss about it. It's early days. Let me enjoy it in peace without your full-blown interrogation about her.'

Crystal smiled. 'I haven't seen a love-struck look on your face in a long time, son. I don't suppose it's the lovely lady who saved your father.'

'How would you know?' Noah shook his head. 'It's annoying when you go all psychic on me.'

'Nothing clairvoyant about it. You talk about Emma all the time. And I saw you kissing her goodbye early the other morning. You brought Hope here and made up a wild story about an emergency at the sanctuary with one of the crocs getting loose.'

'I — um.' He hated lying to his mother. There were enough secrets over the years. 'Emma had a problem. I wanted to help her. It was urgent.'

Crystal laughed. 'Don't get defensive. I'm happy for you. She seems like a lovely girl, and it's about time you settled down again.'

Hugging him to her, she made him feel like a little boy again, but she was much smaller than him now. 'Mum, it's hard to let someone in after what Katie did.' He frowned.

She placed a hand on his cheek. 'Noah, Katie was a mistake you made when you were young. You've had years to find out there are nice women about. Plenty more than the Katie's of this world. You know damn well you're better off without a snobby, selfish, little bitch in your life.'

'Mum, ease up.'

'I know you never badmouth her because of Hope, but I can't help myself sometimes. That stupid woman makes me so damn mad.' She rubbed at the crumbs on her apron, not meeting his eyes.

'Me too. But we have to protect Hope at all costs. It worries some that I'll never find the someone who can love Hope too. Emma says Hope doesn't bother her, but what if she's only saying it? I couldn't bear it if Hope got attached and —'

'Well, I guess at some point you have to take a chance. If you feel this girl has what it takes, give her the benefit of the doubt. She's already shown kindness and compassion to your dad.'

Changing the subject, Noah asked, 'So how's Dad?'

'Doc says he's doing fine. Better than expected, really. Reckons he'll live until he's 100 now. God help me.' She laughed, shaking her head. 'Anyway, don't change the subject. I want to know more about Emma.'

'Nothing left to tell, Mum.' He walked back inside to help Hope with the homework spread over the dining table.

Hope completed her last sum and shut her school book. 'Daddy, I have a friend.'

'I thought you made lots of friends at school.'

'This one is a boy. I have some girls, but Lion, a boy.'

'Lion, now that's a cool name.'

Noah scratched his head, pondering why a boy would befriend his daughter. His heart squeezed, hoping the friendship was genuine.

'Like's animal.'

76

'He likes animals?'

'Yes.'

'That's what you've got in common?'

'Yes. He said he has a cheetah.'

'Really?' Noah raised his eyebrows. The kid must have some imagination.

'Can he visit Stinky one day, Dad?'

Noah ruffled her hair. 'Sweetie, you know we don't let anyone see Stinky. She's not in the circus anymore. She needs to feel safe and not have strangers come poking at her.'

'But Lion love animals.'

'I'm sure he does, but those are the rules, Hopey.'

'Okay, Dad.' With her bottom lip quivering, she put her pencil case and school books in her school bag, slung it over her shoulder, walking to the door.

'Looks like we're going back to our place, Mum. Tell Dad I'm glad he's on the mend when he wakes up.'

Crystal passed Hope a cookie. 'It's for after your dinner, Hope.'

'Thank you, Nanny.' Hope sat on the step petting, Sasha. The dog eagerly enjoyed the attention, licking Hope's ear.

Noah turned to Crystal. 'Let's not mention I have a girlfriend for a bit. Hope will be confused.'

'Your call, son. I am happy for you; you know that don't you?'

Shrugging his shoulders, he grinned. 'I'm kinda pleased for myself too. It's ages since I felt so keen to be around someone. She's different, kinda unguarded and cheerful.'

'A stunning looking girl too.'

'That fact certainly doesn't hurt.' He winked.

***

Emma was too excited to contain her joy about dating Noah. Yeah, she'd told her mum, but it wasn't the same as revealing it to her twin. She only hoped her sister would have internet connection in Kenya.

Waiting for the delay, Emma tapped her computer screen. A blurry picture of her sister cleared slightly. In a jagged voice, Jessy asked, 'What's up? You know I'll be home next week.'

'I know. I'm too excited. I have to share.' Emma paused for effect like a drum roll. 'I have a boyfriend.'

'God, not Wade. Seriously, sis. I think he's a creep.' Jessy's face moved closer to the screen, her eyes wide. Ben, her husband, yelled his agreement in the background out of the screen view. Jessy turned, flashing him a smile.

'Well, your radar was spot on.'

'Great. What a relief. Who then?'

'His name is Noah Cooper. Here.' Flicking her phone, she showed Jessy the picture of Noah.

'Oooh, he's a hottie. God, you look so happy, Emm. Tell me. How did you meet?

They waited for the signal to clear and their faces to refocus.

'Sorry, reception as usual aint great over here,' said Jessy, shaking her head.

'Noah's eyes are a striking sort of green but with blue flecks. He's all sculptured muscle like a smaller version of Thor. Seriously, OMG naked he's a god.'

'Sex?'

'The sex is — none of your business.' She sighed.

'So you've had sex?'

Emma ignored her. 'He's gentle and kind. I feel so protected around him. The sweetest side to him is when he is with his little daughter.'

'God, it makes me miss Jai. You've never dated anyone with a kid. How old is she?'

'A year older but she is Down Syndrome. She's totally adorable, though.'

'Oh, wow. A lot to process. Wife?'

'Divorced. He hasn't said much, but I think she abandoned them.'

'Shit. What a bitch!'

'I guess. They divorced years ago. Hope's only a tiny little girl. I don't get how a mother could leave. Hope's syndrome doesn't bother me. Be a boring old world if we were all the same. She's sweet.'

'Noah sounds like your perfect match. You are a sucker for kids and animals. What went wrong with Wade? Or shouldn't I ask?'

'I'll tell you when you get home. Let's only say you were totally right.'

'Ha, ha. You never admit when I'm right.'

'I just did. Anyway, Noah blew him out of the NRL stadium. Like Mum says, 'you'll know when you meet the one'. I guess I have now.' She grinned ridiculously at her sister who gave her the thumbs up.

They talked about Jessy and Ben missing Jai and how he was coping with them away. When they'd said their goodbyes and Jessy faded from the screen, Emma glanced at the photo on her phone, still smiling. Noah, her everything in such a small space of time.

Pressing the send button so the photo could go to her email, she put the phone aside and waited for her inbox to ping. When it did, she downloaded the photo, enlarged it and sent it to an inkjet colour printer. It spat out the photo on glossy paper. Grabbing it, she stared at the enlargement and the joy on their faces.

As Emma walked down the hall holding the photo, she got the feeling someone watched her. It was silent when she looked around. With wide eyes, she glanced out her windows but didn't shake the feeling. Sticking the picture on the fridge with a magnet made her smile. It would be nice to stare at Noah when he wasn't here.

A chill spiked goosebumps down her arms but she ignored it.

Noah called earlier to say he needed some time with Hope. It was understandable. Though of course, she missed him already. The time alone would be good for her. She needed to catch up with housework, finish an urgent graphic design job and pay some bills, things she wouldn't do with Noah as a distraction.

Walking out the front to check her mailbox, she glanced around checking shadows. Surely there was no need to be so vigilant. Wade wouldn't come back after Noah's threats. It was annoying to feel jumpy anyway. It wasn't like her.

When she returned to the front door, she realised the porch globe had a crack and hole. She wondered how it could have happened. Probably a stray stone from the Jim's Mowing man as he freshened the lawn during the morning. She'd have to call into the hardware store to get a new one at some point.

Stepping inside and shutting the door, again she felt like someone watched her. She placed the mail on the side table. Lifting her fingers, she rubbed her temple on both sides. Perhaps her brain needed to digest both the accident and Wade's weird behaviour. *It was normal, right!* Nothing else could happen, and she needed to trust Noah sufficiently scared Wade.

Wishing Noah could be with her seemed selfish, but she couldn't deny the feeling was there. Turning her attention to housework instead, she cleaned every corner of her home. Thoughts returned to Noah and replayed their lovemaking, making her womb contract. Whistles escaped pursed lips as she worked with a languid smile.

When she returned to the kitchen, while she stared at the photo of him, Noah rang.

'Hey, babe.'

'Hi, Noah. I was thinking of you.'

'I like that. Were you undressing for bed yet?'

The time showed 9.30 pm on her watch. 'I lost track of time. No, I'm not near bed yet.'

'What's kept you up?'

'Housework.'

'At this hour.'

'Well, since you've been around I've done none of it.' She laughed. 'My house was a shambles.'

'Ah. So, about your clothes. What are you wearing?' His voice held a deep, sensual tone.

'Nothing sexy. An old pink t-shirt and cut-off white shorts.'

'Mmmmm. That's done it.'

'What?'

'Mention of cut-off shorts and I can picture your ass poking out and the shape of your hips, your legs, between them.'

Grinning, she joined his game. 'And what do you wear Mr Cooper?'

'Just loose boxers and a boner 'cause I'm talking to my girl.'

'You don't.' She giggled, feeling the wetness between her thighs.

'I do. But it's only for you, babe.'

Putting her phone on loudspeaker, she unzipped her shorts, sliding them down her thighs along with her panties. Luckily she already drew shut her curtains and blinds otherwise she'd be scared Wade was watching. 'I'm taking my shorts and panties off. I shaved for you too. It's nice and smooth, and you'll have a good view.'

'Ahhh, you're killing me, babe.'

'I'm trying.' She teased in a sweet voice. 'Do you still have a boner?'

'Yep. One that could poke your eye out. I reckon I could rest weight on it and it wouldn't go down.' He chuckled.

Her imagination pictured his massive hard-on. 'Oh.'

'Are you heading up to your room?'

'Yes, but as I go, I'm stripping off my t-shirt. My bra is pink lace and makes my boobs look bigger, pushing my cleavage.'

'Niiiice!'

She strode to the front door, double-checking the lock before going up the stairs. 'I'm in my room. I've taken off my bra. Do you still have your boxers on?'

'Nope. It's so hot in here I don't even have a sheet. Jeezus, I want you so much, Emma.'

'I need you too. I want all of you. I want your cock in my mouth so I can pleasure you the way you have me. I'm sucking my thumb.' She giggled.

'Fuck. You're seriously killing me. I've got to hang up before I explode. Love you.'

'Goodnight, Noah.' The words again were on the tip of her tongue. She felt terrible he said them, but she couldn't say them back — yet.

Their sexy talk made her clitoris throb. Her fingers stroked the bud imagining it was Noah's tongue. She placed a finger inside, feeling the wetness his words and smooth sexy voice stirred. Pleasuring herself for minutes, she came swiftly.

Words slipped from her tongue. 'I love you, Noah.'

Chapter 14

Shaun glanced up from his computer screen as Ali walked into their combined office at Moon Under Safaris, the business Ali inherited from Kendwa, Jai's deceased father. Shaun took his spectacles off to have a better look at her. 'Hey, what's up, sweetheart?'

With a thud, she placed a stack of papers on his desk. 'This,' she pointed to the pile, 'is how complicated things are going to get.' She sighed as she rubbed her temple.

'In what way?' He flipped the first couple of pages. 'Oh, I see. Shit!'

'More than shit. It's a whole sewerage plant.' Ali frowned. 'What now?'

'What did the solicitor say after he gave you this pile of crap?' Shaun stood to wrap Ali in his arms.

Resting her head on his chest, she glanced at him with moist eyes. 'That Jessy and Ben will have some rights because of the way they have raised Jai for six years.

'That's good.'

'The business is Toby's, Noah's, whatever he calls himself,' she said with a rise to her voice, 'it's his. All our hard work will go to him and Jai.'

'We always knew the business would be Jai's one day.'

'Yes, in ten years when he turns eighteen. Close to when we'd be ready to retire. Not now!' Ali balled her fists on Shaun's chest.

Shaun clutched her restless hands. 'It's okay. This Noah guy sounds decent. Maybe we should talk to him. We might be making mountains out of molehills.'

'I always wanted to respect Kendwa's wishes. He lost so much, his parents and his wife. It's only fair we cared for his son and his legacy. I can deal with the business loss, but it's Jai I can't lose. Jessy won't let Noah take her beloved son. It would kill her.'

'Come on. Let's go home and talk about it all rationally.'

'I am rational. I'm trying to see the whole picture. Shaun, I'm terrified. It feels like my world is crumbling. And Emma's happiness is at stake too. Every angle I look at it is like dominoes falling.'

***

Emma leant in the back seat to retrieve the box of chocolates and flowers. Balancing them on her hip, she closed the car door and walked down her mother's pathway.

Shaun answered the door. 'Hi, Emma. What's the occasion?'

'Jessy wanted me to thank you and Mum. She worried that by the time they got home from the airport, the chocolates would melt, and the flowers end up droopy. Plus she didn't want to stop to get them on her way because she's too keen to cuddle Jai.'

'It's understandable.' He laughed, letting her inside. 'Jess has never been away from her baby this long. Must be hard.'

'Ben seems the worst. He's such a softy when it comes to Jai.'

'Right from the moment he lay eyes on the cute kid he as a goner. Jai's lucky to have them.' The corner of his mouth twitched. Emma wondered why he'd said it like that, kind of sad or something. 'Your mum's in the kitchen. I'm going back to the study to do the bookkeeping.'

'You're always working even when you're home, Shaun. You need to ease up.' She patted his shoulder. 'We all appreciate how much you do for mum, you know.'

'Thanks,' he said, shrugging his shoulders and strolling down the hall.

Something seemed up with him, and Emma needed to find out what.

'Hey, sweet girl,' said Ali.

'These are from Jess and Ben, to say thank you for having Jai for so long.' She strolled around the kitchen bench to where her mum stood at the sink peeling potatoes.

'Well, that's not necessary. We love Jai.'

Emma noticed her mother's eyes seemed moist when she kissed her cheek, handing over the gifts.

'I'll put the flowers in a vase.' Ali took a while to find a vase, fill it and place the flowers in.

Emma waited as Ali fussed a bit more, averting her gaze. 'Righto, Mum. Spit it out. What's up with you and Shaun? Have you had a fight or something?'

'No.'

'Stupid question. You two never fight. So what is it? Has someone died or something?' Emma asked earnestly, taking her mother's clammy hand.

'No, no. Don't you worry. It's business stuff. A small hurdle the company will have to get over. Nothing for you to concern yourself with.'

'Must be more than a molehill for it to rattle Shaun too.' Emma pulled up a barstool across the kitchen bench from Ali.

'It will be fine. Do you want a cuppa?' Emma knew her mother was only changing the subject.

'No, it's too hot for tea. Got any juice? Or water's fine.'

Cheetah, Jai's dog, charged through the doggy door to leap upon Emma's legs. 'Hey, boy.' She rubbed the eager dogs head. 'Get down. Be a good boy.'

The dog obeyed by laying in front of her feet with its head on its paws. The tail thumped on the shiny ceramic tiles.

Ali opened the fridge. Again taking longer than usual to find juice and pour two glasses. Her hands shook.

'It's not something that's happened to Jess and Ben in Africa, is it?' Emma asked her heart, skipping a beat. 'I only spoke to Jess two days ago.'

'No, they're fine. Please stop worrying. Anyway, how are you and T — Noah going?'

'Great. Awesome. Brilliant.' Emma smiled over her glass of orange juice.

'That good?'

'Even when I'm not with him, I feel a connection. He phones before I go to bed.' Emma felt her cheeks warm at the thought of Noah's sexy phone calls. 'Anyway, it's so easy and natural. Everything about him blends with me. We haven't even had a proper date, dining out or anything yet, but it doesn't matter I'm smitten.' She grinned.

'I can tell.' Ali smiled, but it didn't seem to reach her eyes. Emma watched her mother closely. It wasn't a look of grief, more like fear. Her eyes darted around, and she kept twisting the rings on her fingers.

Trying to cheer her mum up, she said, 'I'll bring him around to meet you.'

Ali bumped her glass. Orange juice spread across the kitchen bench. 'Oh, I'm so clumsy today.' She reached for a damp cloth.

'Mum, seriously, what's up? This isn't like you.'

'I told you, Emma,' her mother's voice was stern, 'you do not need to worry yourself with it. Can you be happy for once? Enjoy your time with Noah.'

Why did it come out like her time with Noah would be short-lived? *What the hell's going on?*

'I — I, okay. I'll drop it. But you know how I didn't want to talk about the accident at first, but you said you'd always listen, well I'm here for you too, Mum. Whatever is bothering you when you're ready to talk, call me.'

The phone ringing made Ali jump. Ali insisted on keeping a landline even though everyone else Emma knew relied on a mobile and internet connection. Ali picked up the phone.

'Yes, I'm Lion's carer. His parents are overseas. I'm his grandmother. Is he okay?' Ali raised her eyebrows at Emma but didn't look too concerned. 'Sure. Hold on.' She covered the phone with her hand and whispered to Emma. 'Can you pick him up? Shaun and I have a Skype meeting in half an hour?'

Emma nodded.

'Yes. My daughter will arrive in about 15 minutes. Give me the address.' She scribbled it down. 'He's been no trouble? Oh, great. Thank you so much.' She hung up the phone and folded the piece of paper.

Emma took the note. 'Where's Jai? What happened? Is he okay?'

'Yes, he's fine. Apparently, he didn't go to Eliah's place and instead snuck over to a girl's.' Ali shook her head but smiled. 'That was the mother, I think. Anyway, she said he is so polite and most welcome, but she didn't have a car to take him home and wanted to make sure he was safe.'

'Okay. I'll put this in my iMaps and go and get him. He can come over and stay at mine tonight.' Emma held the folded note in the air.

'You're not seeing Noah?'

'He had to do something for his dad. We'll catch up tomorrow. We plan to go to lunch at The Boat Shed.'

'Oh, that's lovely.' Ali kissed Emma on the cheek before resting her hand there. 'I'll talk to you about what's going on some other time. Now isn't it.'

'Sure, mum. Love you.'

'Love you too.'

***

Emma unfolded the paper in the car. A smile spread across her face. Noah's house. *What was Jai doing there?* He went to the same school as Hope. Maybe he'd been hanging out with her. Emma grinned broader, thinking of Jai being such a caring boy. He was the kind of kid who befriended people easily.

On driving into Noah's families property, Emma felt the butterflies swarm in her stomach. *What would Noah think of her free-spirited nephew?*

84

Strolling to the main house, she noticed Crystal through the open windows. Crystal opened the door wide. 'Now this is a surprise. You're Lion's aunty?'

'I am.' Emma smiled. 'I hope he's been behaving himself.'

'More than that. He's a charmer with the manners of a butler. Your family should be proud of the young man.'

'Oh, we are. Why did Jai come here, anyhow?'

'Hope was being teased. You know how kids are? He stepped in, and some boy said to prove she's your friend, so he said he'd walk Hope home. He also wanted to make sure no one bothered her.'

'He's always been like that.'

'Hope seems to enjoy his company. They share a love of animals. You should have seen them both with Sasha.'

'His dog goes everywhere with him except school. Oh, did Sasha's paw heal?'

'Sure did. Noah whipped up some concoction to take the bruising out. He's a qualified vet, you know?'

'He did say that, yes.' Emma wondered if Noah told his mother about her. She looked around the warm family home, sniffing the air filled with fresh baking. 'Are the kids inside?'

'No, they are visiting our secret pet. You can too. Go out the back, around a bend and follow the sandy path. You can't miss them. Please tell Hope to get back here before the sun goes down.'

'Sure. I'm intrigued by a secret animal.'

Crystal smiled but said nothing.

Emma walked down the path, wondering about the elephant she thought she saw on the first day she came to the property.

When she stepped in an animal shit the size of a large watermelon, instead of crying at the slop on her sneakers, she felt the joyful anticipation of an elephant around the corner.

'Nothing shits as good as an elephant.'

***

'You'd better come before she takes him home,' Crystal said to Noah.

'I don't understand why it's so important for me to see Emma's nephew. I'd like to of course, and I'm keen to see Emma again, but what's with the weirdness Mum?' Noah glanced at his father in the passenger seat.

'You'll see when you get here,' Crystal said before hanging up.

Noah glanced at the AplePlay screen to make sure the phone was hung up. 'Tell me, Dad. You know Mum better than anyone. Do you think she's acting weirder than normal?'

85

Derick laughed, holding his tender chest. 'Perhaps slightly but I like her eccentricities.'

'Big word, Dad. You know what I mean. Why the hurry?' He raised his eyebrows.

'Guess we'll find out.'

'Are you alright to get to the house?'

'Physio says I need to walk. Here comes your mother anyway. You go, son.' Derick urged as he slowly edged out.

Noah ran past his mother. 'This better be good.'

'Stop, Noah. I want to warn you.'

Noah turned mid-stride. 'Warn me. It's Emma and her nephew for fuck sake.'

'It's him. He looks exactly like you did as a boy.'

'Who? Emma's nephew?'

'He's the right age.'

'The what?' But it slowly dawned on Noah. His mother could only be warning him about one nine-years-old. The child they searched for after Kendwa died. 'Jai? You said his name was Lion.'

'A name is nothing son. You should know that, Toby.'

Noah frowned at her calling him the name he had grown up with, before turning to run to Stinky's grotto.

As he rounded the bend, he could see Emma facing the elephant. The kids were playing around Stinky's legs.

Sasha raised her ears to Noah. She let out a high-pitched bark, running towards him, her tail wagging madly. Stinky raised her trunk and trumpeted noisily, making the children block their ears. Emma turned, smiling wide, with her eyes bright with joy and astonishment. *Elephants could do that.*

It was the boy Noah needed to see. Emma angled her head when Noah walked towards Lion. Noah gave her a nod but stared until the child turned around. Turquoise blue eyes in latte skin. Kendwa's eyes.

'Oh, hey, Mr Cooper. You are Mr Cooper, Hope's dad?' Lion asked.

Hope interrupted by running into her father's arms. 'Daddy, I told you, my friend. My friend Lion.'

Noah let go of Hope after kissing her cheek. Lion reached out his hand. Noah shook it feeling relief and sadness wash over him. It was challenging to keep his emotions in check. *The kid probably doesn't know he's adopted.*

Noah couldn't upset the only person who was his blood other than Hope. 'Nice to meet you, Lion,' Noah managed to say.

In the corner of his eye, he could see Emma watching them. He didn't know what to say to her. *How could she be Jai's aunty?* The precious nephew he'd been searching for lived with her family. It didn't

86

seem possible, but the proof was in front of him. The boy was unmistakably Kendwa's son. *Or an unbelievable friggin' doppelganger.*

'Noah. Are you alright?' Emma touched his shoulder with slender fingers.

He wanted to hug her. Tried to tell her something but his mind tumbled. The shock of seeing Jai made him unable to utter a word.

'Noah?' asked Emma

'Daddy?' asked Hope.

'Why are the adults acting weird again?' Jai said to Hope. 'First, your nanny and now your dad.'

Hope shrugged her little shoulders.

'Aunt Emm. We'll head back to the house.' He rolled his eyes. 'As usual, it looks like you need to talk 'adult stuff'.' He made quote marks with his fingers. To Hope, he said, 'Sheeze, I hate when adults do that. We're old enough to know stuff, right, Hope?'

Hope merely nodded.

Noah smiled at how Jai included Hope. *What a great kid.*

When they were out of earshot, Noah turned on Emma. She stood close. The fragrance of her perfume was intoxicating. It almost softened his resolve. Stepping backward, he asked, 'Is his real name Lion?'

Emma furrowed her brow. 'No. His nickname is Lion. He prefers it to Jai. It's a stage he's going through or something. Why? You're scaring me, Noah. Why won't you come near me?' Her bottom lip trembled. Stinky moved closer, brushing her side. Emma absently stroked the aging elephant but did not take her eyes from Noah.

Noah raked his hand through his hair, looking down. 'Is that shit on your shoes?' he asked, trying not to laugh as he pointed at her brown shoes.

Glancing down, she smiled. Her cheeks coloured. 'A bit of Stinky business. I didn't see until it was too late.'

He chuckled. Only yesterday he would have found joy in her embarrassment, turning it to something they could laugh over. Now the funny things wouldn't help the situation. If Emma's family had Jai, how could he still have a relationship with her?

Her family remained silent about having Jai. They left him to search with no answers. They were to blame for Kendwa's child, never coming home to his real family.

Emma, seemingly urged by his chuckle at her poo-slopped shoes, stepped towards him. She placed a finger on his bottom lip. 'Please tell me.' Her beautiful eyes spoke volumes. He tried shifting his gaze, but she gently pushed his jaw back to face her. 'I'm not going anywhere until you tell me what freaked you out about Lion being, Jai?'

'Jai's birth father? Do you know his name?'

87

'Yes, of course.'

'Kendwa, right?' His jaw firmed.

Blinking twice, she took a deep breath as if something clicked in her brain. She dropped her hand as if he'd burnt her. 'But who's Kendwa to you?' This time she stepped away, shaking her head.

Stinky stroked her trunk down Emma's arm.

'I'm Kendwa's brother.' Rubbing his jaw, he tried not to notice the shock in her beautiful eyes. 'I was stolen from my family when I was a toddler. The lady who stole me was my adoptive mum, Crystal's sister. She and Dad took me in when she died. I didn't know my story for years — until I found out Kendwa was my brother.'

Emma reached for his hand. He pulled his away.

Taking a deep breath, he said, 'You have to go, Emma.'

'You're Jai's uncle?' Emma yelled. 'How can that be? We were told his uncle was dead.'

'Who told you I was dead? I've been back here for a year and well and truly alive. Even when Hope and I were in hiding Metra was bound to tell the people who had him. It was her job to find me at the right time.'

'Metra? Mum's friend from Zanzibar?' The sky was darkening, and Jai called Emma to hurry up.

'Yeah, probably, not many Metra's around.' Noah punched a fist into his hand as he paced. 'This is making me crazy. I don't believe it. You shouldn't see me until I get my head around this.'

Tears pooled in Emma's eyes. It hurt him deep in the gut, but he had to ignore it. Kendwa's son, his precious nephew, depended on him.

'That's fair. I guess.' She gulped, blinking tears.

'Does Jai know I could be alive?'

'No.'

'I'll keep it to myself for now. Tell your family I will not rest until Jai knows who Hope and I am. I'll give them time to tell him.'

Emma's tears slipped down her cheeks. He wanted so damn bad to wipe them away and hug her. What would it accomplish? Make him feel better for a second because she was in his arms? Make him feel worse because he must let her go?

'I'm sorry you haven't had Jai in your life, Noah, but it's not my family's fault. They've loved and cared for him since he was tiny.'

'Maybe they have, but I need to think.'

'It's like Crystal and Derick loving you, like true doting parents.'

'Goodbye, Emma.' He turned from her.

'You say it like it's forever.' She wrung her hands together and stepped in front of him. Her pretty moist eyes pleaded with long-eyelashes blinking.

Watching her hurting, bruised his recently open heart. His breath caught in his throat as he slowly said, 'Maybe it will be.' Digging his hands deep in his trousers barely contained the urge to reach out to her.

Her lips wobbled.

It took all his will not to kiss the tremble away. Instead, he stayed rooted to the spot. The elephant lumbered closer to lend its concern with a stroke of its trunk on top of his head.

Emma walked away. Noah clutched his aching stomach as he watched her go. He'd found love. Why did the circumstances make it impossible? A lump lodged in his throat as he stomped back to the house, hoping the visitors were gone. But also wishing they never left.

Chapter 15

Bats flew overhead heading for their feeding grounds in the valley to the west. Their flapping wings and squeaky cries distracted Emma for a few moments before she burst into tears again.

Jai snored sound asleep in her spare room. The temptation to call into her mothers to ask her to explain didn't seem fair to Jai. Luckily she thought better of it and in time had calmed down, probably due to the alcohol. She glanced at the bourbon bottle on the table with a frown.

Noah's rebuff tore at her soul. The man she imagined and hoped for a future of marriage, love and happiness had hurt her. All the dreams of sharing his life shattered the instant he knew about Jai.

She was confused and shocked by how Noah had found out about Jai. Why would her mother have said the uncle died? How could she keep such a secret from her, let alone Jessy and Ben?

Wiping wet cheeks with the balled up tissue in her hand, she thought of her sister. They were due home tomorrow afternoon. It didn't give Emma much time to get the full story from her mother. She'd have to miss another few hours of work, but she needed to know. And she must smooth the way for her sister. The revelation could shatter Jessy's well-organised life.

In front of her, a half-empty glass of bourbon sat teasing her to drink more and obliterate the pain. Picking it up, she gulped down the last of it before placing the empty glass down with a frown. The spirit warmed her throat, and the alcohol went to her head. Trying to kill the pain in her heart with cheap bourbon was never a good idea. It was also sure make her head thump by morning. *Stuff it!*

She poured another from the small bottle. She couldn't cop it straight so added a small amount of Diet Coke. It wasn't like her to get drunk or to wallow, but she had a right. *A broken heart calls for heartier stuff than a damn cup of tea.*

She blamed her mother because the man of her dreams called it quits. But even in her angry state, she couldn't fathom her mother doing anything deceptive. There must be a good reason the family did not know about Noah's existence.

Pursing her lips, she lifted the glass and took another sip, wondering if Noah felt as bad. The pain seemed evident in his eyes when he told her to go. His jaw twitched in the way it did when he tried to remain calm. He'd kept his hands so deep in his pockets to avoid touching her he'd practically torn them through.

A rustle in the bushes to the right of the waterside courtyard made Emma glance with narrow eyes. *Wade?* Surely after knowing Noah was her boyfriend, Wade would steer clear. She felt ridiculous — sorry, sad, heartbroken and drunk. Rubbing her arms didn't stop the chills. Her eyes shot around the area like a startled pony.

Everything seemed still. Nothing was lurking in the dark. Emma let out the breath she hadn't realised she held, before leaving the glass and bottles on the table to stagger inside. With trembling fingers, she locked the door and pulled the blinds shut.

As she wobbled to her bedroom, she wondered if Noah were feeling as alone and miserable. The queen-sized bed seemed too big for her without his big beautiful physique beside her. Picking up one of the pillows, she placed it beside her, curling into it imagining his body. *Noah.* Fully dressed, she fell into a restless sleep on a pillow wet with her tears.

***

Noah couldn't sleep, so he ran. The clip-on cap light on the peak of his baseball cap lit the way through the bush. A wallaby bounced in front of him, startled by the light. He shooed it off as he kept running until sweat trailed every rivet of his body. Wiping under his eyes with a finger he swore. Tears mixed with the sweat — *not crying.* Just sweaty, so he told himself.

But he cried, sobbing for what could have been with Emma — grieving for the years he'd missed with Jai — howling at his brother, mother and father for leaving him an orphan long ago.

It wasn't his nature to cry except for when Hope was born, but he figured he'd been bottling it up for too long. The dam burst. He never cried over Katie. What was it about Emma to turn his usual sturdy brick wall to a flimsy veneer?

Even while running to rid his thoughts of her, they circled like sharks eating away at him. A jog usually cleared his head. It made his muscles burn and his body sweat, though his mind wasn't cooperating with the plan to avoid thinking. *Thinking?* He couldn't fuckin' stop thinking.

Tearing at his hair, he took in a ragged breath, finally stopping. He'd probably run about twenty kilometres, up Currumbin Creek Road, back through the forest and bush on his property and back to Stinky's grotto.

The old elephant raised her head from a straw bed on the ground. Every few nights, she slept exhausted on the earth rather than standing. The more frequently she did it, the closer she was to death.

Noah placed his hands on his hips, sucking in breaths. 'Poor old girl. You're time's nearly up, huh? Dunno how Hope's going to take it when you go to the big jungle in the sky.' *Another damn thing to worry about.*

When he finally turned in for the night, the clock showed 4 am. He didn't know why he bothered putting his head down. Usually, up around 5 am, it gave him only one hour. No point except for sniffing Emma's scent on his pillow. He hadn't washed the sheets since she last stayed — frangipani perfume lingered. He crushed the pillow to his face. *Fuck, why did it have to be this way?*

Tossing the pillow to the ground, he lay on his back with his arms folded behind his head. Like a hypnotists coin, the fan above whirred around. His eyes dropped closed, but a vision of Emma played on his eyelids. Naked, Emma, smiled her make-love-to-me smile with a sexy tilt to her lips.

His cock hardened. He groaned and yelled, 'Fuck.' He was too damn spent and emotionally exhausted even to give himself a toss. He wondered if Emma pleasured herself alone in her bed. The thought pushed him over the edge.

Rolling over, he reached for his mobile phone. Before he could stop himself, he texted Emma:

I wish things were different. I miss you already.

He didn't add an emoji. It seemed enough. If Emma loved him, she would understand his need to stay connected even if they were apart. He wasn't giving up on her, but a hell of a lot remained to sort out first.

Over the next hour, he checked for her reply. His heart dropped each time he saw no return message.

***

The next morning he didn't hear the message beep, having left his phone behind when he went for a paddle up the tranquil creek.

I miss you more.

***

Damn, why did I send it? Emma regretted texting the message the moment she'd sent it. Things were far from figured out. Now if they never got back together or did and broke up again, she'd be hurt tenfold.

Grabbing her handbag, she shoved the phone down the bottom where she couldn't retrieve it quickly.

'Jai, are you ready for school?' she called, knowing he only needed to clean his teeth.

They'd shared breakfast. Well, Jai ate two bowls of Weetbix while she held her head in her hands, scarcely swallowing a coffee down. The three painkillers barely put a dent in the pain throbbing through her head. It felt like the elephant, Stinky, had trod on her head with one of its massive hooves.

Jai wiped the toothpaste off the corner of his mouth with his shirt collar. 'You might need to get another set, Aunty Emm. I've just about grown out of these,' he said of the school uniform she kept for him for school-night sleepovers.

Trying to smile, she eyed him up and down. 'Seriously, Jai. Stop growing.' The shirt almost popped its buttons and rode up his flat belly.

'Lion, remember.' He rolled his eyes. 'Let's go. The school bell rings in fifteen. If I split my pants today, it will be embarrassing, and I'll blame you, Aunty Emm.'

As she drove along Currumbin Creek Road, Emma glanced at the accident site. Little remained to show anything happened, only the black of the tyre rubber on the road. The flattened bush and grass were already growing over.

Jai noticed her gaze. 'That's where that kid died. You saw it didn't you Aunty Emm.'

'Mmm, I did. I don't want to talk about it.' She didn't want to talk about anything except Noah. It was something she couldn't share with Jai. Her mother, on the other hand, well, she would have to hear her out.

Gravel crunched as she pulled into the side curb. She didn't want to drive past the school gates in case Noah was seeing Hope off. A car pulled in behind them as she watched Jai walk the 20 metres to the school. A door slammed. With pink braids in her hair, a little girl ran passed Emma's car. *Hope.*

Emma's heart tightened. Her fingers trembled on the steering wheel. *Don't look back.*

A familiar, deep male voice said, 'Hi, Emma.' How did he sneak up on her like a cat?

With shaky hands, she turned the key. Noah reached into her open window, putting his hand over hers before she could start the car.

'Look at me, Emma,' he said, sorrow catching in his voice.

94

Lifting her head and her lashes, her heart butterflied when she realised how close his face moved to hers. 'I — um. You, sorry I'll get going. I didn't mean to bump into you here.'

His fingers clasped her hand tighter. Green-blue eyes gazed into hers like tranquil pools of love. 'I'm sorry. Last night I overreacted. I shouldn't have sent you away.'

She watched his lips move, wanting to kiss those thick, delectable lips but he'd hurt her, and she needed to harden her heart. Twisting her wrist, she pried her fingers loose from his. 'No. You had every right. If Jai is your nephew, it must be a shock. It's a shock enough to me.'

'If? If Jai's my nephew? So, you don't believe me?' He straightened, stepped backward and raked his hands through his hair. It had grown longer than when they first met and curled over his forehead and down the nape of his neck. *Just-rolled-out-of-bed sexy.* Biting her lip, she ignored the thought.

'I believe you. It's complicated is all. I have to tell my family today. My sister and brother-in-law will be back this arvo. I —'

'You're worried about them. Don't you care how I feel about all this?' Noah's voice rose.

She wrung her hands in her lap. 'Of course, I care about how you feel too. You know already. Jessy and Ben don't. They'll be blindsided.'

'Fuck, Emma. I only found out yesterday. Don't you think I've been fuckin' knocked for six?'

Tears pooled in Emma's eyes. He'd never sworn at her before. She could feel the venom spitting from his mouth. Trying to keep the shake from her voice, she said, 'I need to see my family. You'd better get out of my way, or I'll run over you.' She gunned the engine and revved it for good measure.

Noah stepped away with his hands in the air in surrender, but he shook his head. 'Tell them I'll come and pick Jai up on the weekend after he's had a chance to understand.'

'I suppose you should cancel our lunch date at The Boat Shed,' she yelled, feeling slight satisfaction at his startled frown.

As Emma drove off, she glanced in her revision mirror. Noah paced, yelling something to the high heavens, before punching his ute, leaving a dent in the driver's side door.

Emma shuddered. Her family had no idea they were about to be torn apart. Noah was hurting too, and it made her sad not angry.

Chapter 16

'Mum, seriously. We need to talk about what you're not telling me,' Emma said as she stormed into the reception of Moon Under Safaris.

Shaun tilted his head around a computer to see what was going on. The customer standing at the counter glanced at Emma with hostile annoyance, twisting thin lips.

'Sorry, Georgie. Could you please give me a minute? This is my daughter, Emma.' Ali's face paled as she ushered her customer to the comfortable reception lounge.

Emma tried to keep her anger in check, but after a restless night and running into Noah earlier, she was wound tighter than a boa constrictor. She could tell by the drop of mother's head and the way she pacified the Georgie woman, she was embarrassed by the sudden intrusion.

Ali grabbed Emma's elbow. 'In my office.' In a whisper, she said, 'What's with you, Emma? I had a customer. You could have waited.'

Emma shrugged her elbow loose. 'It can't wait.'

The workspace resided behind the reception. Ali opened the door to the conference room for privacy. Shaun took concerned glances their way but pretended to concentrate on something on his computer screen. The customer huffed in reception, picking up a magazine to read while she waited. Ali closed the door softly.

'You know who Noah is, don't you?' Ali asked, frowning and leaning back against the closed door.

'How? What? You knew all along he's Kendwa's brother?' Emma held her hands over her face, rubbing them down her cheeks.

'I didn't know he was alive or here for that matter, not until you showed me the photo on your phone.' Ali sat, placing her head in her hands before continuing. 'I wanted to tell you, but I had to see the lawyers first.'

Emma sat across the conference table, allowing space from her mother as she tried to focus. 'Lawyers? For what?'

'To protect Jai. To save the business.' Ali twisted her hands together. 'Remember, when we brought Jai to Australia after Kendwa died?'

'Of course. The poor little guy lost his mum only two years before, and Kendwa died in such horrible circumstances. It's etched in my brain forever. How much Jai cried for his daddy but cuddled Jessy for support. It seemed like fate stepped in because Jessy could never have kids of her own.' She went silent, thinking back to a day six years ago that changed their lives forever. Glancing at the tears pooling in her mother's eyes she realised she was probably visualising the time in Zanzibar.

'Yes, well while you and Jessy concentrated on making sure Jai was happy and adjusted I needed to go through all of Kendwa's paperwork, keep the business going for Jai to inherit and adhere to Kendwa's wishes. I was the custodian of his legacy, and I took it seriously. I owed him at least that.'

'But why does it need to be complicated if Noah's his brother?'

'Because of what Kendwa wanted. He requested for Jai to know his uncle, and he insisted they share the business. It's in writing and signed.'

Emma rubbed her temple. 'You think Noah will take the business out from under you? He's not that type of person. He wouldn't do it.'

'Maybe he won't, but I must put things in place to protect us all. What if he wants Jai to live with him? It would kill Jessy and Ben.'

'You don't know him like I do.'

'How did you find out he's Kendwa's brother? Kendwa's brother's name was Toby.'

'He told me.'

'What? I don't understand. Did you think he looked like Kendwa from my photos of him?'

'No, Mum. I had no idea. He was the guy I'd fallen in love with — an awesome adorable man. How could I know he was connected to our family? When I picked up Jai yesterday, he had visited Noah's daughter, Hope. Noah's mum could see the family resemblance. She rang Noah to warn him. As soon as he saw Jai I could tell something was up. Noah stared at him like he'd seen a ghost.' Emma's lip trembled.

Ali reached across the table to grab her hand. 'They would have met sooner or later because you're dating.'

Emma pulled her hand away. 'We aren't dating any more. He broke it off with me.'

'Because of Jai?'

'Yes, and why wouldn't he. My family have deceived him. He has a right to know his nephew.'

'But I honestly did not know where he was. Metra told me she would tell me when he resurfaced if he ever did.'

'And have you spoken to Metra lately?'

Ali nodded. 'She admitted she knew Noah returned to Currumbin Valley and his parents' property. Because she only thought of Jai's stability and happiness she decided not to tell us or let Toby, I mean Noah, know where Jai was.'

'She's got no right to keep it from everyone.'

'You know what a sweet woman she is. She thought she did the best thing for everyone. Noah's got enough to deal with, bringing up a daughter with disabilities.'

'That's a cop-out. Noah's the best father I've ever seen. Hope has him wrapped around her little finger, but he loves it.'

A knock sounded at the door. Shaun poked his head in the doorway. 'Georgie is getting antsy. Are you two okay?'

'Could you ask her if she can reschedule? Tell her it's a family crisis,' said Ali.

'It is,' said Emma.

'Okay.' Shaun raised his eyebrows, shutting the door.

Ali twisted her hands together.

Emma stared out the window, trying to blink back tears. 'Noah told me to tell you something. You have to tell Jai about him and Hope.'

Ali took a deep breath. 'How much time?'

'You have to talk before Jessy and Ben get home tonight. It will be too much for them to handle. They've been away from Jai for over a fortnight.'

'How do I tell him?' Ali wiped the tears under her eyes.

'Show him the photos. Explain you didn't know Noah was alive. Jai's a switched-on kid. He could have seen the resemblance to Kendwa from the photo on his bedroom side table. It's a constant reminder of what his father looks like. Being a kid, it may not have twigged yet because he'd be too caught up in the present. Maybe it won't even be a shock to him. He knows he's adopted and there's another family somewhere. Rip the bandaid off, Mum. Get it done today.'

'Okay. I will.'

'Do you want me to be there?'

'Yes, I'd like that. If you pick Jai up from school and drive him here. I'll tell him over an afternoon tea with his favourite banana cake.'

'Then we have to tell Ben and Jessy. They'll be here about six.'

'Right. We will. God, I'm exhausted by it already.'

'Mum, when Jai was adopted, was it watertight?'

'The lawyer thinks so.'

'Not that Noah would try and take him from Jess and Ben, but it's good to be able to tell them that. And, the business, what will happen about that?'

'Shaun and I have put a proposal together. It shows our contribution to the business financially. Hopefully, Noah will be reasonable about it.'

'He will be.'

'You're so sure.'

'He's mad as a butcher bird because of the shock, but he hasn't got a malicious bone in his body. I think the shock will wear off and he'll think straight. I'm sure he'll discuss the business with you. He won't steal it out from under you. No way.'

Emma's phone pinged. She glanced at the message. *Noah.* She read the text, smiling.

'From Noah?' Ali asked.

'Mmmm. Yeah, Noah. He's sorry he didn't see my earlier message. He sent kissing emojis. Lots of them.'

'I thought you said you'd broken up.' Ali smiled.

'We have, but I'm hoping it's temporary until all this shit sorts out. We have something special.' Emma stared at the message on her phone. Her heart thumped madly. *I love you, Emma. We'll work it out.*

'I understand. Kendwa and I —' Ali paused, glancing at the door, 'it was special. He was special.'

This time Emma patted her mother's hand. 'I remember how heartbroken you were when he died, Mum. I'm so glad you could find love again with Shaun.'

'I know. Some people never have those connections. I've been lucky.'

'It's weird, isn't it?'

'What?'

'We've dated brothers. We must have the same taste.' Emma giggled.

'It's such a small world sometimes. If I'd never taken my trip to Africa, we'd not have Jai in our family. We wouldn't be connected to your boyfriend.'

'We've broken up, remember.'

'Doubt it will last. A man who keeps in touch even when he's hurt is probably a keeper. Kiss emojis? Not many guys send them, you know.'

Emma blushed. 'He did.' She smiled. 'Mum, it will all turn out. It's going to be an emotional few days, but we'll get through it. There's this powerful woman who always told me we could get through anything if we stick together as a family.'

100

'She also said she's exceedingly proud of the formidable woman her daughter has become.'

They stood and hugged.

'To think I was going to come in here and tear strips off you,' Emma said, laughing.

'I could tell you were mad, but I know it's more your heartbreak at having a separation from Noah, not your anger at us.'

'You're right. I can't think straight. It's the first time I've thought of a guy as marriage material.'

'Really?'

'So much so. We only have to get through this complicated family drama, and we'll be all good.'

'I do hope so, sweetheart.'

Ali opened the door. Shaun stood on the other side, pretending he hadn't pressed his ear against it listening.

'So, you two are all good?' he asked.

'Didn't you hear it all?' Ali said, cocking her head and laughing.

'Well, bits,' Shaun confessed.

'Yes, we're all good. Let's sort all this out this afternoon when I bring Jai from school.'

'So we are telling him?' Shaun asked.

'We have to,' said Ali.

'The sooner we tell Jai, Jess and Ben, the quicker we all get back to normal.'

'The business?' asked Shaun.

'Mum will fill you in. I have to get home. Finish some work and go and get Jai. Bye.'

As Emma drove home, a load lifted from her shoulders. She felt real hope her family would sort things out with Noah. They were all amicable people. *Well, except for Jessy.*

Emma thought about her feisty sister and wondered if Cyclone Jess planned to brew a storm over Noah's head.

Chapter 17

'So, what do they need to talk to me about?' Jai asked, cracking his knuckles — a habit he'd formed when he was about five and realised it made a crazy sound.

'Important stuff you need to know about your African dad.'

'Not the business stuff again. Nana's always reminding me I can join the safari side of the business when I'm old enough. I can't wait to go back to Africa. It was so cool last time.'

A year ago, during the last trip, Jai saw the big five. He remained in awe of the lions he observed, hence his choice of nickname.

'It's about that but also something much bigger. You'll have to make some grown-up decisions today.'

'Yay to that. It's about time. I'm sick of them treating me like a kid.'

'It's only because you're special to them, Jai. All they want to do is protect you. Remember that when Nana is speaking today.'

When they arrived at Ali and Shaun's home, Cheetah waited on the front grass by the mailbox. She approached the car, tail wagging and tongue hanging. A welcome bark sounded as Jai raced to his dog.

'Hey, girl. You miss me much?' Jai asked, ruffling the dog on the back of her neck.

Cheetah circled Jai, barking, before rising on her hind legs to lick Jai's face. Jai giggled.

'Come on, Lion. Nana will be waiting out the back. She's baked your favourite banana cake.'

'Sick! Can't I have a swim first? I need to cool off. It was a boiler at school today.'

'Not sure but I think Nana is pretty keen to talk first. It's important.'

'Righto.'

***

Ali sat next to Shaun at their long timber table. Her stomach churned as Jai and Emma entered the pergola. The table, a teak twelve-seater comfortably fit family and friends when they entertained. Something

103

they often did during the summer months. Kenyan colourful handmade raffia placemats adorned the table. Ali picked at one, her thoughts travelling back to her time with Kendwa.

Shaun smiled at Jai. 'Hey, mate. Did you have a good day at school?'

'It was sick. I got to try out for the Rugby League team. I think I did okay. The comp doesn't start until April, but training has begun.'

'What position?' Shaun asked.

Emma sat across for them and pulled a chair out for Jai.

Ali twisted her wedding ring, trying to compose a smile. The paperwork in front of her seemed toxic enough to poison her.

Jai kissed her cheek before answering. 'Probably Hooker. I didn't miss a tackle, and the other two guys who tried were crapping their pants when the big Maori guys ran at them.'

'I'm sure you'll be a shoo-in.' Shaun glanced at Ali with knowing eyes. 'Anyhow, can you sit mate? We have a few important things to discuss.'

'Sure.' Jai reached for a slice of banana cake. 'Hit me with it. Looks serious. Paperwork and Nana you haven't even cracked a grin.'

Ali tried, she really did but smiling felt foreign when heart palpitations leading towards a panic attack. Lifting the water glass in front of her, she took a sip with shaking hands.

'I'll tell him, Ali,' Shaun said, his lovely eyes sending her a reassuring look.

She patted his hand. 'No. I have to.' She gulped. 'Jai. As you know your real dad, Kendwa, kept some things to give to you when you were old enough.'

'Yeah, yeah the safari stuff,' Jai mumbled with a mouthful of cake.

'It's more than that, Jai. Yes, the business is yours when you turn eighteen. You can start working when you turn fifteen. But you won't own the business alone.'

'Yeah, of course. You guys will still help me.'

'Maybe. You see there's another person who owns half the business.'

'Is that the old African guy who was Dad's friend?' Jai glanced at Emma with raised eyebrows.

'No, he got out of the business years ago. He's employed by the company now.'

'God, Mum, will you put him out of his misery. Tell him or I will,' Emma said, raising her voice.

'I'm trying, Emma.' Ali sighed, shuffling the papers in front of her.

'Aunt Emm, what's got you so upset? You're all worrying me now.' Jai glanced around the table.

104

'What we tell you doesn't change anything? You're still a big part of our family,' Shaun said, receiving a kick under the table from Ali.

'Jai, we were unaware this person was alive, but you have an uncle. Your dad Kendwa's brother Toby.'

'Oh, hey, that's alright. Having another uncle would be rad. I don't get to see Uncle Ritchie now he's playing footy in Sydney full time. What's wrong with me having an uncle on dad's side?'

'Nothing.' Ali tried to find the words. 'It's complicated. This uncle, he was a little shocked to know you were living with us. We don't know if he'll want you to stay with him. He can also take half the business right away. It could ruin us.'

'I'm not leaving Mum and Dad. An uncle's just an uncle, right?' Jai's eyes were wide.

'You are legally adopted by your mum and dad. You won't have to leave them, but this uncle will want to spend time with you. He may demand it.'

'Oh, come on Mum, Noah won't demand it,' said Emma, shooting her mother daggers.

Jai's eyes grew wider. 'What? You said Toby, right? What's Noah got to do with it.

Ali, Shaun and Emma exchanged glances while Jai observed them. 'You know it would be great. If you just spat it all out. I'm not a kid,' said Jai, patting his dog's head.

Emma took a deep breath. 'Hope is your cousin. Noah's your uncle. He was born Noah. Then he was adopted and called Toby. He changed back to Noah a few years ago.'

'I like that dude. Sick. And little Hope's my cousin. Sick.'

'Is that all you've got to say about it?' Ali asked.

'I guess there's more you need to tell me about how the business will work, but as far as having a chilled dude as my uncle I'm down with that. He looks super fit, and he has these sick tattoos. Can I swim now? It's a stinker.'

Ali shook her head. 'Our lawyers think Shaun and I can retain a portion of the business. We have to discuss it with Noah. We're not sure if it will be amicable.'

'Mum, it will,' said Emma, smacking her forehead.

'Well, he did give us an ultimatum to tell Jai about him.'

'Did he?' Jai asked.

'Yes, but don't take it the wrong way. Noah was shocked when he laid eyes on you. You look like your dad and a bit like he did as a child,' Emma again came to Noah's defence.

Ali wordlessly passed Jai a photo from the stack in front of her. She watched her daughter closely. It broke her heart Emma had found love only to have a complicated family mess ruin it.

Jai pointed to Kendwa. 'Dad. His brother. Wow, we do all look alike, don't we? I guess I was so fascinated by the elephant, Stinky, at Hope's place. I didn't look at her dad properly. Wow!'

'What we need to know, Jai, is, do you want to get to know him? Your mum and dad know nothing about this yet. They'll be worried they'll lose you.'

'They'll never lose me. I have the best mum and dad in the world. I do remember bits of when I was little, leaving Africa. I remember dad, but sometimes I think it's because of the photo in my bedroom. I'm not sure. I do know he loved me, but I'm glad I came to Australia. It's never worried me I was adopted.'

'What about Africa?'

'It's a part of me. I feel something there. I wonder if Noah does too. Where did he grow up?'

'Here,' said Emma glancing in the distance as if picturing Noah growing up in Currumbin only miles from her.

'Not Africa?'

'Sometimes, but mostly here. He worked up north with crocodiles.'

'Dad, Kendwa, did that too.'

'Yes, that's where they met before they knew they were brothers,' said Ali. 'Anyhow, what do you want to do?'

'See Mum and Dad. I want to make sure they're fine with it,' said Jai. 'Swim?'

'Sure. Go ahead,' said Shaun, patting Ali's leg. To her, he said, 'You did great.' He kissed her lips.

'I should have let him read Kendwa's letters,' she said, watching Jai run to the spare room to put on his boardshorts.

'He has plenty of time for that. At least he took it well.' Shaun glanced at Emma. 'Are you okay, Emma?'

'I guess.' She glanced at a message on her phone and covered it with her hand.

'Noah?' Ali asked, noting the semi-smile Emma quickly covered.

'Yep.'

'I'm going in for a dip too,' said Shaun, opening the pool gate as Jai sprinted past him, bombing into the swimming pool with a big splash.

'He wanted to know if you told Jai,' Emma said.

'Tell him, yes, but he can't interfere until after Jai sees Jess and Ben. Can he give them a couple of days to get their head around it?'

'I'll text him. I'm sure he will.' Emma tapped her reply and placed her phone face down on the table. 'Mum, Jessy won't take it well.'

'I know. I'm worried about it.'

'I skyped her late last night and warned her.'

'Oh, I wanted her home first.'

106

'It's not a long time to be ready for it. At least they can ponder it on the long flight.'

'I guess so. Did she take it well?'

'No. Jessy's like a mumma bear with Jai.'

'Noah may have to tread carefully if he wants to see his nephew at all.' Ali took a deep breath and frowned.

'I know. The problem is. If Jess goes off like a pork chop, she could ruin any negotiations you have with Noah over the business. You need to have a good talk to her, Mum. Get her to calm down.'

'You usually soothe her better than me.'

'Not this time. She's furious because I've been dating Noah. She thinks I've sided with him against her.'

'Have you?'

'I shouldn't have to take sides.' Emma clutched the table edge.

'Your sister won't see it that way.'

'Neither will Noah. I love him, Mum. I can't help that.'

'I know, honey. We'll get through it.' Though Ali's gut feeling told her Jessy would come home like a twister touching the earth.

Chapter 18

The elephant trumpeted like an untuned clarinet. Hope offered Stinky a handfull of food, but the elephant dropped its trunk, shaking her head, so ears flapped like sails in the wind.

'Stinky, have to eat,' said Hope, frowning as she pushed the mix of grass and fruit closer to Stinky's drooping mouth.

'She's not hungry today, Hopey,' said Noah from the back of the elephant. He inspected the shackle gash on her hindfoot. It festered again where the long-gone chain dug into the flesh. 'I'll give her more antibiotics to fight the infection and a painkiller. She'll be a bit better by morning.'

'I know, Dad. Stinky old.' Hope dropped the food on the ground, brushing her hands together. She glanced at her father with tears brimming.

It broke Noah's heart, but he must prepare her for the inevitable. 'Yes, she is, sweetie. Thing is, she's been happy living with us free in the bush, but her old heart can't go on forever. I'm sure she wants to go to heaven to join Jumbo soon. Don't you think Jumbo's lonely up in heaven without her?'

'I guess.' As he squatted down to fill the syringe, Hope wrapped her arms around his shoulders, squeezing him. 'But you try, Dad.'

'Careful, you know this is sharp,' Noah shielded the needle in his hand.

Hope nodded, stepping back. 'Forgot.'

'It's okay, Hope. Anyway, I can manage to keep her comfortable. I can't promise she has much time. She's very old.' He scrunched his eyebrows in an earnest look, frowning, so she understood.

'Stinky miss Jumbo?'

'Of course.'

'Stinky can go heaven when she wants,' Hope said as she stroked Stinky's grey sagged-skin belly.

Noah stood, holding the syringe high and flicking it clear of air bubbles. He walked past Hope, flashing her a reassuring smile. Eyeing the elephant, he gave the injection under its ear where he found a vein.

109

'It's okay, girl. This will help.' He soothed Stinky. Once finished, he glanced at Hope. 'Are you sure?'

'Yep. Miss her.' Hope's speech faltered; something she did more noticeably when she was scared or upset.

Noah packed the medical kit, snapping it shut before kneeling and taking Hope in his arms. 'Let's make it a celebration of both Stinky and Jumbo's lives when it happens. We can get decorations, cake and music if you like. We'll never forget them, right?'

Hope nodded, trying to smile, but the tears dripped down her rounded, rosy cheeks onto his shoulder.

Noah wiped them from her face with his thumb. 'Sweetie, we have each other to get through these things. I'll always be here for you.' He held her until she stopped sobbing. Reaching for the medical kit, he said, 'Come on. Let's leave Stinky. She needs to rest. Let her medicine work.' He took Hope's hand in his free one, leading her to their modest house.

It seemed about time he did something about the two-bedroom weatherboard. He always planned to build bigger and closer to the creek. The water views would be impressive. He would be able to watch Hope fishing from the verandah or join her for a paddle up the creek.

Hope swam like a dolphin. In the water, you could not tell she had a disability. Swimming was a necessary survival skill. Even if they hadn't lived near a waterway, Noah ensured she could survive in both still water and surf. He first taught her to swim when she was weeks old. Katie and him were still married. She didn't bother attending her daughter's first swimming lesson. At the time he'd been dumbfounded, but soon discovered Katie couldn't care for anything their daughter accomplished.

Perhaps Hope possessed a natural swimming ability, or maybe it was his tenacity correcting her strokes, kicks and breath, making her a good swimmer. He couldn't be sure, but he was proud of her skills. Despite her disabilities, Hope understood fitness, health, survival and resilience were important. She could accomplish anything. Only other people didn't always think so.

Hope skipped up the stairs and inside. He watched her with a smile, noting she'd quickly forgotten her sadness about Stinky. He wished he could ignore things so easily; like Emma. Trying to forget Emma was like forgetting to breathe.

'Hope, time for a bath. You're filthy from feeding Stinky.'

'Okay, Dad.' Hope strode to her bedroom, grabbing her pyjamas before walking to the bathroom.

Testing the bathwater with his hand, he heard her footfalls behind him. 'It's only warm. Get on in,' he said, turning around.

110

Hope, still dressed, pointed to the door. 'I do myself,' she said. 'Hope, too old for Dad in bathroom.'

Noah tried not to grin at her determined little face. 'Sure. You want your privacy.' He stopped himself from asking if she would be alright. She strove for her independence by showing him she no longer needed help at bathtime. 'Wash everything.' He threw a washer in the bath and stepped outside the door. His little girl was growing up.

Though his ears were alert to Hope's noise in the bathroom, he scanned his eyes over the house plans on the dining table. They were curled at the edges because they had been rolled up for weeks. Weighing each corner with a pepper and salt mill, coffee cup and one elbow, he studied each room's size and layout. *Would it be big enough with Emma?*

Though they broke up, deep down, he believed it to be temporary. They could work on themselves after the mess with Jai was sorted. The idea of her living with him appealed to him a lot. It scared him too.

Chewing the corner of his mouth, he tried to concentrate. *What if Emma ended up like Katie?* Katie was the sweetest girl in the world when he first met her. She helped him through Kendwa's parent's death. His parents too, though he'd no idea at the time. He grieved because they were nice people. If only he'd known they were his birth parents, he could have said goodbye rightly, as their youngest son.

Rubbing his temple, he tried to clear thoughts of his past. Wasn't it better to concern himself with the future? *But what was that anyway?* Until he saw Jai again and talked to Emma's family, everything seemed in limbo.

No word came back about the laser light from his commando friend, and his father's court case was only weeks away. Derick hadn't regained his sprite since the heart attack. Crystal was often eccentric but acted weirder than usual. Kids bullied Hope at school though she seemed less concerned about it than him. Stinky, the elephant was close to her last legs. Even the dog suffered an inoperable tumour. The one thing he did not have to worry about was money. He'd been smart with investments and ensuring Hope's future.

Building the house should have been a priority, but too many things were getting in the way. Picking up a pencil and ruler, on the plan, he moved walls for a bigger main bedroom, took some space from the oversised living area for an office with a water view. Emma would love it.

Hope's wet footfalls padded up the hall to her bedroom.

'Did you dry off, Hope?' Noah asked, rolling up the plans, satisfied the changes were perfect.

'Yes,' Hope said, shutting her bedroom door.

111

Noah laughed. At least she tried to be independent. There was a meeting with Hope's teacher on Monday. Was it enough time after his encounter with Emma's family on Sunday? If the family get together ended tensely, it seemed best to reschedule with Hope's teacher. Letting off steam at the poor woman instead of the people he was mad at wasn't going to help Hope through school.

Picking up his phone, he messaged the teacher, asking for an extension to Tuesday. He scrolled through his message.

See you Sunday, Emma xo.

He put the phone down. Merely picturing her beautiful face made his balls heavy. Three days until he could see her again. *Was phone sex breaking the rules after a breakup?*

A bang came from Hope's room. Noah jumped like a goanna up a tree. 'What happened, sweetie?'

'Nuthin.'

Noah tapped on her door with his hand on the doorknob. 'You sure?'

'Dropped my school books. Too many.'

'Do you want a hand?'

'No.'

Noah leaned against the door. 'Do you want a story tonight?'

'No, thank you.'

'Okay. A kiss goodnight?'

'Yep.'

'Can I come in?'

'Yep.'

Noah opened the door, and the rusty hinges squeaked. The doors in his new house wouldn't.

Hope stacked her books on her desk. 'I read myself. Library book.' She showed him a book. *Snugglepot and Cuddlepie.*

'Great. Good choice. Hop in bed.' He pulled the covers back for her.

Once she climbed into bed, she drew up the sheets and covers, brushing his hands away when he tried to help. 'Night, Daddy.'

He grinned, kissed her cheek and said, 'Goodnight my beautiful Hopey. I love you to the moon and back infinite times.'

'Do too, Daddy.'

He kissed her cheek again as she cuddled the book to her chest. The nightlight was on, but he doubted she would read because her eyelids kept fluttering shut. It was funny how she would call him Dad all day but always say Daddy when she went to sleep. He liked it. It seemed sweeter as if she would always stay young and innocent.

Stepping silently from the room, he glanced one last time at his cherub daughter with a satisfied smile, before softly closing the door.

The phone beeped. He reached for it but heard his mother knock on the front sliding door.

'Noah, I'm glad you're here.'

With a finger to his lips, he gave her the signal Hope slept. 'Where else would I be?'

'At your girlfriends, perhaps.'

'We broke up.' Though he said it matter-of-factly, it tore his heart to shreds.

'Over the boy, Jai?'

'You guessed it. You are clairvoyant after all.'

'Don't mock me, son. I have an important reading for you.'

'I didn't ask for a reading, Mum.' Noah ran a hand through his hair.

'It came to me anyway.'

Noah led her out to the deck with his hand on her elbow. 'It's too hot inside. I friggin' can't wait for airconditioning.' He pinched his t-shirt where sweat pooled on his chest.

'Finally, you're going to build your house, son?'

'Yeah. A few adjustments to the plans and I'll put them into the council. So what's so important?'

Crystal adjusted the scarf around her head, so it trailed over her shoulder and breast. 'I'm worried we have trouble coming.'

'You don't think Dad will have the charges dropped?'

'No, he's going to be fine. I think the young man will eventually confess. I've heard there were whispers at the funeral of the driver. It seems someone bragged about using laser lights. A near accident happened in Palm Beach only days before Derick's one.'

'Yeah, Dad mentioned something to the solicitor. It's another avenue of enquiry the police don't seem to be bothered chasing up. Given the sergeant's son is involved, I'm not surprised.'

Crystal flapped her hand in the air. Her bangles sounded like tiny triangles. 'You're dad's fine. It's Hope I'm worried about.'

Noah stood more upright, angling his head at his mother. His heart squeezed. 'Hope?'

'Yes. My vision wasn't clear, but my feeling is; don't let her out of your sight.'

'Mum, I need more than that.' He rubbed his hand through his hair, glancing at the starry sky. Cicadas hummed in the bush. Enough sticky humidity filled the air to run a butter knife through.

'I don't have more. You know sometimes it's only a hunch.'

'And I know not to ignore you. Okay. Hope's going to be with me all weekend, plus I'll drop her off and pick her up from school. Little-miss independent won't like it, but I'll make something up. Thanks, Mum.' He kissed her cheek.

Crystal smiled as she hugged him. 'That's my boy. Now no worrying about your Dad though. I see all good things there.' She went to step down the deck stairs.

'Hey, Mum. Do you know what will happen with Emma and me?'

'That one is up to you, Son.' She smiled with a wink.

***

Emma waited for Crystal to leave Noah's porch before driving further up the driveway and parking in the carport. The automatic light came on. Noah ran to open her door.

'What are you doing here?' he asked as he shut the car door after her.

'Breaking rules.' She smiled at him, loving the way he stared at her with bright eyes and a welcoming smile.

He raised his eyebrows, stepping into her personal space. 'How so?'

On tip-toes, she leaned her face to his to kiss him. His mouth responded. His tongue parted her lips while his big hands wrapped around her waist, crushing her to him. Her fingers trailed through his thick hair as her tongue and lips hungered for him. *How can I stay away from kisses setting every part of me on fire?*

It was risky to come with the possibility he would reject her. Her heart lay open and bare, but she was drawn to him like a koala to eucalyptus leaves.

After leaving her mother's, Emma couldn't stop thinking about how her family were judging Noah without even knowing what he would do. She knew deep down he would do the right thing. There was something about Noah. *Kindness, compassion and sexiness in dump-trucks full.*

'I needed to kiss you.' She confessed, gazing into his incredible eyes, losing herself.

'I've been thinking about kissing you so much I feel like I've willed you here. Man, I've missed your lips — and — everything about you. Will you stay?' he asked, staring into her soul with fathomless eyes.

Trailing her hand along his bristled, hard-edged cheek, she said, 'I wish. No. I need to talk to you.' She sighed deeply, raising her shoulders.

'And kiss.' His lips curved before parting to kiss her again. Her nerve endings lit like a Christmas tree.

When she finally pulled away from a kiss blowing every fuse on the Christmas lights, she placed a hand on his chest. His heart hammered. She knew his cock would be engorged, struggling for release. She couldn't help glancing down. *Oh my, gosh!*

114

'Umm — yes and kiss, but words first —' her voice trailed.

He stole another kiss. It went on and on until she felt like a puddle at his feet. Pulling away again, she stepped back. 'It's ridiculous. I cannot think straight when you kiss me.'

'How's your mind when we do other things?' he asked with a cheeky raise of his eyebrows.

'Stop it.' She placed a finger on his delectable lips. 'Please. I need to warn you about Sunday.'

'Warn me how?' He kissed her cheek. Her legs wobbled.

'Noah, you're killing me. Stand over there.' She pointed to his ute. 'I'll stay here.' Stretching her arms wide, she said, 'See a nice distance. This is serious.' She dropped her hands to her hips, looking mock-serious.

'I'm all ears.' He exaggerated an ear cock.

Leaning against the ute's tray, he crossed his ankles and arms. The tantalising pose displayed his sinuous biceps to their best advantage. *Damn you, Noah. If this weren't so important, I'd fuck you in that ute's tray.*

'Right.' She took a breath, trying to dampen her libido by thinking of horse shit, elephant shit, baby shit brown – anything but Noah's blue-green eyes. 'So, did you know you own half of Kendwa's business with Jai?'

Noah blinked. 'What? Do I? I don't want it or need it.'

'Oh, right. Good to know, I guess, but anyway you have a right to it. It's Kendwa's wishes. It's all in writing.'

'It's nice he included me but as I said I don't want it.'

'My mum and stepdad have built the business up to be a multimillion-dollar company. Does money change things?'

'Nope.'

***

'Well, you aren't exactly flush. You live in a shack on your parent's property.' Emma raised her eyebrows towards the bigger house.

They live on MY property.

'Still doesn't make a difference,' he said, crossing his arms tighter.

Emma smiled her precious smile. It nearly brought him to his knees. 'It's more complicated than that, but it will smooth things over with them if they aren't scared of losing their livelihood. I told Mum you would not do anything to hurt them.'

'Of course, I wouldn't.' He shook his head. 'What I do want is to have time with Jai.'

'I know, but there's a complication with it.' Her eyes dropped for an instant to the ground. He knew her well enough to know she was about to tell him something he didn't want to hear.

'What complications? I only want to spend some time with him, let Hope enjoy having a cousin and vice versa.' He uncrossed his ankles and pushed off the ute to pace at the back of the cars.

Emma moved closer.

'I'm sorry. It's my sister, Jessy. She can be a hothead, particularly when it comes to Jai. She thinks you're a threat and wants nothing to do with you. She doesn't really want you to see Jai.'

'What does her husband think of the decision? Ben, isn't it?'

'Yes, Ben is like you. Kind, silent, thoughtful, measured and with more common sense than Jess and I combined.'

Noah grinned. 'I'm all those things?'

She cocked her head with a smile. 'Yes.'

'Can you talk sense into your sister?'

'She thinks I have sided with you.'

'Have you?'

'No. There are no sides. I want what's best for Jai.'

He wasn't convinced.

'Has Jai been asked?'

'Of course. He wants to see you Sunday, hang out with his Unc, as he calls it.'

'Great, so there's no problem.'

'Jessy insists on coming. She'll grill you. Give you grief. Tell you you aren't worthy of seeing him again.'

'I can handle it.'

'It's not that I think you can't. I'm worried about Jess.'

'She won't cope if I have a relationship with Jai?'

'It's her insecurities about adopting instead of giving birth. She lost her womb young. Jai is her only child. She's terrified. It could break her.'

'I'll be as understanding and kind as I can, but I have to have a relationship with Jai. How do I deal with her?'

'Be yourself. The way you care for Hope melts my heart. If Jessy sees some of that maybe she'll loosen up.'

'Come here,' he said with open arms. He was grateful when she stepped towards him. He'd been afraid she would get in the car and go.

'I know you'll do the right thing.' She rested her head on his shoulder. They fit so well like tight woolly gloves in winter. His body felt her through every nerve, but he tried to ignore it.

Because Jessy and Emma were twins, she would always have a deep bond, which understandably made her torn. He and Kendwa were so in sync they could have been twins. That connection made Kendwa's

116

death feel like a kick to the sternum when it happened and always would.

'I'll do my best,' he tilted her chin, 'and when it's all sorted, I'm going to marry you, Emma.'

Thick eyelashes fluttered as her eyes widened. A sweet smile broke out on her lips. 'I may hold you to that, Noah Cooper.'

Chapter 19

Blood dripped from the girl's swollen eye, where his punch inflicted a gaping cut on the cheekbone. Wade wiped the blood from his knuckles.

'I told you what would happen if you were a bad girl,' Wade said in a low, menacing voice, licking the blood from his fingers. His eyes were narrow slits as he stared her down, shaking his fist.

The girl shielded her face with her arm. 'Stop. I'll do anything. Stop hurting me. I didn't mean to make you mad.' Her naked body shook as she backed away on the bed.

'You'll spread your legs?'

'Yes,' she said in a whisper with tears streaming down her face.

'Good girl. You love it, don't you? You love me, and what I give you?'

She nodded mutely. Wade wiped the blood under her eye with an antiseptic wipe. 'Let me fix your pretty face first.' Slowly and gently, he cleaned the wound as she flinched. He bound it with butterfly clips and plastered a bandage over it. It could have been a kind gesture, but the over-the-top kindness seemed sinister. 'You should take more care next time.' The room smelled of Dettol and blood.

She nodded, shutting her eyes as if she expected further punishment. He kissed her. It wasn't enduring; instead, a possessive mark of his territory.

'Now, where were we?' He tossed the swab and crawled over her on the bed.

Once she slinked from the motel room covering her black eye with her handbag, Wade showered. Her blood stained his bruised knuckles. The scent of her lingered in the room reminding him of her fear. As much as he liked seeing the plea in her eyes, he'd gone too far. Getting caught wasn't an option. He smacked the tiles with a flat palm. 'Fuck it!' he yelled.

Besides he needed to concentrate on Emma.

When he returned home, he passed his mother, picking up the empty wine glass barely hanging from her fingertips. She mumbled incoherently, but he ignored her, placing the glass upright on the kitchen bench and heading to his room.

The door slammed. Wade knew it wouldn't wake his mother from her comatose state. The computer had a USB cord plugged into it. He took the other end, inserting it into his phone and waited for the sound of Emma's voice.

'I'll do my best — and when it's all sorted, I'm going to marry you, Emma.'

That fuckin' guy's voice again. Why was he back?

Wade waited for Emma's reply, thumping his fist on the desk. 'I may hold you to that, Noah Cooper.'

When he heard the distinct sound of kissing Wade ripped the phone from the computer. Thumping his head against the desk, he tried to think of what to do next. His mind churned like a washing machine with muddy clothes.

Downloading the spy app to Emma's phone was more accessible than setting up cameras in her house. Besides, she rarely stayed at the townhouse. The phone brainwave came from an episode of SWAT. Upload the app and record every conversation on her phone. He'd forgotten he'd even done it. They'd been on a second date when she'd gone to the ladies room leaving the phone on the restaurant table. He'd thought the videos would capture what he needed, but the conversations on the phone gave him the best ideas for revenge.

Though jealous as the devil, listening to Emma talking dirty with the fuckwit made him want to fuck. He found the latest girl at the local pub. She thought he was a popstar and he didn't tell her otherwise making it easy to seduce her. But though he'd got his rocks off Emma's face stayed in his head. He pictured fear in her eyes and his cock where it belonged.

Ignoring the gash on his head from smashing it into the desk, Wade picked up the phone, plugging it back into the computer. The child's voice, high and excited discussing seeing his parents after their trip. Emma, laughing and saying, 'I love you so much, Tiger. You're the greatest little kid I've ever met.'

Wade's eyes grew colder. The kid. All along the kid could make her change her mind. In his twisted mind, a new plan formed. It was muddy and unclear, but he'd figure it out as he went. All he knew was the kid, Tiger, Jai, whatever they called him, the curly-haired kid could be the key.

A smirk formed on his thin lips as he glanced at the bruises on his knuckles. It would have been easy to murder the slut, even easier to do away with a kid. The urge to kill boiled in him like lava at the bottom of a volcano ready to erupt.

Chapter 20

Noah paced as he watched and waited for Emma's family to arrive at Winder's Park. An Ocean breeze blew from Currumbin Beach, or The Alley, as the locals called it, along the creek whipping at the tarpaulins and umbrellas erected along the sandy stretch. Families gathered for barbecues, picnics, paddleboarding and swimming. Pelicans perched like guardians of the creek on top of brass sculptures of the same aquatic birds.

A large SUV with signwriting 'Moon Under Safaris' drove around the road loop and pulled up under a tree in the bitumen carpark as a smaller car vacated.

Noah's cheek twitched as he watched the male driver edge within inches of the car in front before straightening up and cutting the engine. The man looked to be in his forties or fifties with think hair and a natural smile. The woman beside him looked like an older version of Emma. She was beautiful. *Emma's mum.* She stared at him as if she'd seen a ghost. People in the back of the vehicle slid across the seats to get out.

'It looks like the whole fuckin' family is here,' Noah said under his breath. *No pressure.*

Jai opened a back door and ran towards him. Though he wore a grin, he stopped short as if he wasn't sure what to do. He glanced back at the woman walking behind him. Nearly as pretty as Emma's, but she scowled and her arms wrapped around her chest as if protecting herself.

'It's okay, Jai. I guess it's kinda awkward since your mum and dad didn't know I'd come back. How about we shake hands?'

'Cool with me. Hey, where's Hope? I thought she'd be here,' Jai said, lifting his hand but curling it to give Noah a fist pump instead of a shake. At least Noah responded quickly, making Jai laugh.

Noah glance at Jessy to see her frown deepen. Her husband, Ben, stood beside her with his arm around her waist, whispering something in her ear, probably trying to keep her calm. Emma's mum and step-dad waved and said hello before walking towards a picnic bench with the weekend paper in the man's large hands.

'I decided this first time it might be best to leave Hope at home,' Noah said, walking towards Ben and Jessy.

'Don't be embarrassed about her. I think she's one of the nicest people I know.' Jai bounced on his feet. *The kid's like an Eveready battery.*

Noah opened his mouth but couldn't speak. Finally, he said, 'Thanks for saying that. I'm never embarrassed about Hope. I'm ashamed of the stupid people who think she's any different to them. I've tried to teach her to embrace who she is and always be kind.'

Jai nodded.

Ben put out his hand. 'Hi, Noah. Nice to meet you.'

Jessy coughed and shot Ben a glance.

'Mum, this is my Uncle Noah. I have a cousin, Hope, too but she couldn't be here today,' Jai said, watching his mum with wide, hopeful eyes.

Jessy took Noah's hand, shaking it firmly like she was at a corporate meeting. 'I won't pretend I'm happy about this, Mr Cooper, or your intrusion on my family but my son decided to spend time with you. I have to respect his decision for now.' She stepped closer, eyeballing him. 'If you set one foot wrong with him, you will never see him again.' She dropped her hand as if Noah burnt her.

'Muuuuum!' Jai pleaded.

'I promise you, Jessy —' Noah began.

'Mrs Stuart to you,' Jessy interrupted.

'Muuuuum! No one calls you that, not even my friends.' Jai rolled his eyes. 'My uncle and I are going to hang out without you.'

'As I was saying. I promise I'll always have Jai's interests at heart. He's my brother's only child —'

Jessy spoke again, narrowing her eyes. 'Was. He's our child. Don't you ever forget it.' Her voice held a don't-mess-with-me tone.

Noah shook his head. He tried to meet Jessy's glare with a kind look. Couldn't she see he was a nice guy who loved kids? No, anger blinded her. She would be a hard nut to crack. Emma warned him. *Dear sweet, Emma.* 'So, where's Emma?'

'Working on a deadline,' Ben said.

'She's not your girlfriend, so it's none of your business,' Jessy said. 'Okay, Jai you have an hour. We'll go sit with Nanna and Grandad until then. Oh and Noah, my mother and step-father will need to speak to you after that.'

'Sure. No problem. Come on, Jai. I have fun planned. Since you love skateboarding I though a little SUP might be fun.'

'Sick. You brought two boards?' Jai said as they walked down to the water's edge.

122

'Mine's a little bigger to carry my weight, but I'm sure this one will suit you.'

'Is it Hope's?'

'Yeah but she's not balanced enough yet, so she usually sits or stands on mine while I paddle. She's getting there though. Do you know what to do?'

'Yep, I've had a couple of turns on Aunt Em's. Stand with your feet braced and paddle each side. Dig in to stop or turn. Right?'

'Right enough,' said Noah as he watched Jai step onto Hope's board. He wobbled slightly but found his feet.

'Do you want me to push you out?' But Jai already dug into the sand, pushed off and slid the board through the water like a pro.

'See if you can catch me,' Jai called over his shoulder.

Noah stepped on his board and paddled towards his nephew, feeling like a part of Kendwa returned. He grinned as he leisurely followed the kid from Zanzibar who'd made a home with a foreign family in Australia. *How did the world work like that?*

Noah paddled beside Jai.

'How do you think this will work, Uncle Noah?' Jai asked.

'By your mother, you mean?'

'Yeah. She's a great mum, but she's overprotective. It's kinda stupid because I can do anything, swim, sport, skating, surfing and even though I'm better than most other kids, even older ones, she freaks out like I'm cotton wool or something. It's why she's mean to you.'

'She's not mean. She's defensive. She's protecting you because she doesn't know me. I guess she's probably threatened because we're blood.'

'I suppose so. Hey, do you know how to steer that?' Jai laughed as Noah's board hit his. He wobbled.

'I do. I'm checking out how good you are at this.'

Jai wobbled some more. His face held a determined line as he moved his paddle and steadied his wobbling knees. He dropped the paddle and dived into the water. He surfaced laughing. 'I wanted to get wet. I did not fall off.'

Noah dived in too. Surfacing beside Jai. 'Me neither.' He dunked Jai's head. Jai surfaced and dunked him back, pushing hard on his head to finally get his nose underwater.

They laughed and splashed until Noah noticed the time on his watch. 'Better head back before your Mum really freaks out.'

'Yeah, I guess,' Jai said frowning briefly. 'I've had fun. Can Hope come next time?'

'I'm sure she'd like to. We'll see. Race you back.'

When they returned to shore, Jessy stood barefoot on the sand with her hands on her hips.

123

'Oh, boy,' said Jai, rolling his eyes.

'Don't let your mum see that. You respect her even if you don't agree. I can sort this stuff out, and I'm sure one day we'll all be one big happy family.' He ruffled Jai's head. 'Drag the board up. I can get it later. Hi, Jessy, sorry we lost track of time.' Noah shrugged, smiling at her.

'Don't be so smug.' She passed a towel to Jai. 'Come on, Jai. We have a barbecue to go to. Noah, please be kind to Mum and Shaun.'

Noah bristled. Jessy bugged him. No matter how hard he tried, she would not let up. He shook the water from his hair and grabbed a towel from the sand, patting down his body.

A giggle ensued from the teenage girls sunbaking nearby. One raised her sunglasses, giving him a brazen appraisal.

'And stop with the macho guy shit,' she said, pointing to his bare chest.

Noah raised his eyebrows. 'The what?'

'You know showing off your pecs 'n' all that.' She waved a finger at him. Her cheeks blushed pink.

'Oh.' Noah finally caught on as one of the teenagers wolf-whistled. *Jesus!* 'I'll put a shirt on before I see your mum. See you next time, Jai.'

'If there is a next time,' Jessy quipped.

Noah strolled towards the picnic bench without looking back. Hackles rose, but he tried to remain calm.

'Hi,' he said as Ben stood.

Ben patted his shoulder as he passed. 'See ya, mate. Don't worry, her bark's worse than her bite.' The little family walked off with Jessy huffing and Jai grinning and waving.

Emma's step-father stood to shake Noah's hand. 'Hi, Noah. I'm Shaun, and this is my beautiful wife, Ali.'

Noah immediately liked the man. His blue eyes held no malice, only compassion, and it was obvious he loved his wife. Ali surprised him by standing and hugging him.

'It's nice to meet you, Noah.' She sat quickly as if embarrassed by her show of affection. Noah sat facing them. 'I — you look a lot like your brother.'

Noah smiled, scratching his head. 'It's so weird, for years we hung out as mates and never even knew we were brothers. We thought it was cool to be mistaken for brothers, but the penny never dropped.'

'Until you had a DNA test,' Ali said, placing her tiny hand over Shauns.

Shaun looked slightly uncomfortable, Noah thought it best to cut to the chase. 'So you wanted to talk about the business. Can I set one thing straight I don't want the business. It's yours, well Jai's one day, but I appreciate the hard work you put into it for Kendwa.'

He noticed Shaun wince at the name.

'The lawyers say it's not so simple. Because Kendwa's wishes were written and witnessed, they stand. We can draft new documents signing your rights to the business back to us until Jai comes of age.' Shaun said. 'There's considerable wealth in the business. You really need to think about it.'

Ali elbowed him. 'Our lawyer drafted new documents for you to look over. They're in the car. I'll get them.' Ali stood. Noah realised how petite she was, a good head shorter than both her daughters.

Shaun leaned in, cupping his face with his hand. 'You don't know about Kendwa and Ali?'

Noah glanced back at the car. Wow, he could see what Kendwa would like in Ali, similar to Emma. 'I thought it must have been Jessy who had been with Kendwa. How did Jessy end up with Jai?'

'It's a long story, but Ali met him and they hit it off, kind of dated while she was on holiday in Africa. She was left with Jai, probably because you couldn't be found, but she'd already raised her children, and Jessy wanted Jai badly. Take it easy on Ali and Jess. They've been through enough.'

'Haven't we all.' Noah sighed. 'I know this is complicated, but I aim to disrupt your family as little as possible. I only want to know Kendwa's son. And I think it's fair for my daughter to have her cousin in her life too.'

'Mate, I agree, but I'm not sure you'll be throwing away the business too easy when you see the figures.'

'It won't matter. I'm doing okay for myself. Hope and I don't need much.'

Ali's perfume wafted as she passed Noah a yellow envelope. 'Take them home and think about it,' she said. She sat next to Shaun with their shoulders brushing.

'I don't need to.' Noah pulled the document out of the envelope. 'Got a pen? I'll sign now and at least put this part behind us.' A large tree provided shade, but the summer heat was stifling even with the breeze. Ali waved a folded newspaper at the side of her beautiful face. Noah kept his hand over the documents so they wouldn't blow, glancing at the ease of the couple in front of him.

'No. We've thought long and hard about this. Our proposal is for you to have a third of the business, we keep a third. The other will be Jai's when he turns eighteen. We keep it in the trust until then.'

'Why? You don't have to do this. I have my own successful veterinary business. Please, I want you to keep it. I believe, from what Emma tells me, you've been terrific custodians to Jai. Kendwa wouldn't have known back then. He probably thought I'd never have security, running around hiding from my ex-wife's family and going bush, but I do.'

Ali smiled at Shaun and back to Noah. 'Emma said you'd be like this.'

'Like what?' Noah rubbed his chin.

'Kind and considerate.'

Noah smiled. 'She said that?'

'And more.' Ali giggled. 'Maybe you two will have a chance once Jessy calms down. I can see why you'd be good for Emma.'

'Anyway, mate. We urge you to take the documents and read them. Don't make a hasty decision. We're rather relieved you weren't going to demand the half. Moon Under Safaris is our life passion. We love the business.'

'Well, that's obviously why it's doing so well.' Noah whistled when he read the net worth. 'Wow, Kendwa would never believe it could have gone this well. Running it from Australia helped I guess.'

'Less red tape and bribery and weird African logic.' Ali laughed. 'Anyway, we've taken up enough of your time. Thank you for meeting with us.'

They stood. Shaun shook his hand. Ali held his arm for a moment and said, 'Thank you.' Shoving the documents back in the envelope and handing them to him.

Noah watched them drive off, clutching the envelope to his chest. *Ali and Kendwa.* He needed to find out more about that. It was time to ring Metra and get the full story — *enough family secrets.*

He strolled back to the sand, washing down the paddleboards and easily lifting, one after the other, to carry above his head to place on the roof racks of his ute. After strapping them tightly, he climbed into the cab, reaching for his mobile phone in the glove box. He wanted to check if Hope was okay for his mum. She'd been sulking all morning because she couldn't come with him to see Jai. She'd never had a best friend and now a cousin too. It seemed history repeated itself. *Me and Kendwa. Jai and Hope. Emma and Jessy.*

He noticed a voice message from Emma. Plugging it into ApplePlay, he played it on loud speaker, and drove towards home.

'Hi, Noah. I wanted to check how you were. I hope you had a lovely time with Jai — um. I hope it went well. You know. Anyhow — after last night, I was thinking about our kiss. Well, kisses, I should say.' She giggled. 'I, oh, don't worry. I'm being silly. Just checking you're fine.'

Noah grinned so broad he felt his face might split. His heart ached for Emma. Hearing she felt the same, in her cute, funny way gave him a boost. Jessy had got to him, making him feel like he would never make inroads with her and sabotage not only his time with Jai but also his love for Emma.

126

He couldn't imagine cheerful family barbecues with Jessy glaring at him with daggers in her eyes. Also, he didn't want to drive a wedge between the sisters. He knew how essential siblings were, especially after losing Kendwa. Most of all, he didn't wish for innocent Jai to be caught in the crossfire.

Halfway home, he said, 'Hey, Siri, call Emma.' He held his breath, waiting for her to pick up.

'Hi, Noah. You got my message?'

'Yeah, thanks. I've been thinking about us.'

'Oh, your tone sounds like something I don't want to hear.'

'You know how I feel about you, but I don't want your sister any more upset than she is.'

'She was that bad.'

'Worse. She may as well have spat at me.'

'What about the others? How was Mum?'

'They're fantastic. I think we could all get on fine. Emma, it's just you know how close Kendwa and I were? I don't want you to ruin things with your twin. She's always going to be your sister.'

'I know, but I'm pissed off with her. She knows how much I care for you, and she's not even giving you a chance.'

'I can understand why she is defensive. Jai's her precious child. The only one she can ever have. It's like she's a wild animal. You know like an elephant will protect its calf even if it needs to attack a lion.'

Emma laughed. 'You're the lion, and she's the elephant. Doubt if she'd be impressed with the analogy.'

Noah laughed. 'You can always see the sunny side, can't you?'

'I try.' She sighed. 'You won't see me until Jessy is onboard, will you?'

'I'm sorry, babe, but I think it's for the best. It's killing me, but we don't want to push her buttons.' Noah tried to keep his focus on the road, but he could hear the tremble in Emma's voice.

'I know, I guess you're right.' She paused. In barely a whisper, she said, 'It's killing me too.'

Could it actually be the end of their love?

127

Chapter 21

Emma stormed through the side gate and found Jessy in her backyard, tending to the vegetable patch.

'Oh, hey. I didn't know you were calling in. I thought you had a deadline. Check out how good my coriander is growing.' Jessy pointed to the green herb, snipping some with small scissors before placing it in an overflowing plastic bowl.

Emma chewed the inside of her cheek, trying to control her rage. 'Why didn't you at least try to be civil?' She stood with her hands on her hips.

'Cool it, Emm. I have no idea what you're talking about. Seriously? I spoke to the guy. He seemed a jerk, showing off paddleboarding with Jai with his shirt off showing all his damn muscles.'

'Most blokes who paddleboard have their shirts off. It's friggin' hot out. He was doing what he does every day, enjoying the creek water. I bet Jai loved it.'

'Well, so did the gaggle of girls watching him from the beach. He sure knows how to get people's attention.'

'The thing is, Jess. He has no idea. Noah's not one bit conceited about his looks. I'm sure he didn't even realise women were watching him. He would have been paying more attention to Jai than anyone.'

Jessy swung the bowl on her hip and faced Emma. 'I saw what I saw. You can't make me change my mind about him.'

'Jessy, why?' Emma wrung her hands together. 'He's Jai's uncle. You can't change that. You're better off trying to like Noah than being mean.'

'Don't call me, mean. You know I'm not. Look, Emma, you're not a mum. You can't possibly understand. You don't know what it's like to share your child with a stranger.'

'I held your hand and cried with you in the hospital when you lost your —'

'Womb, Emma. I lost my damn womb, something you still have.'

Emma ignored Jessy's bitterness. 'I was with you from the start, Jessy. The day you held Jai for the first time and your instant connection with him. I rode your emotional ride with you, and I always support you. Don't you dare say I couldn't possibly understand. I'm your twin, for Christ sake!' Emma's bottom lip trembled.

'Shit, Emm. Don't go crying on me.' Jessy put the bowl down and put her arms around Emma. 'I can't control how I feel when the protectiveness comes over me. To be honest, Noah and Jai were like two peas in a pod paddling out on the creek together, looking like father and son. Have you any idea how much it hurts to see that? What about Ben? He's feeling threatened too.'

'Okay, I'm sorry. I know this all sucks.'

'Anyway, I thought it wouldn't matter to you. You broke up with the guy. He mustn't have been right for you. He was probably a prick about it too.'

'Yes, we did break up, but I know it's only temporary. He's not a prick, far from it.'

Jessy laughed. 'Come on, Emma. You said when you broke up with Harvey Godfrey in year ten. You said he would marry you once he made the Red's footy team, which of course he didn't make. Yeah, and where is he now? Married to stupid Liah Robb with three kids and a boring accounting firm.'

Emma laughed at that. 'Dodged a bullet there, didn't I?'

Jessy laughed too. Lips pursed, she tilted her head to the side. 'Hang on. I know you too well. You do think you're getting back with Noah.'

Emma took a deep breath. She could hide it from her twin and hope things would blow over and Jess would be more agreeable to Noah in the future. Or she could come clean now and risk Jessy thinking she'd taken sides. The problem being, Jessy always saw through her lies. You can't hide some things from your twin.

'Spit it out, Emma. What's going on?'

'It's simple, Jess. I'm totally, head-over-heels, forever-after in-love with Noah. There's no doubt he feels the same about me. He said when all this is over, he will marry me.' She waited for Jessy to respond.

'Holy shit!'

'Is that all you can say?'

'Well, I'm thinking up an appropriate answer. I come back from Africa and get confronted with all this, our family threatened by a stranger who can take Jai away and now you're expecting me to welcome him into the family with open arms?'

'Yes.'

'You know if it was anyone else; a nice, sexy guy who wasn't Jai's uncle, I'd be the happiest person in the world for you.' Jessy took Emma's shoulders 'I want to, Emma, but I can't. I'm sorry. Please just stay away from him for our family's sake.'

Emma let tears fall down her cheeks. 'You don't know what you're asking me to do.' She shook her head.

'I do Emma, but blood's thicker than water.' As words came out of Jessy's mouth, she clamped it with her hand. Emma could tell she wished she'd never said them, considering Jai was not her blood. Emma was. 'I meant —'

'I know what you meant. You said it. I didn't.' Emma ran from the yard, out the gate and onto the street. She only lived two blocks from her sister's house. With tears tracking down her cheeks, she ran home wishing something could change to make her sister realise Noah was a good guy. *The best.*

When she arrived home, she changed into a swimsuit, grabbed her paddleboard and paddle. With angry-stomps, she strode onto the jetty. The wind died to barely a whisper of a breeze, and the humidity oozed as thick as the cicada's buzzing in the bush. The creek water glistened smooth as glass, reflecting the tea-trees and gums lining the banks.

Emma let the tranquillity sink in. She closed her eyes, sniffing the salty-bushland, listening to the lull of water lapping over her board and her paddle slicing the water. She knew the way well. Few vessels were on the water. Most were probably closer to the beach where they'd get a hint of a breeze off the ocean.

'Hey, watch where you're going lady,' called a boy on a canoe, 'ya almost hit me.'

Emma snapped her eyes open and righted her board in time. She hadn't even heard the canoe glide close; being caught up in her thoughts. Emma knew why Jessy remained a mother bear about Jai. She understood the profound inadequacy Jessy felt after her heartbreak of not being able to bear a child. It was taken from her in a terrible twist of fate when an embryo grew inside her fallopian tubes. The day it happened was so bitterly heartbreaking and to make matters worse, their mother was working in Africa having her fling with Kendwa.

Jessy deserved some compassion, and if Emma were honest with herself, Jessy's words were true. She couldn't understand the depth of Jessy's devotion to Jai. Emma was yet a mother. She wished to be one day, of course.

She wondered about her mum being in love with Kendwa before Shaun. Emma couldn't picture her mother with anyone but Shaun. They seemed perfect together. It was unusual, though, to think her mum was madly in love with Noah's brother. The same taste in men ran through their veins. In a lot of ways, Noah was like Shaun too. Quiet, kind, strong, dependable men. From what Ali told her, Kendwa had not always been dependable. She wondered if Noah became reliable when his wife left him to raise their child alone. A lot she still didn't know about Noah, but she dearly wanted to find out.

***

Noah grinned. Again, thinking about Emma made her materialise in front of him. He'd wished he could see her, hold her, kiss her; more — . He wanted so much more. She paddled towards him with her eyes shut, looking to be humming, which made him smile.

'Hold on, Hopey. We're paddling this way,' he said to Hope, who sat at the middle point of the board in front of his feet.

Hope pointed. 'Nice lady.'

'Yes, Hope. Emma. Remember?'

'She bring Sasha. Oh, oh. She Tiger's aunt.'

'That's right, Hope. It kinda makes her family. Hey, don't get too excited. Keep still or we'll fall off.' He laughed as Hope, trailed her fingers in the water and glanced at him with a smile.

Noah glided his board beside Emma's, waiting for her to hear them and open her eyes. He didn't have to wait long because Hope yelled. 'Emma, you awake. Emma we here.'

Emma's pretty eyes snapped open. She did a double-take wobbling on her board. 'Oh, sorry. I was off with the fairies.' She smiled, and Noah's heart tightened.

There was something serene, captivating and adorable about Emma. The electricity burning between them only intensified those feelings — *no way to ignore such fire*. Even with his daughter between them, he remained spellbound enough to forget words and reason.

Half a metre away and he could feel her heat. His nerves tingled in the best way possible. He didn't think he'd ever had the hots for any woman with so much intensity. He drank her in, brazenly raking his eyes over her from tip to toe.

'Fairies?' Hope asked. 'Where are they?' She glanced around.

'Oh, sorry, Hope. It's just an expression for daydreaming. I was daydreaming.'

'Was it nice dream?'

'Yes, Hope. Very nice.' Emma shot Noah a raised eyebrow, nod and a megawatt smile. *She dreams of me.*

'Hi, Emma,' Noah said, with his throat catching.

Hope glanced at him with a questioning look.

'You're out earlier than usual this arvo,' Emma said, shifting the paddle as she drifted to the left.

'I promised Hope since I didn't take her this morning with Jai.'

'Are you enjoying it, Hope?'

'Yeah. It's hot. Water's cold.'

'Refreshing isn't it.' Emma agreed. To Noah, she said, 'Did you read the contracts?'

132

'Not yet. Tonight maybe.' He shrugged his shoulders. 'Did you talk to your sister?'

'I did, but she's not budging. I feel like it would take a miracle for her to change her mind about you.'

'I thought it was that bad? So, what I said, it's what we have to do.'

'Stay apart,' Emma said it with her sweet lips slightly parted as her board rocked against his.

It made him think of them rocking together in bed. He glanced down at Hope who had a befuddled, screwed-up-nose looking back and forwards between them.

'Dad?'

'Yeah, Hope.' Emma's arm brushed his making him want to break all the rules they were imposing on themselves. She reached her free hand to stroke his cheek, never taking her eyes off him.

'Do you like Emma?' Hope shifted her bottom on the board trying to get a better look at the adults.

'I do —' As he said it, Hope attempted to stand, making them both topple off their board.

Emma wobbled on her's but bent her legs and dug the paddle to stay on board. She gasped, but once Hope swam to the board and held on safely, giggling, Emma laughed with them.

'Hope, I told you to keep still,' Noah said with a deep chuckle.

'I hot, Dad. Swim good. Yeah?'

He ruffled her hair and kissed her wet cheek. 'Yes, a swim is perfect in this weather. Do you think Emma needs a swim?' He winked.

'Yep.' They looked up at Emma, who shook her head.

'Stay, Hope.' Noah swam to Emma's board. It's either I rock your boat, or you come willingly.' He grinned up at Emma, reaching for her hand.

'You already rock my boat quite well, Noah Cooper,' she said with a wink, letting him pull her from the board into the water. She giggled as she came up for air.

Noah thought she was probably the most laid-back, easy-going woman he'd met. She joined in on the fun, never complaining, only going with the flow.

Wiping her hair from her face and readjusting the sun-visor, she let Noah wrap his arms around her. He felt her warm body and relished the fact she wrapped her legs around his hips. *Fuck, it felt so damn good.* Lucky their bodies were underwater, and Hope couldn't see the erotic embrace.

'Hey, Hope. You're an excellent swimmer.' Emma smiled at Hope, who climbed onto her dad's board.

'Can't you swim? Dad has to hold you up.'

Noah sputtered. His daughter was observant. Regretfully Emma unwrapped her limbs from his.

Emma swam out a few metres showing Hope a decent freestyle. 'No, I can swim fine. I was just a little shocked when I came off the board and your dad, being the gentleman he is, made sure I was okay.'

Hope seemed to accept the explanation and clapped when Emma swam back to her board.

Noah reached for her hand underwater, clinging tightly. 'I plan on convincing your sister I'm a good guy. We won't be apart long,' he whispered.

Emma climbed on her board. 'I'm glad we all ran into each other. It was lovely seeing you again, Hope. Can you say hello to Stinky and Sasha for me.'

'Okay. Why you not visit?' Hope asked, gripping the edges of the board with her hands as Noah climbed back onboard.

'I — um,' Emma let it trail, sending Noah a you-tell-her look.

'It's complicated, Hopey, but Emma's our friend.'

'Dad's *VERY GOOD* friend,' Hope said, rolling her eyes and giggling.

Emma nearly fell off her board. Her mouth stayed open in surprise.

'At least Hope likes you, Emma,' Noah said with a chuckle.

'She does, doesn't she?' Emma smiled, waving to Hope and Noah as she turned her board towards the jetty.

'Well our swim cooled things off,' Noah said to Hope.

But it hadn't. He was as hot as ever for Emma.

134

Chapter 22

The beach was choc-full of tourists and locals. From Currumbin Alley at the creek entrance to the north, down to the Vikings Surf Club perched on Elephant Rock at the southern end; colourful towels, umbrellas, shade tents and people filled the sand. The biggest huddle of eager beachgoers played in the shallows between the red and yellow flags near the surf club. Beside them, eager nippers lined up for a swim race.

Noah slipped his sunglasses on to watch from the balcony of the surf club. Jai rang Noah on Tuesday to ask if he'd like to watch him compete. Noah wasn't sure if Jessy or Ben knew of his invitation. He thought it best to observe it well away from the parents on the beach.

The colourful carnival was against other Gold Coast surf clubs. Noah quickly spotted Jai. He was tall for his age, darker than the other kids, and his crop of blonde curls made him stand out. Being only nine, it seemed probable he would have the large, muscular frame of his father when he grew to a man. Particularly with his love of sport and adventure.

Watching Jai resurfaced memories of Kendwa. Noah wondered if Ali had them too. The resemblance was uncanny, and it would be more so, the older Jai got — a constant reminder of what Noah lost, but he tried not to see it in such a way. He wanted the fact Jai was in his life to fill the void Kendwa left.

A keen resemblance between Ali and Emma made him see how his older brother would have been mesmerised by Ali. It did make him glad his brother found another love after the grief of losing Sharli so tragically. The knowledge Kendwa was happy before he died seemed bittersweet.

Jai's solid swimming brought Noah out of his thoughts. Jai swam ahead of the pack. Noah smacked the table, urging Jai on. 'Go, Jai. Stay close to the buoy. Yes, that's it.' Jai stroked two-body lengths ahead of the nearest child. As he came around the orange buoy, a set of waves formed out the back. 'Get ready. You've got this.' Noah held his breath as Jai paddled hard to make the first wave. It passed him in a surge of

135

foam, but the next wave rose high. Jai swam into the curve, riding the wave to shore.

Jai stood and ran splashing through the shore to race up the beach and win the race. Jessy embraced him. Ben stood back but high-fived Jai as he passed. Noah stood, clapping and cheering over the balcony, losing himself in the moment because he felt pride for Jai. Jai waited at the finish line congratulating the other competitors. *What a terrific kid.*

Noah's smile faded when he realised Jessy noticed him. She shot a withering look his way and said something to Ben, who glanced towards the balcony. Noah ducked behind a pillar, feeling like an intruder and an idiot for hiding. When he moved back in view, he hoped something preoccupied them. He noticed Jai looking around. Ben turned his shoulders to face the surf club and pointed. Noah waved back as Jai's face lit up. Jessy stormed off.

Noah wasn't sure what to do. They'd seen him, so it seemed stupid not to go down and congratulate Jai. He took the stairs out of the surf club and ran to the beach. Holding his shoes in his hands, he scanned the beach. Jai spotted him, running towards him with a medal bouncing on his chest.

'You saw it? You saw my swim?' Jai asked, fiddling with a damp green club cap on his head. He lifted the medal to Noah.

'Yeah, mate. You were impressive. I could see you stayed calm in the huddle around the buoy and took off like a rocket once past it. You timed your wave perfectly.' He flipped the medal over to study it before dropping it back on Jai's chest. 'Your dad would have been proud.'

'That's two proud dads, then,' Jai said with a grin. 'Mum's pissed you're here though. Sorry. I didn't tell her because I knew she'd be unhappy.'

'It's okay. I'm sure she'll come around eventually.'

'So you keep saying. You don't know how stubborn — hey, Mum. Uncle Noah's here.' Jai's voice changed to false-chirpy.

'Mmmm, so he is,' said Jessy.

Ben stood beside her, giving Noah a slight smile. 'Jai, you'd better go and shower off. We've got to get going. Say goodbye to your mates.'

'Sure, Dad. See ya, Unc. Thanks for coming.'

Noah grinned until he realised Jessy glared at him. 'Bye, Jai.' He waved but dropped his hand quickly. 'Do you have something on your mind, Jessy?'

'How dare you come down here? Nippers happens to be family weekend time.'

'I hadn't seen him in a fortnight. He rang and asked me to come. It's a bit unfair on the kid to say no.'

'You should have run it by me. Give me your phone.' She placed her palm face up.

Noah reached for his back pocket. 'You want my number?' He raised his eyebrows. He knew his humour was lost on her, but what the heck.

'As if. Don't play games. If Jai rings you, you check with me first before you come poking your nose around.' She tapped her number into his phone with an angry thumb. 'And stay away from my sister.'

'What?'

'A friend of ours told me you met on the creek.'

'I — yeah but that was out of either of our control.'

'How convenient.' Jessy passed his phone back. 'Oops! I deleted Emma's contact.'

Noah shook his head. 'You really are a —' *piece of work.*

'What were you going to say?' Jessy narrowed her eyes.

'Protective mother.' He put his hands up in surrender. 'I get it. I'm over the top shielding Hope sometimes. I'm trying to understand from your side of things. Look, I have a lot going on with my family too. How about I don't see Jai for another fortnight and let things cool down.'

Jessy took a deep breath. 'I'm not as bad as you think I am.'

'I'm sure you're as lovely as your sister when you're not protecting your son.'

'Thank you,' she said before striding briskly away without another word.

Noah rubbed his forehead, stunned. He ran his hands through his hair. God, the woman could be exasperating. He thought he could crack her hard exterior, but he wasn't so sure when he noted the last parting narrowed gaze over her shoulder.

Jai would probably be disappointed, but Noah knew it seemed necessary to keep his distance from Jessy. Perhaps she would see some sense if he did. *It sure beats trying to talk to her around.* Noah was becoming exhausted by it.

In the coming weeks, he had enough to do. His father's lawyer wanted to talk about the possibility of dropping the charges. Noah didn't know the details, but he hoped it would be a bright thing in the weeks ahead.

Another scheduled meeting with Hope's teacher and teacher's aide would take place on Tuesday. One of the parents complained about Hope being in a mainstream class. Noah seethed about it for a bit but knew he couldn't help other people's opinions of his daughter.

He'd given Sasha some pain-killers for her tumour. He couldn't have operated again, because each time another tumour grew more substantial than the last. All he could do was keep his father's beloved dog comfortable.

When he returned home, Stinky concerned him the most. Under the shade of Avocado trees, the old elephant lay curled up on a pile of hay. Noah could hear a deep rumbling groan as he neared.

'Not a good day, Stinky my girl.'

The elephant eyed him with blinking long lashes no longer holding the lushness of her troubled youth. A tear dripped from her eye as she reached for his face with her trunk. He let her feel him. He knew it gave her comfort. Elephants didn't like to be alone. She missed her brother Jumbo, and she knew she would soon join him.

The time to put her down grew closer. Noah knew it, but it hurt to acknowledge so even with his extensive veterinary training. And there were Hope and his mum. He had no idea how they would react to the death of their elephant. Keeping Stinky alive and in pain wasn't going to help them in their grief. As he watched the elephant groan, he felt her heart through her ageing skin. He didn't need a stethoscope to know it beat weakly. *Soon girl.* He would put her down over the weekend to give Hope time to come to terms with it and for them to celebrate Stinky's life.

'This weekend?' Crystal asked. He didn't need to tell his mother Stinky's time had come.

'Yeah. It's the right thing to do.'

'And Hope?' She nodded towards Hope, who drew on coloured paper at her desk in the dining room of their modest home.

'I'll find a way to tell her. We'd discussed it weeks ago.'

'Look, Dad. Stinky and you.' Hope held a pencil-drawn picture up to him.

He could make out the elephant with its wide ears, more like an African than an Asian and a stick-figure man, but it was a good drawing by Hope's standards. He always told her they were perfect. When he took the picture from her hands, he tried to keep the wobble from his voice and the tears spilling from his eyes. 'It's perfect, Hope. Hey, look at Stinky's smile.'

Crystal nodded and said, 'I'll head back to the house. Your dad will be getting hungry.' She kissed his cheek and Hope's. 'By the way, Hope's been fine. She's looking forward to school tomorrow.'

'Good to hear. What about Dad? Did he say he would see the lawyer or let me deal with it?'

'He's getting more energy but said if you could find out what's going on and fill him in so he could tend to the chores. He's let the gardening go while he recuperated.'

'Will do. Thanks, Mum.'

Noah sat across from Hope. She picked up a black pencil, drawing with concentration scrunching her button nose. 'What are you drawing now, Hopey?'

'My friend.'

'Jai?'

'No.'

'You have more friends. That's great, Hope.' He glanced over her shoulder. The boy or girl had long dark hair and a noticeable fringe. He couldn't recognise it as one of the children from school, but Hope's drawings were sometimes tricky to decipher. 'Nice picture. But how about you finish up so we can go fishing for an hour or so. I hear from old Pete some big flathead schools are passing through.'

'Fishing. Yay!' Hope dropped her pencil and ran to her room. 'I get ready.'

'Okay, sweetie. Let's have us some fish for dinner.'

***

Emma smiled at Jai. 'You're so clever. Wow, a personal best time?' She eyed his medal. 'You might be an ironman when you grow up.'

'Yeah, by four seconds. Nah, I'll be in the NRL like Uncle Ritchie or maybe move to Africa and get rid of the poachers,' Jai said earnestly as if both were not worlds apart as far as careers go. 'Hey, can I jump on the paddleboard while Mum chats?'

'Sure. It's still out on the jetty,' Emma said. 'Here, drink some water first. You've been out in the sun all day.' She passed him a tall glass of water which he sculled as quick as he could.

He rinsed it and placed it upside down on the sink before turning to Jessy. 'Mum, can I go?'

'Yes, but be careful.'

He rolled his eyes.

Emma laughed.

Jessy shot her a look. They were sitting on the deck with a glass of icy water each, facing the creek. 'He can get hurt the way he goes gangbuster at everything,' she said by way of explanation.

'I know he can, Jess, but he's a capable kid. Look how well he went today at nippers. I think he feels like you treat him like a baby when you tell him to be careful all the time.'

'Oh, so you're going to tell me how to parent now?'

'No, sorry.' Emma buttoned her mouth. Only months ago, she could talk to Jessy with honesty. Now it seemed she censured everything she said — the first time in their relationship things didn't feel natural.

'Did you hear Mum and Shaun now have the third signed off?' Jessy asked.

Emma knew she'd deliberately left out the part where Noah signed the paperwork to make it happen. 'Yeah. I heard. Mum's more relaxed. You should be too.'

'The business is not Jai. It's a different matter. Just because he signed doesn't mean he won't interfere with Jai. Today he had the gall to turn up and watch Jai's events.' Jessy folded her arms over her chest, resting them on the table.

Emma opened her mouth. Words were close to the surface, but she knew it best not to offend Jessy further. Instead, she changed the subject. 'Jai's talented at everything. He could do anything in his future, you know.'

Jessy smiled, a proud smile she always used when she heard someone complimenting Jai. Talking about Jai was her favourite subject. 'I know. Ritchie reckons he'll get picked up with Titan's development soon. He'd rather see him at The Roosters but thinks he should stay local for a bit.'

Jai competed in so many sports Emma lost count. 'What about cricket?'

'It's a summer sport, Emm. He plays cricket Saturday arvos until April.'

'I can't keep up.' Emma laughed. She wanted to ask when Noah would see Jai next but knew if she brought his name up Jess would switch back to her bad mood. 'How's Jai liking school?'

'Loves it when they do sport. Hates it when he's in class. He said he's been helping some girl whose a bit behind in English. I think he might be sweet on her or something. It's kind of him. We've brought up a good kid.'

Emma smiled. She assumed the little girl to be Hope, but she wasn't going to tell Jessy. 'I know. For such a boys' boy, he's a gentle soul. Do you think that comes from his dad?' The words were out before Emma knew it.

Jessy shot her a look.

'Ben, of course. Ben is kind and calm.' Emma smiled.

Jessy's shoulders relaxed. She took a sip of water, watching Jai over the top of her glass as he paddled around in circles. 'Didn't get it from me, that's for sure.' She laughed with a wry frown.

'You balance Ben out, Jess. You make a good team.'

'We do, don't we? Imagine if Jai had not come into our lives. I don't think I can live without our child.'

Emma took a deep breath and placed her hand on her sister's shoulder. 'I know, Jess. He's been a blessing for us all.' *Including Noah.*

140

Chapter 23

Noah strode into the lawyer's office. The ceiling-height windows displayed a broad view over Greenmount Beach at Coolangatta. Ivan Solver rose from behind a desk with a smile on a tanned, wrinkled face.

'Take a seat please, Mr Cooper.' The white-haired lawyer reached across the desk and shook Noah's hand. He shuffled paperwork stacked in a sorting tray and passed a document to Noah. 'There's the proof we need.'

Noah tilted his head towards the windows. 'The surf's picked up. I was half expecting you to cancel my appointment.'

'I was tempted. Unfortunately, work pays the bills.' The old surfer glanced wistfully at a set rolling in. Surfers vied for a take-off position.

Noah nodded as he read the document. 'My mate came through.'

'Very few people, other than those in deep intelligence, know what these lasers are or how to purchase them. Luckily, you knew it to be important. Anyway, he found a place on the dark web, and we've linked it back to Robbie Trobia.'

Noah nodded. 'The kid from the accident. I knew it. Has this information been given to anyone yet?'

'I've discussed it with his lawyer. Don't worry as a professional courtesy he hasn't told Seargent Trobia as yet.'

'What do you think will happen when he knows?'

'He's a man of the law and will not argue. The evidence does not lie. He would be aware of what it will mean to his son's case. Also, by pushing forward an agreement, he will probably keep his kid out of jail. As long as your father doesn't want to press charges. That is.'

'He won't. He's not that kind of person.' Noah tried not to grin, but he felt pretty damn pleased it would clear his father's name. 'What's the process now?'

'Trobia's lawyer will talk to his client once it's agreed your father won't press charges. He'll ask them to drop the case against him and allow Seargent Trobia to discipline his son and keep it out of the courts. Your father could sue for damage to his reputation because the police discarded evidence.' Ivan paused, spinning a pen on his desk. 'If he wanted to.'

'It couldn't be proved unless the woman who saw the officer throw it testified, right?'

'More than likely. Would she?' Ivan nodded.

'For sure, but I don't want her involved.'

'Most people these days choose to sue because of the payouts. Are you sure he wouldn't want to?'

'He's not the suing type. He's old school. Let's leave it at that. I'm sure Seargent Trobia will realise both him and his son are getting off lightly.'

'Probably.'

'Do you think they have any other card to play?'

'Definitely not. They've always known the kid was in the wrong.'

'Why put an innocent man like my father through it then?'

'People do stupid things for their children. Even go against their own values. Trobia's a good bloke. I've dealt with him a tonne of times in law. You don't have to worry. Seriously — celebrate. Your father is a free man.'

'I can't wait to break the good news to him.' Noah stood to shake the lawyer's hand.

'I'll be in touch once the negotiation is completed. When we have an agreement, your father will have to come in one more time.'

'I'm sure he won't mind. Thank you.'

Noah left the lawyer's office, unable to stop a grin from spreading across his face. He flicked his sunglasses from his forehead over his eyes and strode towards the beach pathway. He watched the surfers for a while, letting relief wash over him, and he held the mesh fence. The phone in his back pocket vibrated. It was his mum. He couldn't wait to tell her the news.

'Hi, Mum guess what?'

'Noah, I'm worried.' The tone of her voice made him stride towards the car.

'What's happened, Mum?'

'It's Hope. I can't find her at school. They've put out an amber alert.'

'Fuck no. Wasn't the teacher's aide waiting with her? How could this happen?'

'She got called away for a second. When she came back, Hope was gone. I'm still at the school. Derick said she hasn't turned up at home either.'

'Stay put. I'm leaving Coolangatta now.'

As he opened the car door, his phone rang. He didn't bother looking at the screen. 'Who's this? I can't talk I'm in a hurry.'

'Why because you've taken my son?' It was Jessy, and her voice spat with spite.

'What the fuck? Jessy this isn't the time. I'm in Coolangatta leaving my dad's lawyer, and I have better things to do than hear your accusations.' He hung up, shoving the USB cable into his phone and switching on ApplePlay so he could take messages as he drove.

The phone rang again. What the hell was Jessy playing at? 'Seriously, Jessy? I'm in no mood.'

'Where is he?' She cried. 'Please just tell me.'

Noah's foot hit the accelerator, and his heart smacked the floor at the same time. 'Jai's missing too? From the school?' he said in a low voice sounding unlike his own.

'From school, yes. A little girl's missing too.'

'My daughter.'

'Oh. I — sorry I have to go. I'm at his friend's place to see if he's here.' She hung up — *no apology for expecting the worst of him.*

Noah tried to concentrate on driving, but he broke the speed limit over the Tugun Bypass trying to reach Currumbin Valley and get to his daughter. He almost veered off the road, but didn't ease up until the school loomed in the distance.

Where could Hope have gone? He'd instilled stranger danger. They'd talked about keeping to the rules to stay safe. His mum never arrived late. How could Hope disappear? And if Jai was missing too, were they together? Perhaps they were exploring the bush and heading home. *Yeah, that's it. Nothing to worry about.* Both kids were safe.

Gravel spat from his tyres as Noah skidded into a car spot near the school. No sign of either child on the drive in, and by the time he arrived, he felt sick with dread. He ran to the front gates where parents and teachers were talking in a circle. A police car pulled up near them. In the distance, an ambulance siren sounded.

Noah was tall but couldn't see into the huddle. Was a hurt child in the middle of them. He swallowed the lump in his throat and grabbed someone's shoulder, pushing them aside. The people parted, talking in hushed whispers. On the ground, Jessy curled into a ball, crying her heart out. Emma knelt beside her with her arms around her shoulders. Jessy rocked back and forth.

Emma looked up with tears lining her cheeks. 'Do you know anything about this?' She asked.

The question tore his heart to shreds. *How could Emma ask that of him?* Unable to speak, he shook his head. A hand touched his shoulder, making him jump.

'Son. It's okay. We'll find her.' Crystal said. 'Someone noticed a lady talking to them. The police are checking databases or something.

That's the second squad car to arrive. The other took off up Currumbin Creek Road.'

Noah hugged his mum. 'I'm going to find out what I can do. Can you stay and support Emma and her sister? They don't want me around.'

'They haven't heard about the other person yet. I'll tell them gently.'

'Thanks, Mum.' Noah strode towards the policemen, trying not to see the anguish in both Jessy and Emma's faces. 'I'm Noah Cooper. The father —'

Sergeant Trobia cut him off. 'Hope Cooper.' He placed a reassuring hand on Noah's shoulder. 'Your daughter may have been abducted. The other child —'

'My nephew, Jai Stuart.'

Trobia raised his eyebrows. 'I did not know that detail. Do the cousins take off together at all?'

'No. Well, once they walked home to our property together without running it by adults but my dad's at home and they're not there.'

Orange uniformed State Emergency Services volunteers pulled up across from the school.

'They will form a line through the bush this side,' Trobai pointed across the road. 'They'll scour up to the hill. We have police units doorknocking as well. We'll find those kids. I know what it's like to worry about a child.' He glanced at Noah with a meaningful look.

Noah nodded, unsure how to respond to the man whose son could have sent his father to jail. 'Thanks for everything your doing. I'll join in with the search. I'm going to get my dog. She knows Hope's smell better than anyone, even me.'

Noah turned back to the school. Ali and Shaun arrived and were flanking Jessy and Emma along with a young man he recognised as a rugby league player, Emma's brother. Crystal talked to the teacher's aid, who seemed almost as hysterical as Jessy.

Emma stepped towards Noah. 'I'm sorry. I didn't mean —' She touched his forearm.

Striding around her towards his mother, he tried to ignore the apology in her eyes. He could only think of Hope.

'Mum, I'm heading home to get Sasha.'

'Do you think she's up for it?'

'I'll give her some Macrolone tablets so she won't feel the tumour. She'll find Hope quicker than the SES can.'

'What if they have been abducted? What if it's Katie's people?'

The thought hadn't even crossed Noah's mind or did it, but he didn't want to acknowledge it? 'She's happily married now, Mum. She wouldn't do this now. It's too long ago. I know she's finally moved on. Don't you have a hunch about it?'

'I only knew we had to watch Hope. I wish I'd got here sooner and this wouldn't have happened.'

'Mum, don't talk like that. I've found people in the deep Daintree and gulf areas. I'll find Hope and Jai.'

Emma said, 'I want to help in the search.'

'You'll hold me back.' Noah strode towards his car.

Emma grabbed his arm. 'Look at me, Noah. I'm under pressure too. We were worried about Jai. I didn't think it was you. I asked for Jessy.'

'She already asked, and I said no. Hope's missing that's my focus.' He climbed into the cab. Emma ran around the passenger side. 'Get out,' he said, half-heartedly as she sat in the seat.

'No. I'm coming with you. I heard you say you were taking Sasha. What if she can't continue? I can take her back.'

'I don't need you, Emma.' She'd buckled her seatbelt.

'You do.'

'No, I don't.'

She smiled. It swayed him quicker than he would have liked to admit. Being mad at her allowed him to take his frustration out, but it wasn't fair to her. 'Okay, since you're not getting out.'

'No. I'm staying right here by your side.'

'Don't start getting corny about it.' He gunned the engine and shot her a smile. He liked her being by his side more than he would let on – for now at least.

***

Twisting her fingers around the seatbelt so she wouldn't touch Noah, Emma asked in a near whisper, 'Do you think it's Wade?'

Noah's eyebrows raised in surprise and the steering wheel slipped. Gravel crunched as they veered to the road edge, but he quickly recovered.

'Of course not. What would he want with the kids? What makes you say that?'

'A hunch.'

'Fuckin hell. First, my mother and now you. I'm up to here with hunches.' He placed one hand above his head, keeping the other on the steering wheel.

'Sorry.'

They were quiet until he pulled up in front of his parent's house.

'Hey, Dad.'

Derick stood on the verandah with his dog by his side wearing a harness and lead.

'Son, Emma.' He nodded. 'Sasha's ready. She'll know how to find Hope.'

'Sasha, come girl.' The dog ran towards Noah, her tail wagging, letting out a yap of excitement. Noah reached in the tray of his ute, pulling out his vet kit.

'What are you getting?' Emma asked.

'Pills to make her oblivious to the tumour. It's crushing on her vital organs. It can be painful.' He popped a zip-lock bag of blue pills. 'Two should do it.'

'Won't it hurt her afterwards?'

'Maybe but she'll want to find Hope as much as me.'

Noah fed the dog the pills. Sasha gulped them down as if they were a treat.

'She doesn't mind the taste.' Emma laughed.

'Staffies will eat anything. Come on, old girl. You can sit in the cab this time. Can you open the back door, Emma?'

'Sure.'

Noah picked up the dog. He placed her in the back seat where she paced, wagging her tail. 'Sasha thinks it's an adventure. Let's hurry up before we lose daylight. I need to run over to my place and grab some things. Wait here.'

Emma watched him run, all stealth, like an athlete. Since he'd arrived at the school, she could tell he tried to keep his emotions in check. He loved his little girl more than anything in the world. Though terrified for the children, the more vulnerable side to him was decisive. He stayed calm and wouldn't let things happen without trying his heart out. It showed his caring nature. If only he would love her again with no complications. What if she'd blown it by saying what her sister wanted her to say, instead of asking if he was okay?

She despised herself for the look he shot her — sadness, disappointment and perhaps even betrayal. His eyes were the path to his soul, and his spirit seemed tortured. More than anything, she hated being someone who hurt him. Crossing her heart with her index finger, she promised Noah would come before her own family if they could get through this. If the kids could be found safe. If only everything could turn out okay.

'You're deep in your thoughts, young woman,' Derick said kindly. 'The kids will be fine. Noah won't let anything happen to them. You can count on that.'

'I know.'

Noah ran back to them, carrying water bottles and a backpack. 'Let's go. Hey, Dad, can you call Paul Gopher?'

'The bloke who owns the helipad near the rural fire brigade?'

146

'Yep. I'll message his number. Ask him to ready the chopper in case. Tell him I'll fly it. Hopefully, it won't come to that, but if it's getting dark before we find them, I'm going up.'

Emma shot him a wide-eyed glance as they drove off with Sasha's loud panting coming from the back seat. 'You fly helicopters?'

'Ah, hah! Easiest way to get to places in the outback. I did a fair bit of flying when Hope and I lived up north and before when I was younger catching crocs.'

They neared the school where lines of SES volunteers were fanning out across the bushland. Sergeant Trobia strode towards them as they got out of the car. Noah opened the back door and lifted the dog to the ground. 'What's the intel?' Noah asked.

'We had some witnesses say the woman took Hope's hand and lead her the way the SES line heads. The boy, Jai called out to Hope and chased after them. One of the mum's said you sometimes walked Hope that way, so she figured it was a family member.'

'I take her past the Horseshoe Bend creek to see the tadpoles turning into frogs.'

'So Hope would think it's a treat to walk towards the creek?'

'She knows stranger danger. I instilled it in her. I can't believe she'd go with a stranger.'

'Kids forget those things when adults manipulate their logic. I'd say the person knew about the creek or tadpoles.' Noah liked how the policeman did not mention Hope being Down's Syndrome.

'Other than mothers noticing you take Hope in the direction of the creek, who else would know that?' Emma asked. She imagined school mums watching the sexy father with his daughter. Noah would undoubtedly garner attention at the small valley school.

Noah rubbed his forehead as Sasha tugged beside him, ready to go. 'You. I told you about the tadpoles when we were talking one night on the phone.'

Sexy talk followed. Emma avoided letting her thoughts go there. 'Yes, I remember. I said Jai would have loved seeing the tadpoles. Do you think he followed because of it?'

'No.' Trobia said. 'The witness, after thinking about it for a while, seemed sure Jai looked concerned more than eager.'

Noah's jaw twitched as his eyes scanned the bushland. He ran a hand through his hair. 'I think I'll head to the east. I can see you have police dogs to the north.' Noah pointed with his free hand and pulled Sasha closer with his other hand. 'Soon, girl.'

'Yes do that. Have you got the radio app on your phone so you can hear the search broadcast? You're experienced at search and rescue, right? I've heard some stories.'

147

'Yeah. Most are true. Some aren't. I'll keep in touch. Is Bill Young in charge of this one?'

'Yeah. He's over at Crusty Ridge. I'll call you if we find them.'

'I'll call you when I find them,' Noah said with a twitch to his jaw. 'Emma, let's go. Find Hope, Sasha.'

Emma strode beside Noah, trying to keep up with his long gait. Sasha's nose hit the ground, the front of her body so low it was like she was crawling.

Noah stopped. Sasha turned her head back. He touched a bent tree branch. 'This is recent.'

'Wow, I would not have seen that. So, I look for changes to the bush?' Emma studied the branch.

'Anything at odds with nature. Birds will peel bark and use fallen twigs not snap them like this. Plus the break cuts across, like someone headed this way. Look down.'

Emma did. 'Shoe prints?'

'If we hadn't had that storm a few nights back the bush would be too dry to show us prints like this. They're heavy workboots though, probably the landowner. Not the kids. Let's head the way Sasha is tugging. She's picked up something.'

Emma nodded, following his firm backside in snug blue jeans. The black t-shirt he wore clung to every muscle accentuating his broad shoulders and trim hips. It was difficult to concentrate on the clues in the bush when she couldn't take her eyes off him. She didn't mind the distraction of gawking at Noah because thinking about what happened to Jai and Hope remained too hard to bear.

Chapter 24

Cicada hummed and buzzed like neverending tinnitus. Rozella flew overhead in screeching gusts, and the sun sunk low, hueing the bush in an orange glow. Noah put his phone onto loudspeaker so Emma could hear the SES commander.

'Alpha group are heading back to base. Delta, what's your position?'

'Delta, here. Already at the base. No sign of the kids.'

'Noah Cooper here. We'll circle back too. My dog lost my daughter's scent.' Noah passed the phone to Emma. 'Fuck!'

'All teams will resume in the morning. I'll have a briefing with the police.'

'What now, Noah?' Emma asked. 'The chopper?'

'Yeah. Are you tired?'

'No. I'm okay.'

'Drink some more water.' He took a swig of his water bottle. She did the same.

'Do you think the police may have got it wrong? What if the person who took them had a car up the road and drove off?'

'They roadblocked quickly. They're checking all avenues but consider this to be the most likely.'

'Do you know who'd want to take Hope?'

'My mum thought it could be my ex-wife.' He paused so Sasha could urinate. He poured water into a small canvas bowl and placed it on the ground for the dog to lap up. 'When we broke up, she wanted to put Hope into an institution. She thought I'd love her again if Hope were out of our lives. It got bitter. Her wealth meant she could track us down. I found a way to stay hidden up north and keep Hope safe. I got work training Commandos how to track throughout the north and avoid crocodiles. I can't believe I can't find my own daughter in the bush near our home.' He raked a hand through his hair. 'Anyway, I don't agree with my mum. Katie remarried. I've put her behind us. It's not her.'

'It's odd.'

'Yeah, I don't get why a woman would do this other than Katie.'

'I'm sorry this is happening to you, Noah. I know you've been under a lot of pressure lately.'

'Come on, Sasha.' He smiled at Emma. 'I did have some good news today. Dad's charges will be dropped.'

Emma squeezed his hand. 'I'm so glad. He's a lovely man. I guess he's relieved about that.'

She felt Noah tighten his fingers around hers. 'In all this chaos, I didn't get to tell him yet. Let's move quicker. Sasha's getting tired. I'll carry her.' He let go of Emma's hand to pick up the old dog.

When they returned to his ute, only a dozen SES volunteers remained. A police car drove past lights off. Noah put the dog in the back seat. 'I'll drop her home. Hopefully, the chopper's ready to go. I don't have time to drop you at home, Emma.'

'Do you want me to come?'

'Hey, can I have your phone for a sec? Mine's gone flat.'

She passed her phone to him. His finger poised to send a text when his eyes bugged out. He opened a folder on the phone. Covering the phone microphone with his finger, he whispered. 'Emma.' He put a finger to his lips for her to be quiet. 'What's this?'

'What?' She moved closer, brushing his shoulder. 'That's my sports apps. Hey, what's that one? ClevSpy? How did you see that?' She tried to speak in a whisper, but the shock gave her goosebumps.

'I'm trained in these things.' He deleted the app. 'Someone's been spying on you. They must have heard us talking about Hope.'

'Or Jai.'

'Jai only followed to protect Hope.'

'What if Jai was the target?'

'Wade.'

Emma's heart thumped and twisted but not in a good way, like being near Noah — in a bad, sinking, dreadful feeling.

'Hurry,' said Noah, striding towards where they parked. Emma ran behind him. When they reached the car, they bundled in quickly. Noah turned the ignition, and the ute took off at speed.

At his parent's, Noah screeched the car to a stop spitting up gravel. Leaving the engine running, he grabbed the dog from the back seat and placed her gently on the deck. His mum and dad were sitting in wide chairs on the verandah. Crystal stood quickly and passed Noah a piece of paper. He glanced and it before saying something Emma couldn't hear. Noah ran to the car with determination etched on his face.

'Do you want me to get out?' Emma asked.

'No. If it is Wade, he'll want to see you before giving up the kids. Look at this.'

'He won't hurt them,' Emma said without conviction, staring at the drawing by Hope.

150

'He'd better bloody not, or I'll kill him.' Noah gripped the steering wheel tightly.

'Hope drew a dark-haired person. She wrote 'friend'.'

'We thought it was a big school kid. Mum only just figured it out.'

'It's Wade.'

'I know.'

Noah broke the speed limit driving to the helipad. A cruising police car going the other way did a u-turn. It followed them with lights flashing. After being plugged into Apple Play, Noah's phone had a small amount of charge. 'Sergeant Trobia, it's Noah Cooper. I have police on my tail. I'm speeding to the helicopter pad. I'm happy to take the ticket, but I've got to get on Paul's chopper.' Noah nodded. 'Thanks, mate. Will do.'

Emma clung to her seat with white knuckles. She trusted every move Noah made, but the speed of the car, along with the feeling of dread, caused her stomach to lurch.

Noah spoke to Siri, 'Hey Siri, call Paul Gopher.' He glanced at Emma with a look speaking volumes. 'Paul, great. Yeah, I can hear the engine. We're pulling up. Two of us. Binoculars too. Infra-lights.

Emma had never been on a helicopter. Now wasn't the time to show fear. Besides, she was with Noah. Strong, dependable, calm – Noah. If she could trust anyone with her life, it would be him.

Paul, a guy in his forties with a slender build and freckled face, approached them. 'Come on.' He urged them towards the chopper, ducking as he neared.

Noah grabbed Emma's hand. 'Stay low. Have you been in a chopper before?'

She shook her head and received a squeeze from his fingers and a ' kiss on her cheek.

'You'll love it. I'll take you during the day under better circumstances and show you the beaches.' He grinned, though his face was partly shadowed with night descending. Bats were flapping towards the west, darker shadows in an inky black sky.

'What about the bats?'

'They'll get out of our way. I'll go around them. Don't worry.' He patted her leg as they buckled up. From behind, Paul handed Emma headphones.

'Flightpath cleared. Keep the lights on. Don't go past the creek boundary or Galleon Way. Too close to flights landing at Tugun. You know the drill. I'll be surveying. Emma can watch from the front,' Paul yelled above the rotating blades. He passed Emma infrared binoculars. Noah placed headphones over his ears and relayed their flight departure to air control. He gave the thumbs-up to Paul, flicking switches and pulling the joystick back. With a reassuring smile, he glanced at Emma.

151

'Let's find Hope and Jai,' he said.
Emma clutched her stomach.

***

Jai crouched next to Hope, whispering in her ear, 'This dude doesn't know what he's doing. I'll get us away from him. Don't cry, Hope.'

Tears pooled in Hope's eyes as she nodded mutely, staring at his swollen eye. Blinking to refocus, he could barely see out of it. His cheek stung where a bruise was forming but it was only a black eye. *Worse things could happen.*

'Why did you follow him?'

'Lady. Friend.'

'The disguise? He's been to the school before?'

'Talk nice. Knows my daddy. Friend.' Hope's voice stammered.

'No, Hope. A stranger. I know this dude.' Jai scratched his head. 'Oh, that's right. He dated Aunt Emm before Noah. I mean, your dad, my uncle. I thought he seemed odd. He didn't like kids.'

Hope shivered. 'Scared.'

Jai placed his arm around her shoulders. 'I'm here, Hope. I'll protect you. He'll have to go to the toilet soon. We'll escape then.'

'What are you kids talking about? Shut tha hell up,' Wade yelled.

'I'm just trying to keep Hope calm. You've made her cry,' Jai said, his arm firmly around Hope's tiny shoulders.

Wade paced. The long dark fringe shadowed his face, making him look creepy. A longer dark wig and pale blue dress lay on the linoleum floor.

'This is the old Wilford place,' Jai whispered to Hope. 'It's not far from your property.'

'Shut up,' said Wade, lifting his hand to strike Jai's face.

Jai blocked with his forearm, but the force sent him off his feet and flat on his back. Pushing his hands to the floor, he rose quickly to his feet, widening his stance and facing Wade with closed fists. *I'm not scared of this bully.*

Wade laughed. 'Stupid kid. I could snap you like a twig.'

'Why are you doing this?' Jai asked, his voice a pitch higher than he would have liked.

'You're only bait, kid.' Wade listened to Emma talking to Noah. 'They'll come for you soon.'

Jai understood what it meant. He'd listened to everything since Aunt Emma's concerned voice on the phone spoke to his mother outside the school. He felt terrible his mother had been so devastated, which made him wish he could tell her they were okay. 'Why through Hope?

152

You wanted to get to me because of my aunty, right?' *Why have you been spying on her?*

'If her fuckin' dad had kept his hands off Emma, this never would have happened.' Wade stomped, almost wearing a hole in the old flooring of the abandoned house. 'We were perfect before he came along.'

Jai shook his head. The bastard was a delusional weirdo. At least he knew Uncle Noah would be tracking the right way. He wasn't following the same path, but they were close.

He glanced at the bike trailer the man used to get them to the abandoned house. Because so many of the farmers used similar containers to move lighter things around their properties, the tyre marks may be hard to distinguish between other ones.

Jai knew people were looking for them, police and SES and locals who knew the area. He broke branches and tossed pencils out of his pencil case, hoping to leave a trail to follow, but he wondered if the man realised and picked them up. While Hope and Jai huddled under the tarp, he stopped peddling to walk around the back. Jai peaked out but couldn't make out enough to see what the man did, only seeing he still held a pistol. The cause of Jai's black eye.

The man was well-built. He worked out or something. Maybe he was crazy on the roids or something. Jai stood up for himself against bigger kids, but this grown man seemed mad and held a gun.

He needed to get Hope away from him. If he waited for the right moment, they could escape. Hope wasn't a fast runner, but he knew she swam well. He figured the creek could be better than the bush, darker and less chance of him seeing them. Snakes slithered through the bush, so did spiders, not that Jai was scared of them, but Hope may be. Sometimes bull sharks prowled the creek, but he refused to think about them. They didn't have to swim far, and they were both quick.

But why wasn't the guy letting Aunty Emma know where they were? If they were bait, why wasn't he drawing her into the trap? Nothing made sense.

Jai eyed the gun lying on the dusty dining table. It sat only a metre from the door. Could he grab it on the way out? Was he game? A chill ran down his spine, and he hugged Hope closer as she sobbed on her school uniform.

***

Wade rubbed his temple where a headache throbbed. He couldn't concentrate on what he had to do. Why did he have the kids? He couldn't remember. *Where was Emma?* She should have been begging for the smart-arse nephew of hers.

153

'Stop talking. You're confusing me.' Wade said.

The kid glanced at him with angry eyes. He realised they weren't talking. Voices yelled in his head like a rebelling crowd.

Why couldn't he hear Emma anymore? Why did her phone shut down? He didn't know what to do without her voice. Yeah, so the dickhead spoke sometimes, ruining everything, but at least he could listen to her sweet voice. The sound of it gave him a hard-on.

How could he get her to the house without the big guy? His mind swam. The plan seemed awesome days ago, but where had it gone wrong?

He tore his hair, trying to pull the information from his brain. It wouldn't come. It tumbled like a washing machine full of dirty clothes getting muddier by the minute.

The boy looked up at him, but he could barely focus on the kids. The little girl curled up into a ball with her head tucked low, afraid to look at him. That was good. Fear was good, but the boy didn't have it. When Wade's eyes focussed, he realised the kid's eyes held a challenge. *No fear at all.*

Wade fed off fear. He stepped back from the boy, trying to figure out what to do next.

The girl. It was the girl. The fuckwit would come for his stupid daughter. Yeah. The plan. Should he shoot the guy? Yes. Shoot him. Get him out of the way.

Emma would know he saved her from the fucker. Yes, Wade would be her protector. He would give her the beloved nephew. She would be indebted to him.

She loved the kid, right? Was it how Wade's mother loved him? Too much?

The headache crushed his skull like a falling rock. Wade hunched down, clutching his head with his hands. Grinding his teeth, trying to stem the pain, he squeezed his eyes shut.

When he opened them, the kids were gone.

Chapter 25

Ali held Jessy's hand over her kitchen benchtop. She squeezed tighter when she said, 'They'll find him. Have faith, Jessy.'

Jessy wiped her eyes. 'Mum, you've said it already. Saying it a hundred times won't make me believe you. I need Jai back in my arms. Then I'll have faith.'

Ben took her shoulders from behind. Kissing her cheek, he said, 'Your mum's right. We have to stay strong. Unite as a family to bring Jai home.'

Shaun placed cups of coffee in front of them. Ritchie opened the fridge. 'Mum, what's for dinner?'

Jessy lifted her eyes to him. 'Seriously. You're hungry when Jai is missing. Do you ever not think of food?'

Ritchie shrugged his broad second-rower shoulders. 'Jess, come on. Me not eating won't help Jai. Besides, once I do, us guys will head back to the valley.'

Jessy glanced at Ben, who nodded. 'Why? What can you do out there?'

'Be on the ground. Get updates. We can pass things on quicker that way, and it feels weird not to be doing something,' Shaun said. He patted Ali's shoulder and kissed her lips. 'I'll call as soon as we get there.'

Ali smiled and nodded. Ritchie popped cheese Kransky in his mouth and chewed.

Ben said, 'Ritchie. We've gotta go. Bring the bag.'

'It's not my food choice, but hell, I'm starving. Oh, good, it says they're Keto.' Ritchie ate one more Kransky as he filled a protein shaker with milk. 'This will have to do until we get back.' He grinned. Planting a kiss on his mother's cheek, he said, 'I know Mum will always have something delicious later. Right, Mum.'

Ali nodded. 'You can count on it. All stay safe and bring us good news soon.' To Ben, she said, 'I'll look after Jess. Get going, will you.'

Ben hugged his wife, who burst into tears again. 'I promise we'll bring him home.'

Jessy nodded, rubbing red eyes. Ali hoped she would run out of tears soon. She'd cried too many already. Time to speak to her about handling things better. She probably didn't want to hear it, but Ali wouldn't be the good mother she was by always taking a smooth road with her kids. Honesty seemed necessary.

When the men left, Ali rinsed the coffee cups. 'Jessy, do you think your tears help Jai?'

Jessy's eyes were downcast as she fiddled with her wedding rings. 'I feel useless, Mum. It brings back everything. Not being able to bear a child —'

'Sweetheart, I know that, but you were braver, and it was a permanent thing you dealt with. This isn't.'

'But what if something bad happens to him like kids like William Tyrrell?'

'Don't think like that. Worry doesn't change anything. Jai's the most resilient, clever kid I know. Trust in him if you can't believe in the adults looking for him.'

'I'm trying. I feel dread.'

'I don't. You know very well I would have a gut feeling if something happened.' Ali patted her heart. 'I would know it here. Like I always do.'

'Have you heard from Emma?'

'No.' Ali lied. 'Anyway, you need to listen.'

'What?' Jessy rubbed her forehead and looked at Ali with a rolled-eye look.

'I'm serious. You need to stop your anger at Noah. He's done everything he possibly can to find Jai.'

'He's looking for his daughter.'

'Jess, you know he'd do anything for both of those children. He's a good man. Your sister's out in the bush searching with him because she trusts him. You need to trust him too.'

'What if Jai gets closer to him? Where does it leave us?'

'You don't know your son well, do you? Jai adores both you and Ben. He knows he's adopted. It doesn't bother him because he's always had love showered upon him. By stopping him from enjoying the love of his uncle, you deny him something I believe he deserves to have.'

'And, Ritchie. He's Jai's uncle too.'

'Jessy, what I'm trying to say is, Jai has more than enough love in his heart to share with everyone. You've raised a kind, caring young man. Let him bloom. Don't hold him back. Forgive Noah and move on.'

'I'm tired, Mum. Can we talk about this when Jai's home safe?'

'How about you have a lie-down?'

'What if Jai needs me?'

'I'll wake you the second I hear anything.'

156

'Okay. I do need to put my head down. It's throbbing.'

Ali smiled, glancing out the window, listening to the sound of a helicopter's whoop-whooping blades.

***

'It takes a bit to get used to these infrared binoculars, but this time it's not animals I've spotted. Do you see it, Paul? To our right.' Emma pointed across Noah as he hovered the chopper over a dilapidated homestead.'

'The Wilford's abandoned their hobby farm two years ago. No one should be there. What did you see, Emma?' Noah asked, liking the feel of her hip against his as she leant forward. He also enjoyed that she adapted to search mode easily, listening intently to how to find the kids.

'One or two small, maybe cuddling and one bigger, an adult.'

'Got it,' Paul confirmed. 'Not the house. The tractor shed. Back entrance. What now?'

'They would hear the chopper. Won't he move them?' Emma's eyes filled with fear.

'He'll be watching us thinking we are the police. I'll turn as if we haven't seen anything. I can land over the ridge on a flat area of my property, and we'll have to run in. You can stay with the chopper, Emma.'

'No way. I'm coming too. I want to confront Wade. He's not getting away with any of this.' Emma grabbed Noah's shoulder and squeezed. Her pretty face looked determined as she bit her bottom lip.

'Are you going to inform the police?' Paul asked.

'You can call them when we land, but I'm going in. There's no time. The guy's two planks short of a fence.'

'I'd say the whole fence,' Emma said, obviously trying to make light of a scary situation.

Noah chuckled.

'Hang on. The kids are on the move.' Emma pointed. 'Wade doesn't seem to have noticed. Where would they go? Do you think they've figured out how close they are to your place?' She dropped the binoculars to her lap and gave Noah a hopeful glance.

'Let's get this chopper down and find out,' Paul said. 'I'll stay with the chopper in case they come to it.'

'I'll run between the house and the kids and try to ambush Wade,' Noah said, landing smoothly and cutting the engine. 'It's further but the best option.'

'I'm running to the kids,' Emma said. He noticed a flicker of fear in her eyes.

157

'I reckon they'll swim across the creek to get to this side. They're probably heading towards Stinky and home.'

'God, I hope so.' Emma took the backpack Noah offered her. 'Won't you need it?'

'You and the kids will need it more.' Noah ran towards the old shed.

***

'How will you protect yourself?' Emma yelled after him.

'I have my ways.' He patted his back pocket before leaping over a fallen tree stump and disappearing into the dark bush. Emma nodded at Paul before jogging towards where the children might surface from the creek. A smaller, narrow stream wound down to the main creek, making it only a 10-metre swim.

She stopped when she reached it, gazing into the water and shining a thin torch up the narrow banks. She pulled her mobile phone from her pocket.

'Ritchie, are you guys at Noah's property yet?'

'Ten minutes out. Any sign of Jai?'

'Sort of.'

'What does that mean?'

'Saw them from the chopper, but they've run from the guy and hopefully to where I'm waiting. Noah's gone after him. It's Wade, the creepy guy I told you about.'

'Shouldn't Noah wait for the police?' It was Ben's voice echoing from the loudspeaker.

'Would you if you were here? It's Noah's daughter and nephew, remember.'

Shaun cut in. 'Emm, just let us know when they're safe. We'll arrive soon. Don't do anything stupid. Okay?'

'Me. Never.' She hung up. Something stirred in the water. *Splashing.* 'Jai? Hope?' She almost slipped down the bank, watching the water instead of where she stepped. Lifting the torch to the splashes lit a tiny head. It bobbed up, and she spotted a face. *Hope.* Hope took a deep breath and coughed.

'Hope, keep swimming. Where's Jai?' Emma called. Jai came into view, stroking neatly beside Hope. Hope picked up the pace until they reached the muddy bank.

Emma put a hand out to Hope. Wet, muddy and happy, Hope wrapped her arms around Emma's legs. Jai pulled himself out. He was covered in less mud, making her notice the black eye. 'Jai, are you okay?' He wrapped his arms around them, taking a deep breath.

158

'I am now. Let's get out of here before he finds us. He has a gun, Aunty Emm.' She felt him shiver.

Emma gulped. As goosebumps ran the length of her body, her heart closed in around itself. *Noah.* Dragging the kids with her, they edged off the bank and into the thickness of the trees.

'I have to phone Noah,' she said.

'Where is he?'

Emma shot Jai a look. He understood immediately. 'Come on, Hope. We'll keep going. Aunt Emma will follow us.' Hope's bottom lip quivered. The water cooled them, but the air remained hot on a humid night. The wobble reflected the situation rather than the temperature. Hope was in shock. Emma opened the backpack to pull out a small foil blanket with the phone wedged between her cheek and shoulder.

'Noah. Pick up,' Emma said. He'd left his phone on vibration so any sound wouldn't alert Wade to his presence. Hopefully, he'd feel it, Emma reasoned. If he wasn't already shot. *Don't think like that.*

She turned her ears to the bush. Every noise seemed intensified, making gunfire a sound sure to travel across the valley, louder than cicadas, whooting owls and screeching bats.

'Hey, what's up?' Noah whispered. 'I can see him inside. He's ranting to himself.'

'Noah, he has a —'

'Gun. I know. He's holding it. Did you find Hope?'

'Yes. Hope is fine. Jai —'

'What about, Jai? Is he okay? Jesus!'

'Yes. Sorry, yes, but he's badly bruised. They'll be fine. Hope's unhurt, and she's out of earshot. Please be careful. You can't beat a gun, Noah. Don't be a hero. The police can take him in now the kids are safe.'

'I have a plan. Don't worry. He's not getting away after what he did to you, Hope and Jai. Trust me.'

'I do, Noah. You know —'

'What? Shit. Gotta go.'

I love you.

She followed the kids as they made their way to the avocado grove.

'Do you think the weirdo is following?' Jai asked.

'Nope.' Emma shot Jai a meaningful look over Hope's head as she placed the blanket around her.

The elephant stood from its straw bed, lumbering towards them.

'Hi, Stinky,' said Hope, falling at the elephant's feet with her fingers clutching the blanket to her chest. Stinky stepped forward as if guarding the child under its girth.

159

***

Noah edged with his back against the old metal building. His hand scraped a rusty patch. It came away on his fingers, making a scratching sound like chalk on a chalkboard. Peering over his shoulder, his jaw twitched.

Wade place the gun down. He unzipped his trousers and peed out the doorway, all the while talking to himself like a crazy person.

Noah moved swiftly. With a tranquilliser syringe in one hand, he reached for the gun with the other. The instant he did, Wade turned.

Wade shoved his penis back in his pants and dived for the gun.

In the wrestle, the gun went off, hitting the metal roof and ricochetting near Noah, missing him by a fraction. He concentrated on getting the syringe into Wade's arm. He pressed down, but Wade felt the prick, lifting his arm quickly. Swearing in pain, Wade pulled at the needle. While he did so, Noah raised a clenched fist, slamming it under Wade's chin, making him crash into the wall where metal bent around his unmoving body.

Noah figured Wade to be out cold enough for the police to take over. He grabbed the gun, emptied the bullets into his hand and threw the gun into the bush. He'd tell the police where it ended up later. All he wanted to do was get to Hope.

***

Emma jumped, startled at the sound of one apparent gunshot echoing through the dark sky.

Jai grabbed her hand. Stinky trumpeted. Hope glanced at Emma and Jai from under the elephant with blinking eyes. Emma could not find her voice. *Noah!*

'He'll be okay,' said Jai with a wobble to his usually sturdy voice.

Emma squeezed his hand, still unable to speak. The sound of sirens wailed in the distance. The helicopter blades stopped thwacking. The bush seemed to go silent.

'I hear someone or something coming through the bush.' Jai pointed to the right of the river bank.

Emma blocked him with her body. 'Get behind the elephant in case it's not Noah.' She stepped backwards as Jai did the same. Flicking the torch off, she kept her eyes on the bush. 'Quick.' They stood in the shadows behind the elephant.

Jai grabbed Hope's outstretched hand dragging her to her feet. He shielded her with his body and placed a gentle hand over her mouth. 'Keep quiet, Hope,' he whispered.

'Bad man coming?' Hope asked.

'Noah,' said Emma as his distinctive outline appeared. Emma turned about to run to him when she saw him balk as if he'd seen or heard something behind him. He raised his hand to her in a stop signal, making her freeze.

Her heart pounded, squeezing in on itself in her fear for Noah, but she knew she must get the kids to safety. 'We have to run towards the house.'

'What about Daddy?' Hope saw him too.

'He'll follow. I promise.'

'Who'll follow? Let me see you.' Wade's menacing voice came from the bush. She could see his silhouette nearing. *Where are you, Noah?*

Gulping back her fear, Emma clicked the torch on, facing Wade.

He raised an arm over his face. The other held the gun. 'Turn it off.'

'No. Put the gun down, Wade,' she tried to keep the wobble from her voice. To the children, she whispered. 'Stay in the shadows. Hopefully, he only noticed me. Run back to the house if you get the chance to do so safely.'

Stepping away from them towards Wade terrified her, but somehow, something inside her remained calm as she took a deep breath. She wanted to ask about Noah but knew it would only enrage Wade. If she could distract him long enough, the kids would be safe. Boldly, she stepped closer to him, lowering the torch, so it wasn't directly in his eyes.

He waved the gun. She flinched slightly but stood her ground. 'Drop it, Wade. It's over.'

'You're heeeere aren't you. Thaaaat's all ttthat matters. I've saved you from him.' His words slurred.

Emma shook her head, trying not to let the pooling tears slip. 'I didn't need saving from him.'

'You can be with me now.' Wade's eyes darted everywhere before focussing on Emma. Even from where she stood, she could see his eyes were glazed and red. He seemed to be on drugs or crazy or both.

The elephant trumpeted, stepping from the dark, making them both jump. It moved towards them in lumbering steps, flapping its ears and staring at Wade.

'What the fuck's an elephant doing here? I thought that was a fuckin' rock,' Wade waved the gun at the pachyderm.

'He has no bullets,' yelled Noah from somewhere near the creek.

Thank God. Emma let the tears fall down her face.

'Shut up,' Wade yelled, dropping the gun and searching the ground for something. He found a long thick stick and picked it up. 'Back off,' he screeched at the elephant.

161

Hope ran between the man and the animal before Emma could stop her. 'Leave, Stinky. Don't touch my elephant,' Hope said bravely.

Jai jumped beside her in a shot. The children blocked Wade's path to the elephant.

'Get out of my fuckin' way,' Wade said, snarling at the kids with the stick above his head.

Emma lunged for him, hoping to tackle him to the ground. As if in slow motion, she watched the stick come towards her head. She turned, feeling the sting as the stick smashed into her face. Through the haziness from the blow, she smiled when Jai punched Wade's stomach, making him buckle slightly before lifting the stick again.

The elephant rose on its hind legs as a dog barked from behind. Hope, wide-eyed, stared at the beloved animal with tears slipping down her round cheeks. She pushed Jai to the side as Stinky let out a deep rumble, trumpeted and landed a front foot on Wade's arm. The stick dropped, but the elephant roared. It wasn't finished with Wade yet.

Noah staggered towards them with blood trailing from his head to his shoulder, calling the elephant. 'No, girl!'

Stinky rose again, stomping on Wade. It collapsed on top of his lifeless body. Curled and exhausted, the elephant let out a last rumbling purring sound from deep in its throat.

Footfalls ran beside Emma. 'Emm, shit, Emma, are you okay?' Ritchie bent beside her, touching her face.

'Yes, stunned but okay,' she said in a scratchy voice. 'Noah.' She pointed to where Noah staggered closer as if one of his legs wasn't working correctly.

Jai walked to her, a half-smile on his lips. 'Stinky killed him, I think.'

Emma got to her feet, touching her bleeding cheek and stepped closer to the elephant. She picked up the dropped torch and shined it on Wade's lifeless body. Lifting his wrist, she felt for a beat. 'A weak pulse,' she said, hardly believing it. Wade's body twisted at an odd angle, and blood pooled on the dirt where his stomach split open. She turned her eyes away.

Hope curled in a ball over the elephant's eye. She spoke in whispers in its ear. 'Thank you, Stinky. Thank you.' Her tears mingled with the elephants.

***

Ritchie took Noah's weight as he helped him limp towards them.

'You've broken your leg, I reckon,' said Ritchie. 'I'm surprised you got this far.'

'I had to,' Noah said. 'Are they okay?'

162

'A bit battered, but everyone, except the bloke, seems fine. Yes, the kids and Emma are good.'

'We'll have to get the elephant's leg off him. I don't think she'll get up from this. It would have taken all her strength to stand on her hind legs for any amount of time.'

'Jai said she's an old circus elephant,' Ritchie said.

Emma wrapped her arms around Noah's waist. Hope curled her arms around his good leg. Ritchie stepped aside to take Jai in a warm hug.

Noah wiped the tears streaming down Emma's face. Even with blood on her cut cheek, he'd never thought she looked more beautiful. He kissed her lips. They never tasted so good. He leant on her for support as he hugged Hope to him. 'You okay, Hopey?'

Emma let go of him, stepping aside. Hope lifted a fist, punched Noah's, linked pinkies in a heart shape and high-fived.

Emma grinned. 'A secret handshake, cute.'

Noah cuddled Hope to his side. 'Hopey, I'm here now.'

'I'm okay. You hurt?'

'I'll be fine. Not sure about him, though. Does he have a pulse, Emma?' Noah asked, glancing at Wade.

'Slight.' Emma frowned.

'We have to move Stinky off him.'

'It will probably kill him. Should we wait until the ambos get here, keep the pressure on his wounds or something?'

'Don't feel guilty about it. He raised a stick to an old circus elephant and everything she loves. It was like waving a red flag at a bull. Every hurt the poor elephant ever endured from the shackles they made her wear or the metal barbs they poked her with. To her, the stick was a metal barb. She imagined back to her nightmare life.' To his daughter, he said softly, 'I love you, Hope.'

'Love you too, Daddy. Stinky?'

'I'm sorry, baby. She was very brave.' Noah knelt beside the elephant with his arm around Hope. He closed the elephant's lifeless eyes and kissed her trunk.

Hope kissed the elephant too and sobbed on Noah's shoulder as he held her tight, trying to ignore the excruciating pain of his broken leg. He clenched his teeth, but at least the ache in his heart no longer remained. Hope was safe. Jai was bruised but okay, and Emma stood beside him, smiling through her tears.

'Can you go to Emma for a sec, sweetie? I have to give Stinky some dignity and get this scumbag away from her.'

Hope nodded, reaching her arms towards Emma, who took her, snuggling her head into her neck and kissing her cheek. The gesture caused Noah a twist deep in his gut. Katie should have loved Hope; unconditionally, unquestioningly and easily the way Emma did.

Ritchie said, 'Here comes the cavalry. Though I guess they're all too late.' He helped Noah lift Stinky's front leg off Wade.

A slight groan escaped Wade's pale lips. Blood spurted from the wound in his stomach. Emma picked up the blanket Hope had been wearing, passing it to Noah. He pushed it into the wound, keeping pressure on it, waiting for the nearing ambos with sirens blaring.

The men of Emma's family surrounded them. Shaun and Ben sandwiched Jai, kissing and hugging him until he could take no more and squeezed out of their grip. Paramedics took over the treatment of Wade, each shooting quizzical looks towards the elephant and people surrounding it.

'Jeeeesus!' Shaun said, shaking his head. 'Did the elephant land on him or something?'

'Sort of,' said Jai. 'Stinky's a hero.'

'Stinky hero,' Hope repeated.

'Stinky is,' Emma agreed, squeezing Hope closer. Noah wrapped his arms around them.

'I'm glad everyone is safe,' he said. 'I'm sorry about Stinky, Hope.'

'It's okay. Stinky hero. With Jumbo soon?'

Noah turned to the sound of a pitiful cry.

'Stinky, my baby. Oh my darling girl, no.' Crystal sobbed, sinking to her knees beside the dead elephant. She stroked the sagging, wrinkled skin; her tears fell as if blessing the beautiful beast.

More sirens sounded as three police cars and another ambulance pulled up. A television crew followed.

Derick strolled towards Noah with a lit cigarette in his hand.

'I thought you'd given up,' said Noah.

'I was a little stressed tonight for some reason,' Derick said, taking a long drag. 'You've been in the wars, my son. Better get your leg looked at. Your head too.'

Noah limped to a log and sat down to allow a paramedic to check him over. With a crooked finger, he called Ritchie over.

'What's up?'

'Media. Hope and I don't need it. Can you divert them somehow?'

'Sure. I can manage that. I'll get your mum to take Hope inside, and I'll be your spokesperson.'

'Thanks.' Noah winced as the paramedic inspected his shin.

'No problem.'

***

164

Emma passed Hope to Crystal, knowing she could do with a hug from her grandaughter after the shock of finding their elephant dead and Hope safe.

Sasha circled in front of Stinky's girth three times, before curling under the elephant's stomach. She rested her head on Stinky's back leg where the shackles used to imprison her. The dog whimpered.

Emma watched the grieving dog with tears falling down her cheeks. She turned to see Noah with moisture tracking down his muddy, bloody face. A brave, strong and dependable man with a soft heart for animals and children. *The perfect man.*

Chapter 26

Soft shoes squeaked on the polished linoleum hospital floors like scurrying mice. Emma tried to keep her eyes from closing as she eyed the swinging doors to surgery. She lifted her fingers to the cut on her cheek. It wasn't deep and would heal fine.

Wade died. It should have been a relief, but it wasn't. When the media revealed the whole story about his neglected childhood and time in institutions, Emma felt sorry for him. He had schizophrenia, but the system let him down even after diagnosis, never finding the proper medication to help his mental state. She'd seen glimpses of the man he could have been without the disease — *what a waste of life.*

The doors swung open. Firstly, a male nurse carried a clipboard. Following him, Noah limped on crutches. A bandage wrapped around his head, and a long moon boot stiffened his left leg, but he offered her a smile when he saw her.

The nurse rolled his eyes. 'I suggested a wheelchair to keep the leg as still as possible. You can't talk some sense into him, can you?'

Noah grinned, melting Emma's heart over. 'Doubt it. He's a stubborn man.'

'I told you it's fine. I've used crutches a time or two,' Noah said to the nurse, winking at Emma.

'A time or ten is my guess,' she said with a laugh. 'Come on. Let's get out of here.'

'Wow, you know how to talk Cooper language now?' He laughed, full and throaty.

'I know you better than you think.'

'How come you thought I'd let myself get shot then?'

Strapping a bag over her shoulder, she raised her eyebrows at him. 'You almost did, and I'm not happy about it. No more risks. I want you in one sexy piece.'

'Mmmm. Sexy huh. I don't think I've seen anything damn hotter than you confronting Wade with a torch while he held a gun.'

'An unloaded gun.'

167

'You didn't know it at the time. You were feisty as hell and weren't taking a step back. I was so fuckin' mad I couldn't protect you.' He frowned.

The nurse strolled to the nurses' station chuckling to himself.

'You had a broken leg. Anyhow, I guess I did alright. I was shitting myself, though. It was scary.'

'You didn't look scared. I reckon he was more terrified. That's my girl.'

She wiggled her hips in happiness at the compliment.

'Damn, babe, can we just get to the car so I can lock lips with you?' Noah said. 'Did you change into those denim shorts to tease me or what?'

'I most certainly did,' she said, winking. 'Come on.'

'I'll follow those shorts anywhere.'

She turned to glare at him.

'I mean sexy arse.'

Another glare but a half-smile lingered.

'I obviously mean you. All of the pocket-rocket-hot-sweet-sexy you.'

She shot him a wide grin. 'That's better.'

Once in the car, Emma in the driver's seat and Noah with the passenger side far back to allow for his leg cast, they kissed. The smooch was all-consuming, knee-trembling, and fire-flaming. His tongue twisted with hers, their lips crushed. The intense longing kept buried while they searched for the children exploded.

'Wow!' she exclaimed, pushing his chest with her hands. 'I wish we could continue this, but we have to get back. Crystal said Hope's inconsolable. She needs you.'

'I don't know what to say to her.' He admitted it, taking a deep breath and staring out the window.

Emma drove towards his home. 'You'll find the words. You always do.'

'Do I?' He raised his eyebrows. The bandage around his forehead made his hair tuft out at odd angles.

'Mmmmm. When you do talk, which isn't as much as I do, you only speak when you need to, which I like. I guess I babble enough for both of us. Does it hurt?'

'Leg or head?'

'Both.'

'Neither. Okay, on a scale of one to ten, it's about a four. Satisfied?'

'Not really. I saw you wince when you got in the car.'

'Calling my bluff?'

'Always will.'

168

'I like that. Hey, and anyway, I like it when you chat. You're funny and sweet. Everything you say is music to me.'

'Oh, wow, Mr Cooper, you do flatter.' She grinned. 'On the serious side, you still haven't told me what happened after you thought Wade was unconscious.'

Noah ran a hand through his hair. 'Rookie error. I shouldn't have taken it for granted I got enough tranquilliser into him. He must have pulled it out before I pressed enough in his veins. I should have tied him up and then come to you and the kids.'

'So he regained consciousness and caught up with you?'

'Yeah. I was running through the bush and got snagged on stupid lantana, which slowed me down. The damn weed shouldn't even be growing here.'

'That's why all the scratches.' She gently stroked his shoulder and down his arm, where multiple red welts marked him.

'Eyes on the road, not on the prize.' He joked. 'Anyway, he came from behind. I heard his footsteps but reacted too late because I couldn't see him. Probably a good thing because he missed my temple, and I could have been in all sorts of trouble if he whacked me there.'

'What did he hit you with?'

'A metal truss.'

'Bloody hell. That could have killed you. How did he get hold of a truss in the bush?'

'It's where I'm building my house by the creek. A bit ironic, isn't it?' He shook his head and rubbed the bandage. 'When he could see, I was only stunned and coming toward him, he hit my shin.'

'You can't tell me it didn't hurt.'

'I'm surprised you didn't hear me swearing in the bush. It hurt like all fuck.'

'I knew it, and I know it still aches. You might have to take it easy and let me look after you for a while. Do you think you can do that?'

'As long as I lie on the bed and you're on top of me, I'm sure I'll be not only fine but in heaven. We could move around a little bit.' He winked.

She grinned, feeling tingles from her heels to her hair. 'Stop it. Now I'm too distracted to drive.' *This is what love feels like* — easy banter, longing looks, sexy talk and deap yearning.

***

Hope ran to him as he limped into his parent's home with Emma holding his hand. 'Daddy, is Stinky really gone?' She wrapped her arms around his good leg.

'We'll say a proper goodbye tomorrow.' He ruffled her hair.

169

'Decorations?'

'Ummm. I'm not sure what I can arrange with my leg like this.' He hobbled to the lounge and sat down.

Crystal pushed an ottoman under his foot. 'Rest up, my boy.' She kissed his forehead. 'So you two are back on again?' She glanced at Emma.

Noah smiled. 'Doubt we were ever really off.'

Emma smiled. He patted the seat beside him. As she sat, Hope squeezed between them, grinning. She turned to Emma and said, 'I love you, Emma.'

Noah delighted in the way Emma's face softened. She kissed Hope's cheek. 'What a lovely thing to say, Hope. I love you too.'

His daughter never heard those words from her own mother, but in the short space of time they had known Emma, the words came easily and honestly from her lips.

Noah wanted to pinch himself. How did he meet such an extraordinary woman who could freely love Hope as much as him?

Crystal wiped tears from her eyes. 'Been chopping onions is all. I'll get back to the kitchen. You're staying for dinner, Emma.'

'Only if there's enough. I don't want to impose, just wanted to make sure Hope was okay and get Noah home.'

'You're welcome any time, dear girl,' Derick said, walking in from the back verandah with the smell of cigarettes lingering on his skin. 'Sasha's still sitting next to the body. Won't take her food either.'

'She's grieving like us. Anyhow, Dad,' Noah said, shifting his foot and wincing, 'your heart, remember?'

'A couple of cigarettes to soothe the nerves won't hurt my ticker. It's got a stent anyway.' Derick said, taking his comfy, aged recliner chair in the corner. 'Noah, would this seat be better for your leg?'

'No, Dad. I'm fine here. We'll go home straight after dinner. I'm beat.' He winked at Emma, doubting his father missed the gesture by the grin spreading across his bearded face. 'Since when have you grown a beard?'

'Since I couldn't be bothered shaving every day. After a heart attack, you decide what things remain important and what aren't. Plus, your mother thinks it's sexy.'

'Stop that,' Crystal said. 'I said debonair not sexy.'

'I know what you meant, Crystal. We've been married for nearly forty-five years.' He winked at Noah.

Hope giggled.

'I thought she was inconsolable, Mum,' Noah said, squeezing Hope to him and placing a hand on Emma's thigh.

'She was until she saw you. Once I mentioned the planned celebrations, she put her grief aside. Didn't you, Hopey.'

170

'What celebration?' Emma asked, placing her hand over Noah's and linking her small fingers in his. Hope placed her tiny hand on top.

Crystal wiped under her eyes with a curled finger. 'Will you all stop being so adorable.'

'Mum, I think you're emotional about Stinky, not us.'

'No, son. I've never seen you and Hope happier, despite us losing Stinky. These are happy tears. Anyway, in answer to your question Emma, we plan to celebrate Stinky's life. She's now gone to heaven to join her brother Jumbo.'

'We'll have cake,' said Hope, getting off the lounge and doing a little dance. 'Decorations too.'

'Hope.' Noah glanced at his broken leg.

***

Emma realised the problem. 'I can bring decorations. Are you doing it in her grove?'

'Yes,' Noah said. 'You don't have to trouble yourself. We have a few streamers and things we can rustle up.'

She squeezed his fingers. 'No way. I love decorating. I'm a designer, remember. It will be fun. Please, leave it with me.'

Noah squeezed her hand. He shot her such a deep look of thanks and love with his beautiful eyes her insides turned to mush. Though his family shared the room, her thoughts pictured him naked and her in his arms, equally so. She squirmed on the lounge, hoping her face hadn't turned bright red.

'Your brother did a great job distracting the media from Noah,' Derick said to Emma.

'Yes, we were so grateful. Imagine if Katie saw it on the news. It would have put you into hiding again, Noah,' Crystal said, rubbing her hands together and entwining her fingers.

Noah glanced at Emma. 'I had a word to Ritchie and Sergeant Trobia about us being in hiding for so many years, and we couldn't jeopardise our freedom. It was in case Katie's people saw us plastered all over the world media.'

'Ritchie wouldn't have minded speaking for you,' Emma said. 'He hated it at first but learned how to sway reporters opinions and hold court. He's an old hand with them.'

'Palm of the hand, rather,' Crystal said. 'He had them eating out of it, not to mention sending the pulses racing of every single lady.'

'Was your heart racing?' Derick joked.

'Don't be stupid,' Crystal said, blushing.

After dinner, Emma and Noah strolled hand-in-hand to the smaller house. 'You're building a new home by the creek?' Hope ran up ahead.

171

'I am. I'll show you tomorrow.'

'You have a lot of money, don't you?' Emma asked, biting her bottom lip.

'Maybe. Does it matter if I did?'

'Not at all, but I am glad you're able to look after Hope in any way you see fit or need to. To me, having money means you can look after loved ones and for that, it's money well spent.'

'I guess I'm lucky I can provide well for Hope,' Noah said, not admitting to vast wealth. Emma felt he didn't like to boast.

'Should you check on Sasha?'

'There's nothing I can do for the old dog. She wants to stay with her friend for a bit. She'll do things in her own time, as dogs will.'

'What do you do with an elephant? Do you bury her here? You'll need an excavator or something.'

'We did with Jumbo because Stinky was alive. It helped her grief. Elephants will visit the bones of dead loved ones until they die themselves.'

Hope ran inside the house. 'Get your pyjamas on, Hope. Early bed tonight,' he called.

'Okay, Daddy.'

Leaning on one crutch, he dropped the other to the floor and wrapped Emma in a hug with his free arm. He kissed her deeply, with a pang of hunger like never before. The time they spent apart made them needier for each other than in the beginning. She wanted to breathe his musky male scent into her every pore. 'You didn't tell me what you will do with Stinky,' Emma said.

'I have donated her body to the Queensland Museum. She's the last circus elephant. A reminder to us, wild animals must remain in the wild. They can't be mistreated the way her and Jumbo were. Stinky's story will travel the world, and with that, she leaves a legacy. I hope she would be proud to be the elephant who causes further change. It will help Hope too.'

'Wow. That's beautiful, but how?'

'The chopper will be back tonight to lift her onto a semi-trailer.'

'How does this happen? Surely the government wouldn't cough up for such a thing. A philanthropist must be involved. It's amazing you can organise such a thing.'

He grinned but didn't say anything.

Emma cocked her head at him. 'What aren't you telling me, Noah Cooper?'

'Nothing that can't wait. Between Hope going to sleep and the chopper coming back, I have something else on my mind, and it involves you, me and sheets.'

172

Luckily Hope was exhausted by the two long days. She cried again after Emma read her the story of Dumbo. Noah placed her stuffed elephant toy in her arms. She fell asleep before Emma finished the book. Emma gently shut Hope's door and followed Noah as he hobbled to the bedroom.

He sat on the edge of the bed and lifted the dirty, black t-shirt over his head, exposing his defined chest and colourful tattoos running along the sinewy muscle.

'Should we shower?' she asked.

'After,' he said with fire in his eyes.

Emma took a breath at the sight of him, stepping into his open arms. He lifted her shirt off her shoulders, unclipped her bra and smiled at her exposed breast. 'I have missed that beautiful sight.' His lips closed around one nipple, teasing it to a peak. A hand tweaked the other before cupping the fullness, feeling their weight and dropping his head again for a further taste and tease. His hands slid to her zipper, where he unzipped teasingly slow before dropping her shorts and panties to the floor.

She reached for his fly. 'Now, this could be awkward.' She giggled, trying to help his erection out of cut jeans and underpants and avoid his cast leg.

'Hurry, babe. I can barely hang on,' he said, tugging at the sides of his trousers.

Once they were finally on the floor, she climbed over him, sliding her naked body against him, feeling the press of his cock, throbbing for release. Her breast felt full against his chest. 'I guess it's up to me since you can barely move,' she said, licking him from his neck to his navel.

With deft fingers, he found her clitoris and rubbed the bud. 'I can still manage some stuff.' The throbbing need could be felt everywhere, down through her cervix and into her womb. Each nerve ending ached for more as he dipped his fingers in and out of her wet entrance. She kissed his neck, licking, biting his earlobe, sucking his bottom lip.

'Babe, I can't wait.'

Rising above him, she took hold of his cock, stroking hard and fast until his erection strained proudly against the skin. She could practically see his nerves on fire. Poising over him, she guided the tip in. This time she teased him, slowly down and up, up and down.

His head swayed on the pillow, groaning. He pushed her narrow hips deeper with his big hands until he filled her. She squeezed her vaginal wall around him, feeling each delicious inch as he slowly thrust into her. Her hands curled over his ears, careful not to move his bandage. She tried keeping her body to the right away from his broken leg, but the feelings deep inside were uncontrollable. She was scorched by the rhythm of his cock deep within her core and the warm press of his muscles against hers.

They rocked together, abandoned and frantic, letting their juices flow as one, grinding, touching, feeling, needing, until her pounding pelvis convulsed into an orgasm so powerful she felt like she'd erupted her juices all over him. He grunted and pushed one last time, causing her more tremors as his seed entered her, hot and heavy. She collapsed on top of him, breathing in his ear.

His heart hammered in his broad chest. She left her hand there, savouring the fact his heart was hers, feeling every hammer blend with Emma's own thumping heartbeat.

'I cannot believe we could even keep it on tap for a day, let alone a couple of weeks,' he said, his chest expanding.

She kissed his lips. 'Never again. I want to stay with you forever. I missed you so much, Noah. You have no idea.'

'I do. I missed you too. I could barely breathe when you weren't around. Stay forever. I mean it,' he said, as Emma curled into the crook of Noah's arm away from his broken leg.

'Well, you did say when all this family crap's sorted' She grinned. 'Even if Jessy isn't on board yet. I no longer care. Yes, Noah, I will never leave you.'

His lips crushed hers in the most possessive kiss she'd ever felt. Again he took her breath away, and she was horny.

'I am the luckiest man alive.'

'You bet you are,' she laughed, trailing her hand along the crevices down to his cock where she teased it into action again. 'Ready?'

'Always.'

Chapter 27

Ali knew it was the right thing to do. Surprisingly Jessy was easily convinced. It seemed clear she'd had a change of heart about Noah. Ali watched her hug Jai before he got in the back seat of Emma's car with his dog Cheetah beside him. Jessy climbed in the passenger seat, waving through the wound-down window. 'See you soon, Mum.' It was a relief to see her smile.

Everything turned out alright in the end, with Jai safely in the bosom of the family. Ali waved back with her heart feeling lighter. The business's future seemed secure, and Jessy was finally opening her heart to a different kind of family.

Inside the house, the silence seemed fitting. Shaun was at work. Someone needed to keep the cogs ticking over while the rest of them pulled the family back together. She was too distracted to go back to work yet. She knew Shaun had been feeling threatened and was taking time out to digest things. Noah was another reminder of Kendwa. It seemed to Shaun his wife was linked to a dead man. She'd tried numerous times to tell him he was the love of her life and her salvation.

Kendwa seemed a tiny part for a short time. It was intense, yes, but would it have survived? She couldn't live in Africa, and she doubted he would leave his beloved wilderness life for suburban Australia. It was so long ago. She couldn't even remember if the feelings were genuine, a holiday romance or part of her imagination.

Shaun was her rock. Even before Kendwa, he was the male friend who always turned up when she needed him. He took little from her in return for an unyielding, loyal and total love. She watched him on the night Jai went missing, gathering the men, planning to do something. He couldn't sit idle. She'd found it so sexy. Everything he did ensured she loved her husband even more. She struggled to tell him how much he meant to her without sounding like a broken record. It was time she showed him instead.

The office seemed colder than the rest of the house. She pulled Kendwa's box off the shelf and placed it on the desk. Staring at it blankly for a few minutes, she tentatively unlocked it to peer inside.

175

The diary she kept in Zanzibar was on top, photos and documents below it. She rifled through them to find the letter Kendwa wrote before his death. Her eyes didn't need to scan the pages. She knew it off by heart. She placed it on the desk on top of the journal with shaking hands. A letter she'd written the night Jai was missing lay unfinished on the desk. Picking up the pen Shaun gifted her when she first went to Africa; she studied the mother-of-pearl inlay smiling. It was her most treasured gift. With pen poised, she continued where she'd left off.

So, you see, Jai. You came to this family at the exact time we needed you and when you needed us too. Though you have your uncle and cousin – your blood - family is built on more substantial things than DNA.

Simply – family is unconditional love for each other.

Family is never perfect, but those imperfections make us what we are. Your Grandad Shaun will always be the one you can depend on for solid advice and worldly guy stuff. Poppy Roger may not be around as much as the rest of us, but he is the one who will ensure you laugh often and don't take yourself too seriously. Your dad, Ben, will guide you as you grow into a man. At times, he can be soft, but that only shows how deeply he cares for his son. Uncle Ritchie is your playmate, the one who will continue to steer your sporting ability and keep your mind in a place that will work with your competitive spirit.

Our women have different roles. Your mum, Jessy, will always be your Mumma bear, protective and powerful. I know it annoys you sometimes but remember her love comes from deep within her, and you are lucky to be the recipient of something so strong and pure. Aunty Emma lets you be free and spirited, as she is too. She will always allow you to be your truest self without judgement. Go to her when the rest of the world doubts you.

As for me, you know I love you more profoundly than a grandmother could. The first day I met you, I knew there was something special about our curly-haired boy. You have an aura few people have. Loved ones will drat to you like moths to a flame, ants to a biscuit, seagulls to a chip.

I feel you filled a hole in our family. We didn't know it was even there until you covered the void. You have made my heart full and my family complete. I need nothing else in the world other than your happiness. That is why I am giving you your full story now.

In this box, your birth father, Kendwa's, and birth mother Sharli's belongings are now yours. It is your choice what you do with them. They were never mine. I was only safeguarding

176

them for when you were ready to know the answers to your questions.

Your bravery on the night the elephant died shows you are ready. Move forward, create your own story but always keep us close. Even if you travel miles away, we will always be – family.

Love from the Zanzibar moon and back,
Nana Ali

Tears dropped on the table. Ali was quick to wipe them off in case they ruined her letter. She put down the pen, neatly folded the letter and slipped it inside an envelope. After placing it at the top of the box, she shut it for the last time, locked it and pocketed the key.

The journal and Kendwa's letter blurred on the desk. Blinking her eyes, she tried to refocus, but dizziness overwhelmed her for a moment. Placing her head in her hands, she took deep breaths. The letter to Jai took an emotional toll. She waited for her head to clear. When it did, she felt light as if she were floating out of the office towards the open barbecue in the backyard.

She threw the journal and letter under the grill where wood chip crisscrossed with balled-up newspaper. A bucket filled with water sat beside the barbecue. Ali reached for the lighter on the built-in bench. She tried to flick it on with her thumb, only resulting in a spark.

Ali wasn't a smoker and barely used a lighter. She tried again, and a small flame flickered. She touched the newspaper with it. Flames curled the paper to ash, but tiny flames leapt to the woodchip. They quickly travelled to the corners of the journal, hungering to catch hold.

The letter burned quickly from outside in, curling into itself like a closing flower. Fire licked at the journal's leather, gradually making it buckle and swell, causing a waft of pungent smoke. It twisted into an unrecognisable thing, with the pages inside burning bright as the flames destroyed it.

Ali stepped back, breathing in the burnt leather and paper smoke. She watched until little was left, picked up the full bucket and threw it on the fire. It hissed like an angry snake, puffing up a smoke cloud before settling and dying.

She checked the fire held no embers before turning her back to it and walking inside. Ignoring a message from Jessy, she dressed in a short, sunny-yellow halter dress, Shaun's favourite. It had a low dipping back and clung to her curves. A few more than when he'd married her, but he swore he loved them all.

Shaun arrived home. Absently, he checked the mail as he walked up the hallway, dropping his briefcase on the desk in the office. When he looked around, he smelt smoke and ash. His eyes widened as he sniffed the air. Ali stepped into the office.

'I burnt the journal and letter. The box is ready to give to Jai.'

He couldn't take his eyes off her body. 'I love that dress on you.'

'I know,' she said with a smile.

'Wow.' He stepped close to wrap his arms around her. His lips brushed her's. 'What's going on, Ali?'

'We're celebrating. Just you and me.'

'What are we celebrating?'

'Us.'

He kissed her again, this time deeply, with his hands roaming her bareback. He didn't ask further questions. Shaun understood the gesture meant the connection to Kendwa was severed forever — consumed by fire.

'Can we celebrate in bed first? I love getting this dress off you almost as much as I like seeing you in it.' He didn't wait for an answer. Instead, he led her by the hand to their bedroom.

Ali smiled a knowing smile.

***

Fairylights glittered among the avocado trees. Tiny lanterns hung from random branches. Placed up the tree trunks, plastic butterflies of bright colours took on a surreal look, with bouncing lights illuminating the wings.

Jessy was on a ladder hanging a lantern on an overhanging branch. 'Here?' she asked Emma.

'Perfect.' Emma gave her the thumbs up. 'It's so pretty. I'm sure Hope will love it.

'Trying to keep her away until dusk is our biggest problem,' Crystal said with a laugh. She carried another tray of pink unicorn cupcakes to the trestle table draped in silver.

'It looks magical,' said Jessy glancing down from the ladder as Noah came into sight. 'I love decorating for little girls. It's so different to boys.'

Noah cleared his throat. Emma noticed him run his hand through his hair and stare at Jessy as if he'd seen a ghost. 'You're here? You're helping?'

Jessy smiled at him.

Noah shook his head. 'And you're smiling.'

'I've been wrong about you, Noah. Jai says you're the bravest uncle he's ever known.' Jessy giggled. 'It hurt Ritchie's feelings, but he'll get over it.' She shrugged her shoulders, stepping down from the ladder.

178

Noah shot Emma a quizzical is-this-for-real look. Emma smiled back with a nod. She laughed when Jessy put her arms around him and squeezed him. His arms were at his sides, but he slowly wrapped them over Jessy's shoulders.

'Welcome to the family,' Jessy said.

'Thank you.' It was all Noah could mutter, but you couldn't wipe the smile off his face.

Emma grabbed his hand. 'What do you think?' She swung her free arm around the celebration site.

He squeezed her hand. 'Wow, wow and wow! This will blow Hope's mind. I could not have done this.' He glanced at Jessy. 'Thank you.' He turned and kissed Emma's cheek.

In unison, the twins said, 'You and Hope are welcome,' which made them both giggle.

Noah raised his eyebrows.

'Don't worry. You'll get used to twin-speak eventually,' Jessy said, picking up the last lantern to hang on a branch. 'What happens now?'

'I'll call Dad to bring the kids down from the house. Actually, I'll walk over there because I'll have to carry Sasha.'

'She's no better?' Emma asked.

'Nope. There's nothing I can do either.' He shrugged his shoulders before walking towards the house.

Jessy nudged Emma. 'He's so hot for you. My god. I've never seen you so puppy-dog eyed either.'

'I am not.'

'So are.'

'Stop it.'

Jessy laughed.

***

Hope squealed in absolute delight before crushing her hands to her mouth in shock. Quickly recovering, she ran around the grove, touching butterfly wings and dancing in circles. Noah watched her feeling deep love and utter joy, seeing her happiness. The detail and care Emma, Jessy and his mum put into the decorations and food was overwhelming. They practically set up a fairy garden of every little girl's dreams.

'You like it, Hope?' Emma asked, smiling and letting Hope run into her open arms.

'Beautiful,' Hope said. 'Stinky would love.'

Emma kissed Hope's cheek. 'Yes. I guess Stinky would.'

They heard a car in the distance.

179

'That will be Dad and Uncle Ritchie,' said Jai, sitting down to pat Sasha. Cheetah licked Sasha's face, nudging the older dog to get her to play. On realising she wasn't budging, Cheetah plonked down with head resting on paws.

Derick strolled towards them with Ben and Ritchie. They were laughing like old mates.

Ritchie strode towards Noah and shook his hand. 'Only one crutch now. They breed 'em tough in the valley, huh!'

'I couldn't do enough with only one hand. I manage,' Noah said. He and Ritchie hit it off. There was something about a famous guy who didn't show a hint of vanity for his sporting prowess. He loved his family before sport, fame or anything else.

'You'll be back flying choppers and chasing crocs in no time. I've heard a story or two.' He slapped Noah on the back.

'Nah, I have more settled things in mind,' Noah said, watching Emma put Hope down and follow her to the cupcakes on the trestle table.

Ritchie nodded. 'Ah. I see. Should I get my suit and tie ready then?'

Noah laughed. 'Nah, mate. It will not be like my first wedding. Might even be barefoot. My brother —,' he faltered. 'Anyway, I was once at a barefoot beach wedding. It sounds more up Emma's alley wouldn't you think.'

'For sure,' Ritchie said. 'The way she looks at you. My guess is she would marry you in a laneway if she had to.' Ritchie chuckled. 'I think I need to taste those cupcakes.'

Ben strolled over to Noah, casting his eyes downwards before reaching his hand to Noah. As they shook, Ben said, 'Thanks for saving my boy. I owe you one.'

'I think I owe Jai one. You should have seen how he punched the guy in the guts. You have raised one hell of an awesome kid.'

'Thank you.'

'I mean it, Ben. Without you and Jessy as Jai's parents, Jai would not have turned into the incredible human he is. I guess it means I'm in debt to you.'

Ben laughed. 'How about we make it even. Welcome to the family.'

Noah grinned. 'Thank's mate.'

Crystal picked up a chime and dangled it in the air, making a tinkling sound, getting everyone's attention. She walked to the spot where Stinky died, and the two dogs lay near a pile of cut flowers. 'We have come here to celebrate the life of our elephant, Stinky.'

Everyone fell silent as they listened to her. Hope walked between Noah and Emma taking a hand of each. They glanced down at her and

180

back at each other. Love shone from Emma's eyes. Noah gulped down the lump in his throat.

Crystal continued. 'Stinky remains the last of the Australian circus elephants. She was a baby, chained and mistreated until our laws changed. When we took her in, she was sick and septic, but our son, the animal whisperer, brought her back to health where she and her good friend and brother Jumbo lived out the happiest days of their lives.'

'Hero, Nanny,' Hope yelled.

'Yes, Hope. Stinky died a hero, saving those she loved most, Hope and her new friend and cousin, Jai. To Stinky the hero.' Instead of raising glasses, they all held a party popper. They formed a circle around the dogs and flowers, lifted their poppers to the sky and called, 'To Stinky.'

Cheetah barked, and Sasha howled. Crystal sobbed as Derick hugged her. Hope danced around the circle. Jai took her hand to spin her as she giggled in delight.

Jessy and Ben stood arm in arm, looking the happiest Noah had ever seen them. Ritchie bounced an NRL ball in his hands, ready to throw it around with the kids.

Noah turned to Emma. Taking her face in his hands, he kissed her. 'Thank you for everything.'

'It was fun,' she said simply. 'So worth it to see Hope's face light up.'

'She's never been this exuberant. I want to show you something.' He took her hand. 'Follow me.' To the others, he said, 'We'll be back in a minute.'

Crystal shot them a smile and a knowing look.

He led Emma past the avocado grove towards the creek. He stopped to lean on his crutch.

'Are you okay?' she asked. 'Is your leg hurting?'

'No. Listen.'

The sound of the creek water bubbled over rocks, whip birds with their distinct high-pitched whip cracked in the trees, cicadas hummed.

Emma breathed in the sweet lemony eucalyptus, grasses and water. 'It's beautiful.' In the clearing, she gasped. 'This is your house.'

'Sorry I didn't take you this morning, but I wanted to surprise you today.'

'You and Hope will love it here. The view, wow, it's divine. Oh my gosh. The house will be huge.' She stepped onto the raised slab. 'What's this?' she asked. 'Other than the deck view, this room's outlook sweeping across the creek is stunning.'

Noah grinned. 'Open the toolbox.' He pointed to a red toolbox sitting on the room floor with only frames for walls.

'What's going on?' she asked, raising her eyes as she lifted the lid.

181

'Note first, please.'

She saluted as she lifted the note. Rose petals fell from it, and the sweet scent lingered. Glancing at him with a quick smile, she read.

> *You already own my heart. I wanted to share with you a piece of mine in this labour of love. This is your new office. All you have to do is say yes. Yes—that you'll have both Hope and I and hold us in your heart always and share our lives. Please marry me, Emma Jarvis.'*

Emma dropped the note and held her hand to her mouth as tears pooled in her beautiful eyes. *Why wasn't she talking?* Noah held his breath. *Say yes. Please say yes.*

Still silent, Emma took the small velvet box from the tool chest. She snapped it open and gasped.

It felt like an eternity. 'I'd drop to my knee, but this damn crutch —'

She jumped up, wrapped her arms around his neck. Tears slid down her cheeks.

'Emma?' *She's nodding. Nodding is good.* 'You're saying, yes?'

She kept nodding, crying and clutching the box and note to her heart. Finally finding her voice, she said, 'I'm too overwhelmed to speak.' She gulped. 'That's the most romantic —'

He kissed her lips. His hand brushed tears from her cheeks. 'I doubt if I've ever met anyone who cries so much when she's happy. You had me worried for a minute.'

She kissed him and grinned. 'Yes, Noah Cooper, I will marry you and Hope.' They kissed deep and long.

His heart thumped and swelled to an incredible size. *Emma included Hope.*

Emma was his heart and soul. The lover who'd alluded him until now. She was the only woman he'd ever met who had a heart big enough to take not only him but his cherished daughter too. He could never guess he would find such love, but she'd said yes. *She said yes.*

'I love you to the moon and back, my fiance,' he said, breaking his lips from hers.

'Well, you'd better put a ring on it.' She grinned, snapping the blue box open and sticking out her ring finger. He gladly complied, letting happiness consume him as the diamond ring slid on her dainty finger.

It was a perfect fit – like them.

Dedicated to:

My mum who has given me compassion, resilience, courage, inspiration, support, praise, confidence, curiosity, defiance, determination, positivity, hope, empathy, gratitude, pride, nostalgia, patience, advice, kindness and most of all unconditional love.

Mum has taught me; I can do anything I set my mind to, it's okay to be the emotional one and wear your heart on your sleeve, when times are tough there's always someone worse off, look after yourself, style and proper grooming makes you feel better even if you are unwell, don't judge people, avoid gossip, keep your sense of humour, it's okay to talk about sex (which does help me write erotic romance), be kind and genuine, smile often, there's nothing wrong with being small, your heart can always be open to love, there is only one you — and so much more it would take a whole book.

The Author

Donna Munro was born in Sydney, Australia. She moved to Port Macquarie for most of her school years and to Gold Coast in her late teens. Her first family home was in Currumbin (the setting for Elephant Creek). She moved for a quieter life on the Sunshine Coast with her real-life love (husband), and Mahli the sooky Staffy.

She is the author of four novels and two non-fiction books. She first achieved fiction success with a short story published in *Woman's Day*, which established her freelance career.

She enjoys long walks smelling salt air and eucalyptus, the humming sound of summer cicadas, the morning *poop-kak* alarm of wattlebirds, elephants, dogs, warm hugs, kisses and the taste of Peanut Butter.

You'll often find her on a beach with a book in her hand and her toes in the sand.

Visit her blog at: donnamunroauthor.com

Follow her on Social Media: linktr.ee/donnadmunro

***

Acknowledgements:

My readers. Without you, my words would be empty. Thank you for reading my stories and keeping this writer's dream alive.

To my editor, proof-reader and beta readers, Debbie, Rebecca, Janet, Tracey, Toni, Valerie, Karen and Leesa; fellow writers, Katrina and Sandra; my brave long-time friend Angie and anyone else who helped or gave me guidance during the production of this book.

Fabulous Australian author Michelle Somers for a critique that inspired encouraged and improved the story during a fantastic Skype session.

My Sunshine Coast writing friends (and yes, we need to meet up more regularly).

The circus elephants of Currumbin Valley, Queensland, Australia. Though few records of their existence remain, I know they lived out their last days free, loved and safe. They were the inspiration for this story, and though not all exotic circus animals were oppressed (many circus families love animals) I am glad the practice is banned. The tale of my elephant, Stinky, was of my own imagination and was not an actual elephant.

My tribe at RWA (Romance Writers of Australia). I have learnt so much, both working for the organisation, and as a member. The knowledge and encouragement have influenced my writing craft in many surprising, wonderful ways.

Lastly, my husband and family for putting up with writer vagueness and encouraging me, even though you sometimes don't get this writing gig.

Croc Brother Romance series

Croc Brothers Romance - Book One

A
Summer
in
Paradise

Donna Munro

Summer in Paradise: Book One

This book was previously published as *The Zanzibar Moon*.

A magical adventure romance to have you wishing you were on a Zanzibar beach.

A Summer Before: Book Two

Kendwa's earlier life is the prequel to *A Summer in Paradise*.
It was previously published as *Kendwa's Secret*.

A thrilling adventure romance to have you wishing you were on a Borneo beach.

A Summer of Hope: Book Three

The sequel to *A Summer in Paradise*.

It was previously published as *Elephant Creek*.

A family adventure romance to have you wishing you were on a Gold Coast beach.

Coming March 2022

A stand-alone contemporary women's fiction with romantic suspense

Pepper Cassidy can wield a drop saw like most women use a nail file. But when she returns to Blueshell Beach, the last thing she needs is a sexy, unfriendly neighbour to distract her from the family cottage renovations.

Keegan Dallas left the city for a peaceful coastal life—surfing, yoga and a chance to regain custody of his son, Joe. His PTSD is improving, but he's not quite there yet.

She doesn't need or want a quiet, stubborn man who can't even use a hammer, let alone a seemingly damaged guy.

He would rather be alone but can't help falling for the beautiful, clumsy, sunshine-optimistic neighbour.
After a tragic accident renders Joe mute, can they come together to bring back his voice? That's if they don't nail each other to a renovated wall first.

When it seems impossible for love to save them, the past might hold the keys to a happy future after all, but not before a threat to those they love most.

If grief renders you mute, can love find the words to save you?

Beach Cottage Haven

'I absolutely loved this book! Thank you for choosing me to read it. The book was well-written with well-rounded and wonderful characters. I was pulled into the story from the beginning and kept hooked throughout. I really didn't want to put it down once I started reading. The backstories of each of the main characters was well-done and gave you clues to the people they became. I really enjoyed how Pepper read her father's diaries and began to understand the man behind her father.' - Darla J Taylor

'A wonderfully rich read, great depth of characterisation, movement, and well-crafted threading of story within story.' - Sally Ryhanen - writer

Extract next page:

Chapter One

2019

Pepper Cassidy's nostalgia hit her like a nail gun to the heart. Cutting the car engine, she stared at the blue beach cottage. *Home or is it?*

To her right, on the idyllic Queensland beach, waves surged over rocks, booming and rhythmic like a heartbeat. Seagulls screeched above, gliding in a baby-blue sky. They swooped into the ocean, pinching fish from a school of mullet close to the shore. Lemony eucalyptus and frangipani blended with salty air in a fragrance so familiar it hurt deep in Pepper's chest. Yesteryears' memories swirled, making her dizzy. She steadied her wobbly legs, placing a hand on the hot car bonnet, glancing at Livia to check she missed the stumble. *Why, after all this time, have I chosen to come back here?*

'We're finally home.' Liv glanced around and yawned, stretching one slender arm over her blonde head.

'It's a bit cliché returning to my hometown. I honestly never thought we'd settle back here,' said Pepper, giving Liv at least some of her thoughts. Leaving the car, they strolled to the cottage. She brushed the dusty weatherboard surface, and dry, faded aqua-blue paint came off on her fingers. *One thing noted on the list of things to do.* Rubbing her hands down the side of her jeans, she bit her bottom lip before saying, 'Oh, well, new year, new life, I guess.'

The stand-alone garage on the left-hand side came into her vision, even though she told her eyes not to stray there. Goosebumps popped along her arms. She quickly averted her gaze, avoiding Liv's questioning look by walking towards the veranda, gulping back her fear. Lantana trailed over the rail and into the gutter.

195

'Your hometown, Mum. My sea change,' said Livia, pulling an earphone from her left ear. 'The beach is amazing. I'd forgotten it's this close. What was I, about four last time we came here? It seemed miles away when I was little. It's like right there. Wow!'

'Nearly five.' *The same age as me when Dad went to war.* 'You can hear the surf. It's beautiful at night. I remember it lulling you to the most peaceful sleep.' Considering how much Pepper dreaded moving back to Blueshell Beach, finding one pleasant memory was reassuring. A two-hour drive north from Brisbane with crawling traffic for the first hour hadn't helped her apprehension. *Too much time to think.* She inhaled a deep breath of salt air, stretched stiff shoulders, and stepped on the timber stairs. The second one sunk and creaked. *Another thing noted on the list of things to do.*

Livia strolled to stand beside Pepper, taking in the ocean with wide eyes like the first beach she had ever seen. Her young face was hopeful. 'Oi, check him out.' Liv pointed, grabbing Pepper's shoulder to make her face the north. 'Bit old, but what a six-pack and those arms,' Liv said, elbowing Pepper's ribs.

Pepper gazed at the fine specimen of a man jogging shirtless along the goat-track path winding around the beach in front of their home. A large dog with pointy black ears and tan fur ran in front of him close to his feet. It wore no collar or lead but didn't stray far. The man glanced at her, holding her gaze for a second before facing the track. A small smile tugged his lips. The barking dog loped towards them, seeming excited by the prospect of new people. The man whistled, and the big dog stopped, tilting its head towards his master, triangle ears raised at the command.

'Awww, he's so cute. Hello, boy.' Liv grinned at the pet.

The dog hunched low, returning to its owner with his tail between his legs. They jogged, but in the dog's exuberant state, it circled back to happy-bark at them, causing the man to trip over the mutt. He righted himself in one fluid movement, said something to the dog, patted its head and glanced over his shoulder with irritated eyes.

Pepper stifled a giggle and placed her hands over her mouth.

Liv enthusiastically flapped a hand towards him. 'Hi.'

He shook his head but didn't wave; instead sprinted the rest of the track with the dog following closely.

'Not very friendly.' Liv laughed. 'That was pretty funny, though. Mum, mum?' She waved a hand in front of Pepper's face. 'Earth to Mum.'

Her mind was still holding a vision of the guy in her head. Her dropped jaw was having trouble returning to her face. To cover her weird reaction to the guy, she asked, 'Since when have you noticed six-packs?' She ruffled Liv's hair, ignoring the weird something stirring deep inside.

'Who doesn't?'

A tiny niggle of worry about Livia's comment stayed with her. *Don't grow up, Livy.*

At fourteen, Livia already developed a womanly shape, much to Pepper's concern. Unlike Pepper, Livia took after her father's side — tall, with long angled limbs and her mothers-in-law's enviable model body. At least Liv didn't have their snobby, mean disposition. *She takes after you, always wearing a bright smile.* The thing mother and daughter shared most was the unique colour of their violet eyes. People always commented on their eyes—eyes the same as her father.

Pepper opened a screen door and inserted a key in the intricately carved timber door. It would have looked more at home in a place like Bali or Zanzibar. Her mother had imported it from Morocco, and her dad lovingly installed it. A recollection so happy, Pepper smiled. In 1970, the year Pepper was born, he'd devotedly built the house. *In a time before he changed.*

'Come on, Mum, open the door already!' Livia said, startling Pepper from her thoughts. Liv glanced at the mobile phone in her hand. She smiled before tucking it into the back pocket of her jeans.

'I'm trying. The key's a little stubborn. It hasn't been used in months since Nana went to the nursing home.' Pepper jiggled the key, and the lock clicked. She pushed the door wide open. The hinges didn't even creak. At the same time, a gush of memories surfaced like ghosts circling over her head.

The mudroom flowed to the sunroom facing the veranda, where faded cane lounges took in the picturesque view. Beyond, the main lounge room housed the old purple velour sofa and a huge Persian rug that never seemed to match the décor, but the carpet held favour with her mother.

Daylight streamed on the kitchen benches from a circular skylight. The cabinetry, dated lime melamine with curved metal edges, was art

197

deco at its best or worst. Pepper wasn't sure which, but she knew she had shitloads of work to do renovating it back to a proud little beach house. At least the modifications would keep her busy enough to forget things. A folded note sat like a tepee on the bench.

She unfolded it. *Welcome home, Pepper. I'm so sorry for your loss. Meg was a dear friend. It's terribly sad. I've been feeding Chloe until you arrived as I said I would. Poor thing seems to be pining but must be eating all her food because she's looking on the chubby side. She's an adorable cat. I just loved looking after her. Any questions, just give me a call. Mrs Charlotte Walters.* A phone number at the bottom was written in a different pen ink as if an afterthought.

'It's all so old,' said Livia, running a hand over the velour lounge. 'Jeez, who'd put purple with that rug?'

'Your grandmother,' Pepper said with a catch to her throat. The rug seemed to lift and roll. She steadies her feet. No ocean breeze to do that, and the rug was heavy. *Odd.*

Liv didn't seem to notice. 'Oh, sorry, Mum. Are you okay? You look a little rattled?'

'I'm fine. It's just strange being here after all this time.'

'You didn't come back much because of Granddad, right?'

Pepper glanced away, trying to ebb the flow of tears pooling in her eyes. Changing the subject, she opened a door. 'This will be your room. It was mine growing up, at least when I wasn't at boarding school. The bay window has views of the beach.' She strolled over to where a bench seat tucked under the windowsill. The view wasn't as clear now that the native bush had grown. 'I read here, escaping into books when Dad was —,' she trailed off, taking a deep sigh. 'Anyway, what do you think?'

'It's so huge compared to my room in Brisbane. I can put my bed here.' She spun around, pointing to a blank wall. 'My Five-SOS poster could go up here.'

'Sure, but after I paint. What colour do you want your walls? I'm doing shades of white everywhere else, but you can choose in here.'

Livia shrugged her shoulders, but the smile remained. 'I'll think about it.'

Liv's room led to an adjoining patio taking in the backyard. A double cat bowl for food and water sat near the door; a small pet bed wafted of cat piss and mould. A couple of deck boards were rotted black like stumps burnt in a bushfire. *Add it to the list of things to do.*

'Chloe, here pussy,' Pepper called, but there was no sign of her mother's cat. Probably under the house in the shade, where their old dog Mahli used to sleep.

She strolled to the second bedroom, the one her two brothers shared. She could see the overgrown backyard from the grimy window where they would chuck a football or wrestle each other and her on the freshly moved lawn. Having boisterous brothers made her robust even though she was small. Fighting with them taught her how to beat boys and later men at their own game. She never backed down when she knew she was right while working in construction, which helped her business thrive, and the primarily male tradesmen respected her.

The room would be a spare room or an office for her company, Pepper C Construction, at least at the start. Anyhow, Rob wouldn't be coming back to the house any time soon. Tim definitely wouldn't.

Pausing at the door to the main bedroom, Pepper sighed. She opened it slowly, hearing the familiar creak of the hinges. Her mother's scent wafted. Pepper lifted a pillow and held it to her face, sniffing deeply. *Lavender mixed with the spicy vanilla and sandalwood Coco perfume.* The tears came. She muffled them with the pillow, but they dampened her face until she felt Livia's thin arms wrap around her shaking shoulders.

'I miss her too, Mum.'

Pepper dropped the pillow to hug her sweet daughter. 'I know, darling. It will get easier one day. This house brings back all the memories.' The sooner she packed up her mother's things, the easier living in the house would be—*another thing for the list.*

'I could take this room instead.'

'No, it's okay. Once we renovate, it will be fine. We'll have to camp out in the lounge or outside while we get at least one room habitable. We'll do yours first.'

'Why don't we stay in the garage instead. It looks like there's a loft?'

'No.' Pepper said it too abruptly. 'It's um, dirty, and it's locked.' She glanced at the floor, scuffing her feet over a worn section of laminate flooring. *Add it to the list.*

'We could break the lock and clean things,' Liv said. 'It looks like a Miami condo, well, if you renovated it.'

'I said, no, Liv. Just drop it. The garage is out of bounds.' Livia was clueless about what happened in the garage, and Pepper planned to keep it that way. She couldn't face it yet, either. What happened in there could never be erased from her mind but moving forward meant it had to be. *One day at a time.*

Buy Donna's books on Amazon, all good bookstores

or
www.donnamunroauthor.com

If you would be kind enough to provide a review of *A Summer of Hope* please email the author or place the review on

Facebook
https://www.facebook.com/pg/donnamunrowarmwittywords/reviews/

Amazon
https://www.amazon.com/dp/B09JTTS876

Goodreads
https://www.goodreads.com/author/show/16547319.Donna_Munro

Book Bub
https://www.bookbub.com/books/the-zanzibar-moon-by-donna-denise-munro

Thank you, beautiful readers.

www.ingramcontent.com/pod-product-compliance
Lightning Source LLC
Chambersburg PA
CBHW030631120726
47904CB00006B/2114